Also by Susan Dunlap

JILL SMITH MYSTERIES:

Sudden Exposure
Time Expired
Death and Taxes
Diamond in the Buff
A Dinner to Die For
Too Close to the Edge
Not Exactly a Brahmin
As a Favor
Karma

KIERNAN O'SHAUGHNESSY MYSTERIES:

High Fall
Pious Deception
Rogue Wave

VEJAY HASKELL MYSTERIES:

An Equal Opportunity Death
The Bohemian Connection
The Last Annual Slugfest

A JILL SMITH MYSTERY

SUSAN DUNLAP

COP OUT

A DELL BOOK

Published by
Dell Publishing
a division of
Bantam Doubleday Dell Publishing Group, Inc.
1540 Broadway
New York, New York 10036

ISBN 0-440-22479-9

Reprinted by arrangement with Delacorte Press

Printed in the United States of America

Published simultaneously in Canada

March 1998

10 9 8 7 6 5 4 3 2 1

WCD

For Judy Davis,
who gave me the idea

ACKNOWLEDGMENTS

Once again I am indebted to the Berkeley Police Department, especially to Sergeants Kay Lantow and Mike Holland for their unfailing willingness to help. And to Officer Abbie Cohen for her generosity and literary sensitivity.

Thanks to Mary Alice Gorman of Mystery Lovers Bookshop for her thorough research and quick response.

And to the Blue Buddha Tattoo Studio for suggestions I would never have considered.

And for their continuing guidance and support, to Jackie Cantor and Dominick Abel.

CHAPTER 1

"OTT, YOU ARE AN ASS."

Ott said nothing. He didn't even look abashed. What he looked like was a molting canary perched on an ostrich's egg—and all the time swearing there was nothing in his nest.

"Nothing!" I continued. "When you called me an hour ago, you were sitting on something so big you couldn't wait to give it to me. Too big to keep till tomorrow when I'm back on patrol and being paid for wild-goose chases like this."

His arms were bent, and he moved them in and out, winglike, as if he were a giant yellow bird perched precariously on that big egg of what he had decided he couldn't tell me and had to flap like crazy to keep from falling off.

Which brought me back to my original thought. In fairness Herman Ott, private detective to the counterculture, looked as uncomfortable as I'd ever seen him. And here, on the grounds of Berkeley's venerable, elegant Claremont Hotel, it was hard to say whether he looked more disdainful-than-thou or just awkward.

I'd been to his sorry Telegraph Avenue office more often than I cared to recall. Never had he let me in before my third knock, never had he answered a question without a battle, and never, never had he been dressed in anything but garments in various hues of yellow—and all from Goodwill. Now he stood in the farthest corner of the landscaped parking lot behind a luxurious fan palm, overlooking two silver Mercedeses. His sparse blond hair was combed back, his white shirt was ironed, and a handkerchief peeked out of his jacket pocket. The man was almost overdressed.

"Ott, don't tell me you went out and bought a black suit—"

"Used." He pulled a handkerchief out of his pocket, spilling a tiny tin cross that came to a sharp bottom point.

"You got a funeral suit and religion too?" I couldn't quite conceal a smirk.

Ott stuffed the wee cross back in place and gave a ferocious blow into his white hankie, wadded it back up, and plugged it into the pocket, thus destroying any decent line the trousers might have had.

"You're dressed to kill—"

"Smith, you been a cop too long." He glared.

For an instant I took that look to be a sartorial indictment of my jeans and Polartec jacket. Then I remembered to whom I was talking. "You've never had the urge to get gussied up and meet a cop at a fancy hotel before. But here you are, decked out like a penguin. All so you can tell me that what you called me here for isn't important anymore. Come on, Ott."

Ott shrugged.

"If it's so unimportant, why not just tell me what it is?"

This time he didn't even bother with movement.

"Fine," I snapped. "The next time you've got an

emergency, when you don't want to deal with a Berkeley police officer who isn't as incredibly tolerant as I am, I'll remember this masquerade." I turned toward the driveway. "I'm missing the Raiders game, and I've got a houseful of guests waiting for me to—"

"Smith, just bear with me, huh?" Ott's sloping shoulders rose. To the untrained eye he'd have looked almost normal. To mine, his stance shrieked fear. "I can't tell you now. Maybe I should've waited before I called you. Look, I'm sorry you're not home to be the perfect hostess—"

"Don't give me that condescension."

He shook his head. "You're a cop; you don't need a gridiron to watch overpaid brutes shortening each other's lives."

I started toward the driveway.

He grabbed my arm and said words I didn't think his mouth could pronounce: "I'm sorry." Then he added, "Just give me till tomorrow, and I'll explain the whole thing."

He sounded pitiful, desperate, trying his best to hold off overwhelming forces pushing in from all directions. His whole being implored: *Surely one day's grace is little enough to ask.*

But I had given him grace periods before. I'd put investigations on hold, and my reputation on the line, only to discover the next day that Herman Ott hadn't answered his phone or opened his door. I unpeeled his hand. "Wait till tomorrow? Right. That's the kind of agreement that ends up with someone getting killed before sunrise."

I said it as a riposte. I never expected it to be true.

CHAPTER 2

OTT GRABBED AT ME ONE last time, as it suddenly came home to him just who would be watching the Raiders game at Seth Howard's and my house. "Don't tell all those *cops*—"

"Don't worry, Ott. I'm not about to confess that I spend my Sunday afternoons with you." I stared at his odd black suit and tie. "I'm giving you an hour. That's plenty of time for you to get me this great secret."

"I can't—"

"Of course you can. You call me by five o'clock, or even a disguise as good as this isn't going to save you." I hesitated, but I couldn't resist a final dig. "I suppose you're waiting for the valet parking attendant to bring your car around."

For a moment I thought he'd gone mute with horror. "Emma in a *pay* lot?" With that he stalked off, doffing his jacket as he went. By the time he reached the sidewalk it was wadded up under his arm, leaving the tail of his overlarge shirt hanging rumpled to his knees.

Ott was a self-righteous pain in the ass. And the worst part was there was nothing I could say about it. Had he been anyone else, I could have gone home and regaled the very cops he had disparaged with this afternoon's farce, right down to his car, Emma, which had been named for Emma Goldman. We could have had a ball speculating on the famous anarchist's reaction to that vehicular tribute. My guess was she'd have reacted the same way Ott had to the idea of parking in a pay lot.

But that wouldn't happen, because while Ott was a pain in the ass, he was *my* pain, and I felt a ridiculous protectiveness toward him. Other cops rightly saw him as a pest who relished impeding their work. But for me, Ott was a breath from a bygone era of hope and promise. He was the private eye to artists, old radicals, the strung-out and worn-out, clients from whom no investigator could make a living. I couldn't guess how scant his living was; there were months he probably got more threats than dollars. He ate off a hot plate in his office, slept on the floor there, never compromised his principles, and answered to no one.

As it turned out, there was only one visitor's car in the driveway of the shambling brown shingle Howard leased and loved and I lived in and tolerated. I glanced at my watch: 4:27. The game wouldn't have ended till 4:00 or later. The speed with which the majority of our guests had abandoned ship spoke ill for the Raiders. When I walked in, the living room looked the way the Oakland Coliseum must have by the fourth quarter: huge, nearly vacant, and littered with empty cans, broken chips, and the detritus of mixed nuts. It smelled similar. And it probably wasn't much warmer.

The living room was a large, high-ceilinged L connecting with the dining area. Like a ladder folded down from an attic the staircase from the second-floor balcony dropped into the middle of the room. Clearly more than one of our landlord's predecessors had remodeled, and had done so without the assistance of an architect.

"Beer?" Howard offered, unfolding his six-foot-six frame from the Danish modern sofa. He was halfway to the kitchen before I nodded. This rambling house with its cavernous green living room and too many bedrooms was perfect for a man who craved a downstairs area bulging with friends, bedrooms bulging with children, and weekends bulging with structural renovations. People talk about the police being "family." Howard, who grew up largely alone, flourished among dozens of brothers and sisters in blue. Others had dreams beyond the department, but for Howard, the Elysian Fields were here.

Sometimes I wondered what had attracted him to a woman who bristled at departmental orders, had lived on a back porch for two years, and still hadn't unpacked her boxes here. He offered me a grin, handed me the beer, dropped back onto the sofa next to me, and wrapped an arm around my shoulder. "Too bad everyone's gone."

"Hey!" Connie Pereira barked. "What am I, crab dip?"

"Almost," Howard said, laughing.

Connie Pereira was perched on the edge of a leather ottoman, whose companion chair had vanished with a tenant before my time. The ottoman was surprisingly uncomfortable, but it gave Connie easy access to the pretzels and crab dip on the coffee table. The standing joke between Howard and me was that Pereira was the puppy we'd never had.

"So, Jill, what was it with Ott that couldn't wait?" I could hear the edge in Howard's voice.

"He changed his mind."

"He what?" Howard's indignation was endearing in its way.

I sighed. "I gave him till five."

"And you really think he'll call you?"

"We'll see."

"Jill—"

"Lay off," I said. "I've already had it out with Ott. He'll call, or I'll deal with him."

Howard leaned forward as if to speak, then shrugged and sat back on the sofa. There was no point in going on. We'd snapped about Ott before; nothing new was going to come out today.

"*A Fair Deal*'s coming on." Pereira grabbed the remote and switched to the public access channel. "They always do cases where somebody's pissed off at some bureaucracy, but today is a special deal. Today's case is the Telegraph Avenue street vendors against none other than Brother Cyril and the Angels of Righteousness."

Howard straightened up. Now that he was a patrol sergeant, the denizens of Telegraph Avenue—Berkeley's answer to Greenwich Village—had a new spot in his heart. "Brother Cyril's being mediated? What for? That guy's not on the Avenue looking for converts; he's looking for trouble."

I curled my feet under me. "Cyril and his band of thugs. If that bunch is holy, it'll be a real miracle."

"The miracle will be if Bryant Hemming can mediate anything with them," Howard said. "Compromise is the last thing they want."

Pereira held a well-loaded chip inches from her

mouth, contemplating it like an intriguing idea. "Hemming's never blown a mediation, not since the show began."

"It looks like this might be a first time."

"Ten bucks says he isn't. Ten on Bryant Hemming."

Howard laughed. "Ten says the righteous punks take out Hemming before the first commercial."

On the TV, game show music announced *A Fair Deal*. I took a swallow of my beer.

Bryant Hemming burst onto the TV stage like a running back. He had an ordinary face and light brown hair, but when he smiled, the man looked like a star. He virtually glowed. And he aimed that glow right into the camera—right, it seemed, at me. Pereira was holding a loaded chip and smiling back.

Hemming sat and leaned toward the camera. "On *A Fair Deal* our goal is not for some outside judgment but a *solution* everyone supports. It's a matter of listening to the other guy and ourselves, of acknowledging what we both really want. Then we come out with a plan we all support. That plan works, it lasts, because we're all in it together, which is what makes it" —he paused and the camera drew back—"*a fair deal.*"

"The guy's had death threats," Pereira said.

"From Cyril's boys?"

"Probably. They're not likely to have been from the postmaster or the head of A.C. Transit—they were on the short end of Hemming's last two mediations—but any crazy in town could be after him. Bryant Hemming's turned into the gonzo frog of Berkeley public access TV."

"Biggest frog in the puddle eh, Connie?" Howard asked.

On his bare-bones set Bryant Hemming was smiling as confidently as if he'd made it to a network feed. "Well, my friends, what would Berkeley be without a clash of wills, of thoughts, of hard-held beliefs? A real shock, huh?" He chuckled. "And it'd be downright boring. But not to worry, you're in no danger of dozing off here. Not with our case tonight, our toughest case of the season. No matter what your convictions, this dispute's going to bring you up cold." He leaned forward. "We all know Berkeley's commitment to freedom of speech. The free speech movement was born here. But what about freedom of commerce? The city's had a rep as being down on business. When freedom of speech comes up against freedom of commerce, which side are you on? Don't be so sure you know!" He wasn't rubbing his hands together, but I guessed it was sheer will that kept him from it.

With a flourish he motioned toward a woman with long, wiry brown hair and jeweled bangles on every enclaspable portion of her body. "Demanding freedom of commerce, we have Serenity Kaetz, of the Telegraph Avenue Street Vendors. She has a display on Telegraph."

"She *is* a display on Telegraph," Howard muttered as the lights bounced off her silver breastplate.

"Where else is she going to get free advertising broadcast to households all over town?" Pereira said, scooping up a hillock of dip with her chip. "The reason people come on the show is publicity. Getting their problems mediated, that's just the chance they take."

But when Serenity Kaetz started to speak, she wasn't jiggling her head to show off her earrings. And she looked anything but serene. She poked her elbows into her thighs, hands out at the ready. "Here's the thing. I design this jewelry. I won't tell you how long it takes me to make one inlaid cuff. But, so what, I'm an artist; that's what I do," she said, palms up, voice so clearly Bronx that I smiled. She reminded me of my great-uncle's neighbor in the apartment on the Grand Concourse, a buxom, bustling woman with the face of a determined cherub. "You want I should come back from the deli with half a bag?" she'd say, staring accusingly at Uncle Jack's sparsely filled kitchen shelves. She must have been half the age of my great-uncle and his friends in the building, but her comments were greeted with thoughtful nods, and she was always addressed as Mrs. Bronfmann. And one day she met a Spanish exchange student on the crosstown bus and never came back.

"Bryant," Serenity Kaetz was saying now, "I'm an artist, but I also run a business. I have to jump the bureaucratic hurdles just like anyone who wants to add a porch to his house or an awning over his display window. The city made me go before a board to prove I am the maker of this necklace, this ring. That's fine; good the city should be so committed to art. I had to wait three years for my license; I'm not complaining."

"On *A Fair Deal* we go beyond complaining to finding solutions."

If she noticed the little whine in his chiding, she ignored it. She gave him that same smile Mrs. Bronfmann used to offer to Uncle Jack when he insisted that he didn't need nice fresh carrots. "Every two months Berkeley runs a lottery for spots along Telegraph. A week each, eight total. Some weeks I don't make the list at all. Half the time the slots aren't worth having. So I'm talking one, two weeks a month max when I can sell my work. Serenity's Jewelry," she added.

"So what you're asking us is?"

"Telegraph Avenue—the street—is my store. I pay for my license. I want the city to protect my rights. A couple years ago we had the nudists, stopping at the tie dye stalls, resting *their* wares on *our* wares, and you know damned well they weren't planning to buy shirts. Then we've got the drug dealers . . . and the panhandlers begging for money they're just going to plop in the hands of the dealers. This year we've got these religious assholes moving down the Avenue, running off our customers. And the city just lets them go screaming and pushing—"

Hemming put a hand on her arm.

"We demand our rights."

The camera panned the audience. The half cheering theatrically were women in tie dye, men with Crisco'd Mohawks, girls with hair every shade food color will provide, guys in turbans, berets, fedoras, and one with six snakeskin belts encircling his chest and a snake over his shoulder. Across the aisle close-clipped scowling men in black looked anything but righteous. The angels they resembled were Hell's Angels. They sat as if they were straddling hogs, legs apart, hands poised to rev up and mow down anyone in their way. Patience and forbearance looked like virgin ground for these guys.

Bryant Hemming's brow tightened. There'd never been a free-for-all on the show, but his expression said: There's always a first time.

CHAPTER 3

With what must have been practiced effort, Bryant Hemming relaxed his face back into an encouraging half smile. But his voice was tight as he said, "And who is it that Serenity Kaetz says infringed on her rights?" He let the question hang long enough for the unknowing viewer to consider Telegraph Avenue's usual suspects: students, street people, environmentalists, the old radicals, and, of course, us—the police. Then, turning his attention to his left, he said, "Demanding freedom of speech and freedom of religion, we have with us Brother Cyril of the Angels of Righteousness."

Howard and Pereira shook their heads. The first time I had seen Brother Cyril, I'd laughed. What I'd expected was a street thug who'd been cleaned up for trial—big near-shaven head, round face, and muscles that screamed steroids. But Brother Cyril was a slight middle-aged man with thinning light brown hair. Seen on the Avenue, he'd have been taken for an undergraduate's father, the type who would hesitate before suggesting his son change majors and die before asking his daughter about birth control. He looked like a man who would wait at the end of the line forever. Now I could see his pale eyes were a bit too close together, his nose a bit too narrow, lips thin, chin falling too quickly back toward his neck.

He looked like a man his half of the audience would have kicked out of the way. They were the street thug models I had expected Cyril to be: young, muscled, surly, with black pants and shirts and bulbous arms that sported tattoos.

"How does Cyril keep 'em in line? Fire and brimstone?"

"More likely drugs and sex, Howard," Pereira said. "Maybe hypnosis. I can see him with candles and a swinging watch."

"More likely a computer password or a delete key," I said. Cyril reminded me of the nerds I'd known in school before nerds became stylish. Then they were just bright, pimply guys, seething at the ludicrous unfairness of being shunned by brawny guys, pretty girls, all clearly their inferiors. And when they got even, they dished out excruciating humiliations that echoed loud and long.

Howard gave my shoulder a squeeze. "I hope ol' Bryant's got plenty of security off camera. If the Righteous leap the aisle, they'll pound the vendors into parchment before he can call nine-one-one."

Bryant Hemming must have had a similar thought. His clean-cut smile looked brittle, and when he spoke, his voice had lost that easy, hopeful tone. He patted Cyril's chair. "In one sentence, Brother Cyril, tell me what you want."

But Cyril didn't sit. He looked directly at the camera almost shyly, as if he were surprised a nerd like him was allowed to speak. His voice was soft, his tone thoughtful. "They seem so innocent, these out-of-time hippies with their feather necklaces and their peace symbols, but what do we know about them? Let me tell you"—his words were coming faster, his voice higher—"they are money changers. They allow drugs, licentiousness, baby killing. They are money changers. And what did Jesus do when he saw them in the temple? He cast out all them that sold and bought and overthrew their tables and"—he glared at the vendors with an intensity nothing in his bland face had foreshadowed—"he obliterated their tables and their caged pigeons." He started toward them. The camera preceded him, focusing on Serenity Kaetz and her graven bird breastplate. She shrank back as if Cyril had struck her there. Colleagues shoved closer, their faces narrowed in anger. But even they reflected a fear left by Cyril's piercing accusation.

There was a rumble of muffled voices as the camera shifted. At the side of the screen black-clad biceps jerked up and bruised forearms thrust forward in a jumble of movement. Cyril was at the edge of the stage before Hemming caught him.

"Berkeley's as foreign ground as he could find for that tirade. What's he after?" Pereira asked.

"If he were crazy, the Avenue'd welcome him," I said. "He could shriek and shout and dress in a coat of many colors. Citizens'd line up to defend his rights. Then he couldn't offend people enough. He'd be right up there with Hate Man or the guy who sold acres on the moon."

" 'Course people'd blow off his message," Pereira said. "But they will anyway. What we got here is just another wacko out for the limelight."

I shook my head. "Looking for attention, sure. But wacko, no way. This guy gives me the creeps. It's like his parts don't mesh. I can't tell what's real and what's costume. Or what's behind it all."

Howard was strangely silent on the subject.

On the screen Hemming was still smiling, but now the smile seemed real. He looked not at the camera but at Cyril. "Brother Cyril, in one sentence what is it you're asking for? We don't expect our viewers to remember more than that. They're watching you."

I thought Cyril bristled at Hemming's subtle condescension—Hemming was exactly the popular jock type that nerds hated—but he held himself so stiffly I couldn't be sure. The audience was silent. The silence lengthened. Finally Cyril thrust his inadequate chin forward. "We *demand* a platform for our free speech rights and rights of assembly, right on Telegraph Avenue, the home of free speech."

Serenity Kaetz jumped to her feet, rattling metal. "If he's there yammering and haranguing, we might as well move out. Our customers aren't going to put up with that."

"Yeah, what about *our* rights?" came a female voice from the audience.

Hemming put a hand on the shoulder of each adversary. "Let's sit back down. It'll make things easier for the cameraman," he said, again reminding them of the greater audience judging them. "Remember we're here to find middle ground. So," he said, settling between them, "Ms. Kaetz, you would like Brother Cyril to stay off Telegraph?"

"And stop hassl—"

"Right, Ms. Kaetz. And you, Brother Cyril, want your voice to be heard on the Avenue?"

The preacher was poised to retort but seemed to think better of it.

Hemming let a moment pass, then spoke directly to the camera. "This is one of those issues that make you say: How can you possibly come up with a solution that pleases everyone? And that's the trick—no, *trick's* a bad word, because there's no trick to mediating. The reason mediation works is that we're all basically decent, honest people who are willing to give a little as long as we know we're getting . . . a fair deal." With that Hemming looked at each adversary. He offered them that small smile of understanding. But when he sat back in his chair and let his eyes close, he seemed to lose control of his face, and his mouth tightened into a greedy little grin. The not-quite-quiz-show music played in the background. The audience knew the routine and waited.

As one, Howard, Pereira, and I reached for crab dip. Howard selected a chip, held it in abeyance. "If he can get Cyril and his blackshirts on Telegraph and off Telegraph at the same time, he can forget this mediation business and take over Cyril's church."

"With that kind of miracle, he can take over the pope's church." I took the chip from his hand and popped it in my mouth.

"He's got to have the fix in. The last thing a guy like Cyril wants is to make peace." Howard's voice was tight. He should have been lounging happily, still warmed by the afternoon among friends. I glanced over at him; his jaw was set firm, his tense gaze square on the TV screen.

Bryant Hemming wasn't precisely smiling but it looked as if he couldn't keep completely at bay the satisfaction or maybe the triumph he felt. "This dispute seemed insoluble, right? But the wonderful thing with mediation is that there are no views so divergent they can't be brought together. If the Israelis and the Palestinians can talk peace; if the Irish can sit down with the Brits"—the grin took control of his face— "then well-meaning people even here in Berkeley can come to agreement."

The camera panned the audience: tense street vendors sitting with their arms crossed tightly over their ribs and the black-shirted Angels poised to shoot from their chairs. If either group sent good wishes across the aisle, no glance revealed it. All eyes were straight ahead, all lips pressed hard together, all brows sullenly lined.

The camera moved in close on Bryant Hemming as he lifted his head and smiled again at Kaetz and Cyril. "Ms. Kaetz, Brother Cyril, there are some things you have in common. You're both concerned about the drug dealers in People's Park right off Telegraph and the pernicious influence they have on the Avenue, right?"

It was a moment before each nodded, Kaetz looking confused, Cyril suspicious. Drugs weren't either of their main complaints. And they, no more than we, expected dealers to be swept off the Avenue for good.

"And you both want your message, your product, as it were, to reach the shoppers on the Avenue, right?"

This time the nods came more quickly.

"So here's what we'll do. You're familiar with Hyde Park Corner in London, their sacred ground of free speech. Why not have a Hyde Park Corner here in Berkeley? We have speakers in Sproul Plaza on campus, but no place set aside in the city itself. And Telegraph's the primo place."

"Aw right!" Whistles and bass cheers from half the

audience seemed to startle Hemming. Beside him Brother Cyril's thin lips curled up into a disbelieving smile. Not much of Serenity Kaetz was on camera, but it was enough to show a fist clamping down hard.

Hemming held up his hands. "Let me finish. Telegraph Avenue is primo but not perfect. Perfect is the corner of People's Park, near enough to be seen on Telegraph, and with a speaker system every word can be piped out there."

"Hey! What the—" came from the audience.

Brother Cyril's thin smile vanished, his narrow features sucked in tightly, and his Adam's apple bobbed as if desperate to plug the venom about to spew forth. His fingers squeezed into fists. He didn't speak, and the only thing that revealed his fury was a slight, uncontrollable bobbing of his Adam's apple. I felt I could see a hard black knot smoldering behind it; he would never be able to swallow without its blocking his windpipe.

Hemming reached a hand toward the preacher's shoulder, then seemed to reconsider. "And here's the added good you'll be doing, Brother. You'll fill the park with righteous men, believers. You'll create the kind of atmosphere drug dealers hate. Your message will be cleaning up People's Park."

Serenity Kaetz's expression turned to one of amazement.

But Hemming didn't see that. His eyes never left Cyril. Perhaps it took the brother a minute to realize how bad he would look refusing the deal. Or perhaps he spotted unintended possibilities in Bryant's offer.

"A fair deal, right, Brother Cyril?" Hemming's voice fluttered.

Cyril stood stone still for a moment before extending his hand to Serenity Kaetz. By the time she shook it, she was smiling. Cyril's sucked-in expression never changed. The theme music rose, the camera moved in close on the clasped hands, and the credits rolled.

I stretched. "How long do you give that deal?"

Pereira tucked a foot under her thigh. "It's four days to Thanksgiving. If Brother Cyril doesn't manage to empty the Avenue of buyers this weekend, the truce could make it for two weeks. But if he ruins the biggest shopping weekend of the year, I'd say we're out there in uniform, batons in hand, by Sunday."

Howard groaned. "And by Monday both the vendors and the brothers will be 'victims' and we'll be the bad guys." He glanced at me. "Or we will be if your friend Ott has anything to do with it." He didn't move, but his hand resting on my shoulder tightened. "So, Jill, it's five o'clock. Shouldn't the phone be ringing?"

"Come on, Howard," Pereira said, "Ott's a Berkeley person; his time is fluid."

"Right, fluid like water under the dam. Jill, when has he ever called back? Ever?"

Howard was right, more or less. And when he got around to telling me I should have known better, he'd be right too. But understanding that something is your own fault rarely makes you feel better.

I glanced at the detritus of chips and dip. "We're going to need something for dinner. Vietnamese?"

"I'll keep a pen handy so I can take a message when Ott calls."

"No gifts are necessary," I snapped.

"My gift, Jill, was not telling anyone but Connie where you went this afternoon." Howard was still standing next to me, his hand stonelike on my shoulder, his voice as cold as I'd heard it in interrogations. "I didn't tell your friends that you rushed out to accommodate a guy who shits on them."

Connie grabbed her jacket and headed for the door. "I gotta go. Bryant Hemming's going to be interviewed on the local news tonight. Be interesting to hear his take on the mediation. He's on at six. I gotta rush." She was jabbering, trying to propel herself away before things got worse here.

As soon as she was out the door, I pulled loose from Howard's hand. "I've had enough hassle already today. I don't want to deal with your attitude about Ott. Call in the order to Da Nang, and they'll have it by the time I get across town. If I hurry, I can get back in time for the interview."

I was out the door before he could answer. No one in the department liked Ott, of course. Plenty of officers held him in a special contempt. But Howard's reaction was different; I could see it in his suddenly pale face, hear it in his icy voice. He should have felt the affinity I did for Ott's commitment to his principles. Howard, the King of Sting, should have applauded Ott's maneuvers, but their similarity in that regard just scraped him closer to the bone.

No one hates conflict more than Howard, particularly conflict in his home and most particularly with me. There was a level to his scorn of Herman Ott that I didn't understand. If I hadn't been so annoyed, I'd have done the wise thing and found out what caused it.

CHAPTER 4

I STOPPED AT A PHONE booth on University Avenue and called Herman Ott. He didn't answer. *Of course* he didn't answer. He wouldn't have picked up the receiver if Ed McMahon had been calling. "Ott," I said into the phone, "you contacted me; you dragged me to a meeting for nothing. You said you'd call me by five—half an hour ago—and now you don't even have the courtesy to reach over and pick up the receiver. I know you're there." I *didn't* know, but I was too pissed to deal with that. "Call me at home. Tonight."

Maybe he's *not* there, I thought, as I drove across town to the Da Nang Restaurant on San Pablo Avenue to pick up dinner. Maybe he was going out of town, and he wanted someone to know.

But I couldn't believe that Ott would leave town. And if he did suddenly, why would he use me as his tether? Surely he had friends and associates he trusted more than a police officer.

But that was the thing: he didn't. His associates were not the types you would trust with your files, much less your life.

I pondered that while I picked up the coconut satay and chicken brochettes, and if I hadn't had the food in the car, I would have swung by Telegraph Avenue and bearded Ott in his den. His reason for not getting back to me wasn't the issue; even the animosity he'd spawned wasn't it. The bottom line was that a police officer doesn't keep her sources by allowing them to blow her off.

When I got home, Howard was sprawled on the couch, left arm hooked over the back, right leg stretched across the coffee table. He looked back to normal. The truth, I knew, was that he didn't want any more dissension. That was fine with me.

"Bryant Hemming's already on," he said, nodding toward the TV. He hadn't looked up. That was fine with me too.

I put the cartons on the table and plopped on the ottoman. On the television screen Bryant Hemming was smiling. The man looked so pleased it was hard not to be pleased for him.

Next to him at the news table Jason Figueroa, the young anchor, made a quarter turn toward him. "What's this we hear about your being called to mediate in Washington? You'll be focusing on your specialty—disputes with bureaucracies, right? So, does that mean the Berkeley way has finally become legitimate?"

Bryant Hemming nodded. In a light denim shirt and chinos, he could have been a Cal professor or a checkout clerk at Andronico's Market. A man giving you something. "This is an important—a vital—project, if I do say so myself, and I'm delighted such a prestigious foundation in Washington is getting behind it."

"The Mutual Respect Project," Figueroa slid in. "We'll be following your progress with it, Bryant, in a weekly segment here on the evening news. And we—"

"Here's why it's so vital." Hemming leaned forward. "People are pissed off all over. Like these homegrown militiamen, and the radical right, and the radical leftists; everyone is pushed to the wall. But the thing is they're not bulldozed by one big force, 'the government.' They're pecked to death by a flock of smaller, often unintentional tyrants. Phone company marketers interrupting their dinners. People just want to mail letters and use the phone and get on with life. But see, these bureaucracies keep pecking. And when the citizen tries to deal with them, there's no one to take responsibility. All people want is to be treated fairly and with respect. Bureaucrats want to be viewed as serving the public, but most of the time they just don't know how." He was looking right at the camera, imploring me to understand. Just as he'd done on *A Fair Deal* and just as effectively.

"And are they happy when you point them out?" Figueroa asked, barely controlling a grin.

Hemming had his smile in place too. "Well, Jason, a bureaucracy that sloughs off its clients isn't likely to treat its workers much better. It's demoralizing to represent a department people hate or, worse yet, scorn. What's the TV image of the postal worker? Do you think letter carriers like to be portrayed that way? Of course not. Wouldn't they rather work for a place they could be proud of?"

Howard laughed. "Are we talking utopia here?"

"—Washington power brokers," Figueroa was saying. "Won't you be stepping on toes asking them to compromise?"

Howard held up a finger. "Translation: Those guys don't want to compromise; they want to win. Hemming better watch his ass."

On the screen Bryant Hemming simply smiled. "Good mediation means everyone benefits. The Mutual Respect Project is a great breakthrough. If it takes hold, think of the difference it'll make. We can nip people's fury in the bud. The project will save lives, not just through a lessening of tension in everyday life . . ."

Figueroa didn't utter the word *overblown*, but the sentiment was barely masked on his face.

Hemming took a quick breath, a debater's breath. "If people thought the government, the IRS, the post office, were fair . . . If people treated each other with respect . . ."

"What about Brother Cyril—"

"No," he snapped. "Let's focus on the greater impact of the Mutual Respect Project. This is critical," he said, back in stride. "Because, really, what choice do we have? In an age when anyone can buy a gun, when you can blow up a building with fertilizer, how are we going to protect ourselves? More police, more metal detectors, more roped-off areas—if you think that'll make you safe, then you're really talking pie in the sky. No battalion of guards or miles of barbed wire can keep out a crazy committed to killing.

"The only chance we've got is to go at conflict from the other end. When you've got a disgruntled employee with a bomb, there are two things to look at. We know there's no way we can prevent him from making the bomb. Maybe, though, we can keep him from becoming so disgruntled."

"An inspiring concept, Bryant. But all great gener-alities come back to the particulars. Brother Cyril. What happens when he's preaching half a block off Telegraph and the street vendors bring in a band and drown him out. What happens to your mediation set-tlement then?"

Hemming's smile looked fragile. "Mediation stresses the integrity of the parties involved"—he paused for an instant—"but occasionally people do have second thoughts, and we are prepared to consult with them. It's part of our service—"

"But you'll be in Washington. Gone."

"Bryant Hemming will be gone, yes. The Arts and Creativity Council, the umbrella organization for our mediation service, will still be here, headed by my fine assistant, Roger Macalester, an old-time Berkeley hand."

"Lucky Roger," Howard said. "Hope he's got a mop."

"I never heard of Brother Cyril till he started marching down Telegraph like it was Palm Sunday. Who is he anyway?" I hadn't meant the question to throw us into shoptalk. But if I had mapped out the evening with the goal of improving it, I couldn't have taken a better turn. When I was going through my divorce years ago, and Howard and I were bent on ignoring the attraction that itched beneath every epi-dermal centimeter, we clothed our unacceptable urges in the garb of talking cases. We spent long, intense evenings palpating the pulsating questions of warrant data, digging our fingers deep into the hidden mean-ings in suspects' interviews. Looking into forbidden eyes, brushing against fingers, talking ever more intently till our words barely bobbed above the sea of wanting.

Talking shop had served us well. It still could.

But Howard took the bait only halfway.

CHAPTER 5

HOWARD HEADED UPSTAIRS. NONE OF the tenants was home, but any of them could burst into the living room at any time, with any number of friends. Howard was the chief lessee of the house, and it was his— in theory. Practically, the only rooms he controlled were his bedroom and the section of mine in which he stored his excess stuff. He longed to buy this place, which was entirely too large for us, and have space for every friend traveling through town, plus a study, breakfast room, library, game room, and never to have a whim he couldn't house. It unnerved him that I could go on comfortably without so much as putting my mark on his bedroom, where we slept, or unpacking my cartons in my furnitureless room next door.

I checked for messages, though Howard surely would have told me if Ott had deigned to call (he hadn't). Then I followed Howard upstairs.

He settled on his California king-sized bed and leaned back against the headboard.

"So, Cyril?" I prodded, punching my own pillow into sitting shape.

"Cyril's been around Monterey County for a while. Had a storefront church, one of those that make you wonder how he comes up with the rent.

Then he hit on the idea of soliciting guys from the halfway houses to hoist and carry for minimum wage."

"Hoist and carry what?"

Howard shrugged. The product wasn't his point. "I know this type of guy," he said, his voice lower, "from when I was a kid."

This, I realized, was why Howard had moved upstairs. He rarely mentioned his childhood and never without a flurry of embarrassment as if he had exposed a raw and suspicious rash. He had grown up in a series of valley towns to which his free-spirited mother had flitted, alighting for months, weeks, or on more than one occasion fewer than seven days, yanking her son from the hope of security time after time. For Howard, the lure of stability grew so seductive that he chose a career protecting the kind of life he'd never had and a house he could spend the rest of his life rehabilitating. As if she understood the symbolism, his mother had never even been to this house. She still moved so often that Howard had no address for her, and his annual contact was likely to consist of a box of cookies she sent on a whim—with no return address. But she held sway in his mind, the ultimately alluring absent parent.

Now he said, "Those preachers with their tiny missions always had their fangs out for us. Sometimes they'd come after me to join the youth group or the choir, but it was my mother they wanted."

"Physically?" I'd seen an old picture of her. She'd been tall like Howard, with his high cheekbones, blue eyes, and red, curly hair. In the photo she wore a gauzy dress that flowed as if she'd been floating free on the zephyrs. "Or did they envy her freedom?"

Howard flinched at the word. I ached to take it back, to keep from reminding him that the freedom she desired was also freedom from him. He swallowed and said, "They envied it, sure; they lusted to capture her and keep her like—like a pigeon in a cage."

I put my hand on his arm and felt the muscles tense. "Pigeon?"

"In the Bible they kept pigeons in cages."

"So they could never fly off?"

"So they were there for sacrifices."

Before I could ask more, he shoved himself off the bed and headed into the bathroom. He ran the shower long after the water had to have gone cold.

Patrol teams work four ten-hour days. That's the price of three free days: three from 4:00 P.M. to 2:00 A.M. and one from 10:00 A.M. to 8:00 P.M.

I got to the station at twenty to ten on Monday morning. Dressing in uniform takes a while, particularly in winter, when it's good to have a few layers on under the bulletproof vest. November's tricky, and today was going to be only a thermal T-shirt day, but still, adjusting the Velcro so the vest protects but doesn't fit like something out of *Gone with the Wind* takes time. So do the lace-up ankle boots, the leather belt, the equipment belt over it with the baton and flashlight. I don't wear much makeup—I'm from *Berkeley* after all—but I do like a little shadow over the eyelids, a touch of rouge, a couple of swipes of lipstick when I'm going on patrol. Most times on duty I'm working to cut the tension, to ease the fear of witnesses, to calm the suspects. The blue uniform screams authority. A little bit of makeup reminds people the officer in blue is a person too.

I climbed up to the second floor, checked my mailbox—nothing new—and my voice mail, hoping for a message from Herman Ott. There wasn't one. Howard and I hadn't mentioned Ott again last night. Nor had he called. Today I'd have to deal with him; have to make a bigger deal than the issue merited just to remind him what the pecking order was. But that would come after my beat assignments. For the moment I was assigned to Howard's team, not the best of arrangements at the best of times. Even with a sergeant as well liked as Howard, it's hard for a patrol officer stuck with chasing teenagers off Telegraph not to wonder if the sergeant gave the better beat to his girlfriend. Howard bent over backward to be fair, and I ended up covering the beats with armed truants, drug deals, and endless ringing alarms.

The team meeting was in the second-floor squad room, an almost windowless square, the architectural equivalent of Russia perpetually seeking access to the sea. In our case the saltwater ports were occupied by the chief's office suite, the sergeants' office, a meeting room, and telephone and typing rooms. The squad room had been left a Vladivostok of a window by the back of the building. If a photo of the room, with its old plastic wood-grain tables and gray plastic chairs and cardboard boxes of forms in the center were to be captioned "Moscow 1950," no one would question it.

Howard assigned those of us who were floaters to beats; mine today would be 16 between the freeway and San Pablo Avenue, an area of light industry, the chichi Fourth Street shops, the sari shops and Indian restaurants on University Avenue, and the tip of

Aquatic Park. He passed around the hot car list and held up a flyer from Pasadena; someone had stolen the equipment from a marching briefcase brigade in the Doo DA Parade (Pasadena's alternative to the Rose Bowl Parade). "Pasadena assumes anyone who lifted twenty-five fake briefcases with trapdoors would naturally be headed here."

By ten-thirty I had checked out a radio, snatched one of the new patrol cars, and was driving to a burglarized self-storage unit off the frontage road to Route 80. Berkeley is the tenth most congested city in the nation, but down between the Southern Pacific tracks and the freeway, some streets are patch-paved or not paved at all, dry grass waves, and barren stucco rectangles sit atop hard clay soil looking as if the wind could blow them on to San Joaquin or Salt Lake. Storit Urself was half a block filled with four-story prefab cubes. Inside, narrow cement-floored halls ran past plywood doors five feet apart. There was no natural light, nothing to distinguish one hall from the next. Like a cut-rate mausoleum.

Perhaps it was the sight of the complainant, Margo Roehner, planted in front of 207, that sparked the thought of sarcophagi. She looked like one of those Chinese tomb warriors, single-mindedly defending the emperor in life and petrification. She was small, trim, brown in hair, eyes, and clothes, but the overwhelming impression she gave was square. Square face, square shoulders, and she was facing me square on, foot tapping impatiently. "I've got a grant application that has to be in the mail by Wednesday night. I've got the roofers at home finishing up. Yesterday they dropped some sort of tool and knocked off my suet feeder that the red-breasted nuthatches just started using. I don't want them to leave before I check things. I have two new coordinators I hired last week who have to be trained. And that's on top of my regular work; I'm on call eighteen hours a day."

I pulled out a pad. "So what's missing from here?"

"Nothing's gone, probably. There's nothing here but files, and now they're all over the floor. Nobody'd need them but me. And look! Useless! I don't have time— But you expect a report anyway, right?" She shot me an accusing glance, seemed to think better of that, and aimed her hostility at the mélange of papers inside the storage unit. If we had been anywhere more spacious than this dark, narrow hall, she'd have paced. As it was, she tapped her finger on her wrist next to her watch.

"What kind of papers?" I asked, glancing into the five-by-nine plywood cubicle.

"Medical. Printouts of disease progress, what symptoms you can expect, what your doctor should be doing for you, how soon, what steps to take if he isn't."

"Are you a doctor?"

"Hardly." Her mouth quirked, as if she'd considered a laugh but thought better of it. "I'm the head of Patient Defenders."

I restrained a smile. If she was the *patient* Defender, what did the Impatient Defender do, grab for the throat?

Margo Roehner certainly wasn't smiling. "Life is too short for levity," I could imagine her saying. She flicked a glance at her watch, stopped her finger tapping momentarily, and then, with a puff of breath— the sigh of the rushed—said, "I see you haven't heard of us. Means you haven't needed us—yet."

"And us is?"

"Look, you get sick, you go into your HMO like a lamb to pen or slaughter, as they wish. When you get a diagnosis, you don't know if it's the right diagnosis, much less what competent treatment is.

"Look, if their choices are, treat you aggressively and expensively and cure you in a week or send you home to suffer for a month and then get well on your own, what do you think they're going to do? Right. Doctors are pressured to cut costs. You have a doctor who orders 'aggressive and expensive,' he's taking money out of not only his own pocket but the rest of the white pants around him. I grew up with money, until my father married his trophy wife"—she shrugged off that misfortune—"so I know what good medical care can be. But now, with HMOs, it's not all malice; a lot of times it's ignorance. Or sloth."

"How—"

"How'd I get into this? I had a sharp metallic taste—" She waved off her words with a brusque flip of the hand. "I don't have time— *Briefly*, I had a medical problem. My doctor decided it was nothing serious, gave me a palliative, didn't answer my calls, referred me to a department that didn't handle the condition. Bottom line was she couldn't be bothered."

"But you're okay now?"

She smiled.

I didn't look away, but I wanted to.

She held my gaze. "You're better than most. It's only a crooked smile now, not the grotesque sneer pulled halfway across one cheek, as it was in the beginning. People don't gasp anymore. But then I've trained myself never to smile."

"If the HMO—"

"If my doctor had treated me right away, would it have averted the paralysis? I'll never know. What help I got is from time and friends."

If her father hadn't remarried and she'd still had his money, would she still have a working face? Surely she had wondered that. What had she been like before? Had this stolid little warrior grinned over shared secrets, laughed explosively, smiled at a lover? I shivered, peeking into the black void where humor is the enemy and slamming the door to it so quickly Margo herself would have been impressed.

My face must have betrayed me. Margo Roehner cringed—but only momentarily—then plunged on. "Everyone doesn't have knowledgeable friends, but everyone can have Patient Defenders. We're there— free of charge because when you're too sick to fight, you're too sick to decide whether a defender is a sensible expense. We go with you to emergency or urgent care, and we stay as long as needed. When we go home, we're on call. Medical care's real 'life or death'; you make the wrong decision, you wait and see, and you can die. I could tell you stories."

God forbid.

"I'll tell you, they don't send *my* clients home 'to see how things go.' " Another woman might have smiled in satisfaction. True to her word, she didn't. Her lips merely pursed together and even in that motion pulled crookedly to the right.

Again I didn't look away. Nor did I run for a mirror to check that my own face was still normal, though I was desperate for that reassurance. "This," I said, motioning toward the mess of papers in the storage unit, "will it affect your work?"

"It'll cost me time, time I don't have. If I don't get the grant application finished— I gave them our bank statement and signed the papers yesterday. Their money will pay the salaries of my new coordinators. Then we'll be organized enough so we'll never have to turn down a sick person."

"Can you think of any reason why someone would break into your locker here?"

"None. It's insane. It's going to take me hours to clean up. And all this paper wasted!"

Wasted paper, indeed. Within her warrior's breast beat the heart of a Berkeleyan. I almost grinned, but before my face moved, I found myself shuddering, as if like Margo Roehner, I had a finite number of smiles in this life and I needed to husband them so they would last as long as my face.

I stepped inside the storage unit, a sort of San Quentin for possessions. Papers were strewn two feet deep, boxes tossed helter-skelter. Nothing here that anyone but a doctor, Defender, or masochist would choose to read. Except for the poster on top of the rubble.

I laughed. Relief swept over me. I walked outside holding the plastic-wrapped picture of a pig in a raincoat flashing his round belly. "Eye on the Future" was the caption. There was something at once smug and silly about the porcine expression. Some viewers would howl, some sneer, but Margo Roehner could do neither, and the poster seemed an added slap in the face to her. "Is this yours?"

"Oh, that. It belongs to a friend."

"That's what they all say," I would have said to someone who could smile in return. Normally it's a waste of time to take prints in a place with this much

coming and going, for a case with no loss but the door lock. But somebody was looking for something. Maybe in the wrong unit. Prints from the door couldn't hurt, I told myself. Maybe I just didn't want to divert this woman's angry focus from doctors to cops. I called the dispatcher, got a case number and time, and put the storage unit on the list for the ID tech. "If you hear anything about other break-ins or suspicious activity here, call me." I wrote the case number on my card, gave it to her, and walked back to my car to write up the report and wonder if I'd done anything more than create more wasted paper.

The second call was from Aquatic Park. The university rowing team was harassing a water-skier. Or a motorboat and water-skier were trying to capsize the rowers. Take your pick. I could have used Bryant Hemming on that territorial dispute. Tempers were not cooled by the proximity to the pond. Both sides were anxious to press charges. It was only when I told them they'd all have to come to the station and give me their statements one by one that they moved their dispute to the higher ground.

Next up was a fender bender at Fourth and Hearst. It took me twenty minutes and three reinterpretations from a woman in a blue van and a man in a red Miata to conclude that the woman, driving south on the busy block of Fourth Street, spotted a rare and wonderful parking spot on the opposite side of the boutique-jammed street. She knew it was illegal to hang a U, she insisted righteously, so she made a circle turn in the intersection. *Assuming the chance to block four lanes of traffic instead of two makes it legal?* Then she cut sharply into the prized spot. And crashed into the red Miata that was backing in at full clip, because, the driver insisted with equal righteousness, he was late for the back class at the Yoga Studio. *It'll be even more valuable to you now.* The comments you have to choke down when you're a cop could feed you for a year.

At one o'clock I called the dispatcher. "Adam sixteen here. Can I go code seven?"

"Wait a bit, sixteen. We've already got three units on lunch break. And you've got to go on a welfare check on Alston Way. Regina Wilson. Her son called from New York. She hasn't answered her phone in two days."

I found Mrs. Wilson on her bathroom floor. More than two hours passed as I called the medics, called her son, talked to her neighbors, hunting for a friend who could stay with her till her son arrived. Failing to find one, I thought fondly of Margo Roehner and Patient Defenders and ended up going to the hospital myself.

Regina Wilson was lucky, luckier than Howard's mother would be if she slipped in her bathroom and broke a hip. Howard's mother would be too new a resident wherever she lived for her neighbors to think about her, to care whether she'd fallen to the bottom of her pigeon cage. And her police department would never get a worried call from her son. He wouldn't know how to find her.

The afternoon with Regina Wilson had numbed my stomach, but as soon as I called in for code seven —very easy to get at this hour—I was starved. Before dealing with that issue, I called Herman Ott on my cell phone. He was now over twenty-four hours past deadline with me. Not surprisingly he didn't answer the phone.

"Jerk!" I muttered as I hit "off." I still didn't know

whatever he was *not* telling me, and now I was going to have to waste time finding out. Worse luck, it probably wouldn't turn out to be important. But the principle of the thing mattered to me, and enforcing it was going to be more of a nuisance for me than for him.

Unless I could reverse that.

I didn't have time to drive across town, park outside Ott's building, run up the flights of stairs, and stand banging on the door he wouldn't answer. "Lunch break"—it's lunch no matter what hour of day or night—is a break, not time off. The beat officer's still on call as her fork moves to her mouth, so the rule is you eat close to your beat.

The apartment behind Ott's rented parking slot was no nearer. But if I got a take-out burger and got lucky, I could see if the bird had flown the coop entirely.

CHAPTER 6

USING THE PHONE—I WASN'T about to go through the dispatcher on this—I called Howard.

"Sergeant Howard."

"What a sexy-sounding sergeant. Berkeley must be a lucky city."

"Some citizens are luckier than others." His voice dropped mid-sentence. I was alone in the car; clearly he was not so in his office.

For years Howard and I had shared a tiny office. I still had trouble picturing him in the sergeants' office that he now shared with someone else. It was as if his curly red hair were too bright for the drab metal desks, and the long, lean body I knew and loved out of place in such a public room—separated from the meeting room by only a window. When he was grinning, as he would be now, his blue eyes sparkled.

They might have sparkled at me while I ate. Downing a burger on a French bread roll, laughing about the red Miata and the blue van crashing together into their parking spot were just what I needed now. Then I said, "Howard, I've got to use lunch break to check on Ott's car."

"What?" I could hear the anger in his voice and

the muffled sound as he tried to swallow it. "Why? Did something happen to him?"

"He's still not picking up his damned phone."

"Now there's a surprise. Herman Ott doesn't answer his calls, so you're racing out to check his car?"

"Uh-huh," I said, cutting off whatever comment was coming. There was no point in listening to Howard tell me that Ott was a pain in the ass withholding information whenever possible, with the goal of strengthening the hand of his clients, who were also our clients, and who remained on the street longer until they burglarized or boosted or botched things up so that even Ott couldn't help them. I was checking on Ott in spite of all that.

"Howard, it's just a welfare check."

I could almost feel his outtake of breath over the phone. Behind him his fellow sergeant, Stetsky, would have discreetly turned his back and walked his desk chair to the farthest corner of the office. Sotto voce Howard said, "What makes you think he's faring any less well than his usual high standard?"

Ott's usual living was done in two rooms—office and home—in a run-down building on Telegraph. His stonewall lips garnered him trust in circles throughout the city. And allowed him to continue breathing. Still, considering the caliber of Ott's clients, it would take only one breach . . . "That's not the point. The—"

"What is your point then?"

"The point, Howard, is that Ott made a deal with me. I can't let him blow me off."

Howard was silent. He couldn't disagree with that. It was a moment before he said, "So you're assessing his welfare by checking his car?"

I could have explained the logic, could have soothed Howard's pique. Instead I snapped, "Right."

"That's a long way from your beat," he said icily.

"Not with lights and siren," I iced back.

"Look, I can't be making exceptions—"

"Howard, it's not an exception. If I were on another team, the sergeant wouldn't think twice."

His rasp of breath struck my ear. "Fine. Go. But remember your beat."

"Right," I said, failing to keep the sarcasm from my voice. I wondered again why Herman Ott infuriated him so much. Any other welfare check would have been fine.

Yanking the wheel, I turned onto Dwight Way.

Had I ever heard of Herman Ott leaving Berkeley overnight? Not on a case; for that he could call on a statewide ring of private eyes who had come of age with the counterculture. His ancient Studebaker could be cited for noise violations any time it moved (which made it clearer why he didn't tail suspects out of town, or in town for that matter). As for vacation, *if* Ott ever considered indulging in anything so bourgeois, his leaving Berkeley for pleasure would be like my choosing a resort with bad coffee. For Ott, crossing University Avenue into North Berkeley was a trip worthy of a passport.

I couldn't picture Herman Ott walking out of his office into his Studebaker and driving to the wine country for a week of mud baths and massage. Certainly not just to avoid me.

I drove up Dwight, made a right on Telegraph, and in a couple of turns came up behind the eight-unit apartment. If the corner slot was vacant, I would forget about Ott and assume he was taking the waters in a spa above his element. I'd be surprised but—

I wasn't. Ott's Studebaker sat snugly at the end of the carport. I pulled up by its fender.

Behind me the lights were on in the third-story apartments, but the first two levels were dark, and the spotlight that might have illumined the carport in back was out. On the patrol car we've got overhead lights, wigwags that blink, "alley lights" on the end of the light bar up top, and swivel lights by the side mirrors. I left the headlights on and aimed the swivel light down the row of stalls. The far two cars—a VW bug and one of those aging Toyotas or Hondas that have taken over the Volkswagen's place in American society—looked empty.

I walked to the back of the carport and shone the light in front of them and Ott's Studebaker. In the world of the homeless, carports are a boon, but citizens who are happy to give spare change to a transient on the street don't want him sleeping in their own backyards. Uninvited guests often have different standards from their hosts. I understand that; still, it doesn't make rousting the sleepers any more pleasant.

Tonight no one was sleeping against this cement wall, and I turned back to Ott's car and shone my light in the window.

There was a body on the backseat.

CHAPTER 7

I STARED INTO THE STUDEBAKER.

The body there wasn't Ott's.

Long strands of brown hair looped out from a red serape that covered the curled body like a shroud. A pale, long-fingered hand clung to one edge. There is a skill known as watching with your ears. Those of us who grew up in busy, urban societies learned to block out whole levels of sound. Leaves rustle, VCRs hum, people breathe nearby; we don't notice. But if you listen . . . It didn't take too much concentration to hear the forced flow of breath in the car, like the snore of a little pink pig. I tried Ott's door handle and was not surprised to find it locked.

"Police," I called. "Move your hands out where I can see them."

The serape flew up. I jumped back out of immediate range. I didn't expect him to have a weapon, but in my business you guess wrong, you die.

"Put your hands out slowly."

Fingers, palms, and finally wrists slid into view. The serape fell back, revealing a face I'd seen on the Avenue in the last few weeks sitting against the wall selling Free Advice. "If it's not free," he had told me, "it's not worth anything." It had been a clever and harmless riff, the kind that makes Telegraph Avenue fun.

I eyed him. "Let me give you some advice," I said, "free advice. Don't use someone else's car as a crash pad."

I was ready for him to insist indignantly the car was his and, when I axed that, to declare with undiminished outrage that he had permission to sleep there and finally to announce with great righteousness that he wasn't harming anyone and if the city of Berkeley provided beds for its citizens, he wouldn't have to be sleeping in a backseat that was way too short for him anyway. Blame someone else, it's the way of the nineties. But he surprised me. He said nothing and sat up.

"Now move out here slowly. Keep your hands where I can see them. Okay," I said as he got out, "now hands spread on the car. Do you have any weapons on you?"

"Not hardly."

"I'm going to check you, okay?" It's a thin line here between a witness's rights and my safety. You never know what you'll find: a knife taped to the inner thigh so close to the groin you wonder if the suspect was planning a sex change or an uncapped hypodermic under the sock.

But he was clean. And he had a driver's license: Charles Edward Kidd. Twenty-seven years old. Address: a trailer space number in Portland, Oregon. I let out a breath I hadn't realized I'd been holding. I should have been relieved that it wasn't Ott in the car, that Ott wasn't dead. But I knew Ott. The man was a leftover from the hippie era, but when it came to his car, he was a neat freak. No papers were ever left in it, no client of questionable hygiene allowed inside, and even a passenger who passed muster would never be permitted to put parcels or, God forbid, feet on the fine leather seats. No way would Herman Ott allow Kidd to use the Studebaker as a crash pad.

If he knew.

Maybe Ott *had* left town. Yesterday afternoon he'd looked worried. Worried enough to call me.

"Where are your car and your trailer, Mr. Kidd?"

"Didn't have a car. If I'd had the cash for a car, I wouldn't have lived in a trailer. Here's my free advice: Don't live in what you can't stand up in."

I glanced questioningly at Ott's car.

"So I don't always follow my advice. No loss; it's free."

Relief blew over me. Kidd wasn't stupid. He wouldn't kill, maim, or abduct Herman Ott and then doze off in his car.

The radio on my shoulder crackled. I cocked my ear. I didn't want to miss a beat call, not for what might well turn out to be a housekeeping problem. But the call was for Adam 2 on a beat in the hills.

I concentrated on Charles Edward Kidd. I'm a sucker for guys like him, not the ones who threw spitballs in school but the ones who came out with the quips. Add to that someone who has heard the song of the open road and written his own chorus, and I can feel the wind in my hair. It makes me think of driving down Ashby Avenue, turning right onto Route 80, and having the whole country open up ahead. What's beneath that freedom? I always want to ask guys like Kidd. Are you running away, or have you slipped your bonds to walk unfettered? Does the road rise up to meet you? And when there's no more open road, will you regret having driven so long and far that you can never find your way home again? Or will you know things in your soul the rest of us can only dream of?

None of that feeling was I about to let Kidd see. "You're in a lot of trouble here, you know that, right? Your only chance to make things better is to be completely straight with me."

"And you'll let me go?" he said, leaning back against Ott's car as if he owned it.

"And I'll do what I can for you."

He laughed. " 'Up to twenty percent off'? That means nothing."

"Wrong, Mr. Kidd. Nothing is what you've got if you don't cooperate. Nothing plus breaking the law. Now how did you get in this car?"

He was a tall, rangy guy. He looked at me, behind me at the driveway that led between the buildings to the street, and then, without moving his head, at the six-foot cement wall between this parking area and that of the next building.

"Don't even think about it."

He smiled sheepishly. "Okay, I'll tell you. It's no big thing. I did take the keys, but it's not like I stole this old jalopy of Ott's. I just wanted a place to sleep, and I knew he wasn't going to be using it."

My throat tightened. "How'd you know that?"

"Because I saw him getting in someone else's car."

"When?"

"Last night."

"Are you sure?"

"Yeah, 'cause it was real foggy by then and I was cold and didn't want to spend another night sleeping outside. I mean I looked at him getting into someone *else's* car and bingo—lightbulb—it came to me he wasn't going to be in *his* car, so—"

"What kind of car was it?"

"Brown or gray or like that. Or maybe it just looked dark. It was dusk, so I couldn't see good."

"But what *make* of car?" Please, I prayed to the gods of interrogation, don't make him one of those dropouts who pride themselves on the ultimate un-Americanism: not knowing cars.

Idols beseeched in desperation rarely deliver. And what this one gave me was about as much as I could hope for.

"Big. Lumpy. A van, or a station wagon, or one of those four-wheel-drive things for people who'd never consider an unpaved road."

That limited the possibilities to half the vehicles on the freeway.

The radio crackled. Again it wasn't for me. But I'd used up the time I'd normally have spent at lunch. I had to wrap up here and get back to my beat. "Was Ott alone?"

"No. Someone was driving."

"What did that person look like?"

"Dunno."

"Come on, don't start that now."

"No, listen, this is the truth. I was across the street, and I just saw this blur of pus yellow and looked up, and there was Ott getting into the van or whatever. Well, really what I saw was mostly his butt. It was on the other side of the street—Telegraph—did I say that? Then a bus pulls by in the near lane. I'm lucky to've spotted him."

"What was he wearing?"

"Ott? Yellow—"

"No, the other guy." To say Ott was attired in yellow was akin to announcing the fog rolls in at 4:00 P.M. here or grass is brown by August. Ott wears only yellows; he shops only at the Goodwill and Salvation Army, which means he has a remarkable collection of garments other people can no longer bring themselves to wear. It's only through knowing him that I realized how popular mustard polyester was in years gone by.

"All I saw was a sleeve. Dark. Loose, like a coat, not a sweater."

Amazing how much they remember when they've just got finished swearing they couldn't have seen anything. "So how did you come to have Ott's car key?"

"I did some work for him."

Ott had gofers from time to time, amicable transients not on drugs or with axes of their own to grind were his employees of choice. "The key?"

"I got it out of his file drawer."

My breath caught; this was worse than I'd imagined. "He left his files unlocked?"

"He must have left in a hurry. 'Cause the dead bolt on his office door was off. I mean, I just walked up after I saw him. I thought about—well, never mind about that—but when I got to his office, I walked right in."

Which meant Kidd had already helped himself to the keys to Ott's office and his files. But I ignored that for the moment. Because the idea of compulsive, anal Herman Ott walking out of his office without locking it stopped me cold. Ott could be carted out by the paramedics and he'd stop to double lock. Only with a gun to his head . . . I stared at Kidd. "Why didn't you just spend the night there?" It came out more sarcastically than I'd intended, and for a moment I assumed Kidd's shocked expression was in reaction to that.

"I thought about it," he said. "But, well, the place is not a palace. I mean my standards aren't high, but—" He shuddered. "I mean the only place to sleep is on the desk, exposed like a dead fish in front of the door. If anyone burst in . . ."

"And so you opted for the backseat of a Studebaker?"

My skepticism could have stopped him cold. But Kidd was a Scheherazade of the transient set, and he'd probably been on his end of the questioning as long as I'd been on mine. The edge of the serape dangled by his hand, and now he ran it between his fingers. "Actually, I'm glad you're asking. You know, he'd kill me if he thought I went to the cops, but the thing is I was really kind of worried about ol' Herman."

Worried didn't half cover it. I glanced at my watch. It was past time to be heading back to my beat. Instead I called in to the dispatcher, giving her my 10-20 (destination), and asking for Leonard, the beat officer, to meet me there.

Less than five minutes later, I left the car behind Leonard's in front of Ott's office. Ott always hated that; he figured we were out to besmirch his reputation.

I yanked open one of the double doors to Ott's building. The bulb in the lobby was out. The place was going downhill—again. It mirrored the socioeconomic state of the Avenue. Built in the twenties for fashionable offices, it had a double staircase, and its circular hallways had been ready to accommodate the rush of commerce. It must once have been a lovely building with its old open-grille elevator, but not so appealing that businesses stayed on Telegraph Avenue. And so began its decline. There were periods when the two-room office suites became illegal crash pads and the Ott Detective Agency was its most respectable tenant. Asian refugee families moved in, and the building improved. A gym followed on the top floor. The refugees prospered and moved on; the gym failed. Now Ott's floor housed a hodgepodge of cottage industries. Whether the proprietors were living in their cottages was a question I was glad I didn't have to deal with.

Ott's office was at the far corner of the third-floor hall. I came abreast of Leonard midway up the first flight of the once-grand double staircase.

On Telegraph Avenue Leonard is as much of a fixture as Ott. Gray-haired and shambling, he looks out of place in uniform. Suspects tend to dismiss him, and they tend to be sorry when they do. As we headed up the next staircase, I started to brief him on Kidd, but before I finished a sentence, he was shaking his head as if he already knew. "Seems, Leonard, that Kidd did a little low-level watch-out work for Ott. In Kidd's case it sounds like charity on Ott's part as much as need."

"Maybe Ott wasn't such a hot judge of character with this kid. Drugs create a lot of Mr. Hydes," Leonard said.

"You'd think Ott would know that. I'm inclined to believe Kidd, Leonard. He knew where Ott kept the car key."

"I'd believe Ott was forced before I'd picture him giving Kidd a tour of his hiding places."

We were rounding the landing toward the second flight of stairs. There were still tenants living illegally here, but fewer than were here a year ago, and the halls had the night-empty feeling of an office building. As we rounded the second landing and headed down Ott's hall, I was five steps ahead of Leonard.

"Smith, what's your rush? So Ott goes off in a car. A case could have taken him out of town. He wouldn't much like leaving Berkeley, but it's the logical explanation."

"And you think he'd leave his dead bolt off?"

"*That's* the reason you got me risking a heart attack? The guy hasn't dead-bolted his door!" Leonard was panting, but still, he edged in front of me. This was his beat. "Or Kidd *says* he didn't dead-bolt it."

Before I could answer, the smell hit us: urine, shit, blood, decay.

Leonard tried the doorknob. Of course it didn't open.

I pulled out my baton and smashed its end through the *O* on the OTT DETECTIVE AGENCY sign. The opaque glass held for a moment, then sprayed like white fireworks.

I reached through and opened the door.

The body was inside.

CHAPTER 8

I DON'T KNOW WHETHER I was more relieved or shocked. The body lying dead in the doorway between Herman Ott's office and back room was not Herman Ott. It was Bryant Hemming. And he'd been dead awhile. There was what appeared to be an entry wound in his chest.

I didn't let myself think of Bryant Hemming alive —not now.

Automatically Leonard and I moved back into the hall, and Leonard called in a DBF (dead body found). Chances were the killer was long gone, but you can't be sure. I didn't want my headstone to say: "Dumb Cop Assumed Everything Was Fine."

"I'll lead," I said. "I know the layout."

Leonard nodded and covered me as I moved back into the two-room suite. The nauseating smell of death struck me again; I blocked out all speculative thoughts of it, and of my reaction to it, and concentrated on the search. I surveyed Ott's office: no closet, three tall file cabinets, big old wooden desk with chairs on either side. I edged around the office, keeping my back to the wall, till I could see under the desk. Nothing. Not even dust balls.

"Window?" Leonard said.

"Faces the air shaft. Probably hasn't been opened since V-E Day. Hasn't been washed since the Great War."

I had to step over the body to get into the other room, Ott's bedroom. "Doesn't have a closet."

"Jeez, Smith, it *is* a closet."

What it looked like was the box at the bottom of the laundry chute. Clothes, and blankets, and towels, cloth items I couldn't classify formed a compost on the floor. Bookcases, overflowing with newspapers, magazines, cups, dishes, and paper bags, covered three walls, and one floor-to-ceiling bookcase jutted in the room next to the sprung lounge chair in which I assumed Ott slept. (Or maybe he just nested in the clutter on the floor.) Under the window was a hot plate, and under it a cabinet holding tea, sugar, instant coffee, and three boxes of caramel wafers. "The room's okay, Leonard. It's emp—unpeopled."

I took a shallow breath and looked down at Bryant Hemming.

Bryant Hemming was a collage of the colors of death, all shaded with sepia as if to remind us that he was already part of the past. The chest wound was just to the left of his sternum, a shot right into the heart. Blood was caked around it, but not much. His heart would have stopped immediately, pulsing no more blood back out of the hole.

"Jeez, Smith, he looks like he's doing some kind of relaxation technique, straight out on his back like that," Leonard said.

Death had swollen Hemming's features into a cruel parody of the eager face that had glowed as he had mediated the hardest case of the year. But still, there was something about his half-open mouth, the angry creases between the brows that death hadn't eased. "He looks not so much frightened as, well, offended."

" 'How could this be happening to a good guy like me,' huh, Smith?"

I nodded. It was a reasonable question. One that Homicide Detail would be asking a lot. I edged around Hemming back into the office room and wrote down our time of arrival on the scene. In a few minutes Ott's little office would be jammed with personnel: scene supervisor, Homicide detectives, ID tech, and later, when we were through with the body, the coroner. We'd be knocking on doors on every floor in the building, rousting the tenants who didn't officially live here, who would be more worried about covering their housing violations than a neighbor's demise. Maybe I'd be interviewing them; more likely I'd be here answering questions.

Leonard moved to the wall of the office, as far from the corpse as space allowed. "So whadda you think, Smith? Hemming was here in the office, he cops to it that the bad guy's gonna shoot him, and he starts backing into the bedroom?"

"Bad choice," I said, realizing it was something of an understatement. "Why not head for the hallway?"

"Maybe he didn't know the bedroom wasn't gonna let him escape. Maybe he figures he can get inside and slam the door. Maybe he sees the door out to the hallway, figures it's like a back door and he can zip out. Or maybe he panics and doesn't think." Leonard was a big proponent of "the average crook is not bright" theory. And "the small-time crook is not bright big time."

"Hemming was on his TV show Sunday, and,

Leonard, the guy relished going headfirst into conflict. He's a big guy. I don't see him panicking or backing away. His flaw would be being too sure he could deal with any problem."

"You don't mediate with a murderer."

"Yeah, but maybe the other guy wasn't a murderer then, not till it was too late for Hemming. If Hemming had talked him down, what a great story he'd have to take to Washington. Think of the triumph."

"Or, Smith," Leonard said without missing a beat, "Hemming could have been in the bedroom when the killer walked in and startled him."

"Why would he be in there? Anything could be living under that clutter. Could be so many generations of mice they see themselves as the landed gentry."

Leonard peered into the room, looking for an answer. But it was Hemming's feet that gave it to me. "Leonard, I've seen Ott walk across that room. He shuffled, because even he couldn't be sure what was at the bottom of his clutter—a sticky remnant of yesterday's lunch or a slick magazine that could send him flying. And by the time Ott made it from hot plate to chair, he looked like he'd been trudging through seaweed. Bryant Hemming could never have made it through that morass unflagged, certainly not if he were moving in panic."

Leonard moved back to the far side of Ott's desk. It was useless; there was no way to get away from the sight of Bryant Hemming's body, much less the smell of it, in this small office. Leonard glanced longingly at the bare desk but didn't take the chance of sitting on it. A shiny surface like that was a natural for prints. If the killer were one of Ott's clients, he might have balanced his butt on the edge of the desk and put a hand back onto the wood to push himself up. I'd done it plenty of times myself, mostly because it infuriated Ott. Maybe Bryant Hemming himself had perched there. But why? "Leonard, did Bryant Hemming even know Herman Ott?"

Leonard stood peering out the dirt-caked window, as if the air shaft held the answer, as if he could see the air shaft. "Bad luck, bad judgment, take your pick. Maybe Hemming was too cocky to keep an eye on Ott." His acid tone could have etched the glass. He made no move to turn toward me even when I didn't answer.

I'd forgotten—or momentarily chosen to forget— how much everyone else on the force hated Ott.

"Chances are they shared clients." An olive branch he was offering me.

I snapped it up. "Of course! Serenity Kaetz and Brother Cyril. Either one could be Ott's client. But why would Bryant Hemming come here? The man was just about to leave for a whole new life in Washington. He said on the news that he was flying out Sunday night. He'd barely have time to swing by here on the way to the airport. If he had one stop to make, why Herman Ott?"

"If that stop was voluntary, Smith."

I looked back at Hemming. In death he was bear-like; he'd been a big guy, a guy in good shape. "It would have taken a sizable person to force him. Or a weapon. But that still leaves the question why here. Why would anyone abduct him and bring him to Herman Ott's office?"

"Because, Smith," Leonard said with the kind of sigh I'd heard him use with particularly zonked-out suspects, "Herman Ott had something on him. Ott called him here. And Ott killed him."

I stared at Leonard. He knew the Avenue scene better than anyone. Merchants confided in him, old rads remembered him from college. He'd been on Beat 6 so long that he blended into the walls transients sat against as they begged for spare change. Leonard was honest, fair, and committed to Telegraph and making it an avenue everyone could enjoy. He was, in his way, the departmental equivalent of Ott. Maybe that was the problem. But while there was a certain respect between the two men, they didn't like each other, and as if looking into the depths of their own souls and the secrets they'd managed to conceal, they didn't trust each other. "Leonard, you don't think—"

"Yeah, I think, Smith. Ott makes a big thing about his code of ethics. Gets on his high horse about not talking with us, using us, lying to us, setting us up and being so damned righteous about it he's lucky no one's taken *him* out in here. Well, okay, I don't like it, but I understand it. We've all got codes. But you know what the other side of those codes is?"

"What?"

"Prices. And we've all got those too."

"Are you saying you can be bought, Leonard?"

"Oh, yeah. Just not cheap. I go for more than anyone on Telegraph or in Berkeley's gonna pay for a beat cop pushing fifty. A lot more."

"And me? You're saying I'd sell out too?"

"Maybe not for money." He turned toward me, his brown eyes sharp. "Would you sell out if it meant Howard's life? Or for principle? Maybe that's your Achilles' heel, Smith. Yeah, if you sold your soul, it would be to defend a principle or a right. A small price to pay to lose your reputation if it meant preserving freedom in Berkeley, right?"

I laughed uncomfortably. "A little melodramatic, Leonard. Burning at stakes and witch dunking have been passé for centuries."

"But you admit I'm right, Smith?"

"I don't know."

"I'll take that as a yes. And if I've got my price, and you've got yours, and we've sworn to uphold the law, of course Herman Ott has his."

Suddenly the smell of death seemed stronger, murkier, and unavoidable. I looked past Bryant Hemming's body into the cluttered room in which Herman Ott had lived for at least twenty years. "If Ott sold out, he'd be living better." Before the protest was out of my mouth, I knew the answer.

"Ott wouldn't have sold out for money. My guess is it would be for something even we wouldn't think of. But the bottom line is it doesn't matter what I think or what you think. Ott's missing, and there's a corpse in his office. Let me give you some advice, Smith. You're a friend of Ott's; it's not to your credit, but there it is. If you're any kind of friend, you'll get him to turn himself in before the coroner's got Hemming's body out of here."

I shook my head. "If I knew where Ott was, I wouldn't be here tonight."

Leonard shrugged.

Leonard was right: Ott needed to be found. I glanced around the office. In a couple of minutes the room would be packed and I'd be in the hall. Carefully I opened Ott's desk drawer and, using the eraser end of a pencil, shifted the papers in there. But there was no calendar, no address book. I tried the side drawers. The top one held a copy of the California penal code. The middle one was devoted to INS regulations. The bottom file drawer must have had twenty manila folders.

"How typical of Ott!"

"What?" Leonard had opened the door a crack and appeared to be peering out; at least his nose was to the crack.

"Not one folder's got a name. They're all numbered."

"Is there a master list?"

"In his head." I lifted a file out. Inside were sheets of lined paper, filled with notes in Ott's tiny scrawl. I flipped from page to page. "Lots of short reports. Years apart. Here's one on the resale of stolen T-shirts from a vendor's table on the Avenue and another on vandalism to display tables. Doesn't look like there's anything major, but there's no name or address on the file."

"Must be a regular customer."

I nodded, replacing the file. "And Ott'd know how to reach him."

I plucked another file. "Pot thefts."

Leonard laughed. "Ott is hard up. Even we give marijuana low priority."

"No, not drugs. Flowerpots. And some kind of chemicals, missing along with the pots. And no name or address."

Outside, footsteps resounded on the stairs.

Leonard moved back, opened the door. The draft wafted under Ott's big desk and tossed an eight-by-eleven sheet, a printout of a newspaper article, onto my foot. I scanned the sheet. There was no header, nothing to suggest which newspaper had been copied.

Historical Review Subject Chosen: Famous Mine Case Disinterred. Mediation to be tried this time.

At a meeting of the Historical Society last Thursday board members J. Reynolds Remington, Martin A. Burbacher, Christian Jensen III, Devlin P. O'Malley, Dr. Thomas Ashford Everett, Eldridge Everett, Cornelius E. Whipple, and Kyle Lovington Jones reviewed the records of suitable local cases for the third annual historical review to be presented this next spring in the community meeting hall at City Hall. It was decided that the

Presumably the article continued on a following page, but that was a page I didn't have. I bent, eyed Ott's floor in all directions. It offered no other sheet.

"Looks like Hemming brought it himself," I said.

But Leonard's attention was already on the hallway.

I turned the sheet over. Blank. I read it again and wondered why the printer couldn't have started at the top of the page so the entire article fitted on it. So much for the benefits of technology.

"Smith!"

I glanced up at Inspector Doyle, my old boss from Homicide Detail.

"Jesus, Mary, and Joseph. Smith! I guess it's no surprise to find you here in Herman Ott's office. So the little rat finally bought it, huh?"

"No, not Ott, Inspector. Bryant Hemming."

"In Ott's office? Where's Ott?"

I shrugged. "Out. No sign of him."

Doyle sighed. "Isn't it just like the little rat? Leaves a corpse in his office, hightails out, and holes up. And how many man-hours'll he eat up till we dig him out?"

"Aren't you talking 'scenario before evidence' here?"

He didn't answer, a tacit yes. "Well, Smith, you can go on back to patrol."

That would have been the safe thing to do, the smart career move. I glanced at Ott's desk, seeing not its clean surface but remnants of the sparrings he and I had had over the years, many I'd lost, some I'd won, but none I'd left without baring bits of Ott he wouldn't otherwise have exposed. Encounters like Sunday afternoon's that had bared the "thing" Ott couldn't bring himself to reveal. He wouldn't tell me what it was, wouldn't—or couldn't—return my calls, and now a man was dead in his office. I didn't know whether my words came from outrage at Ott, or worry, or just plain foolhardiness. "Inspector, no one knows Ott as well as I do."

"You saying you can find him, Smith?" Before I could answer, he said, "Well, then, you go ahead."

CHAPTER 9

I GOT INSPECTOR DOYLE'S OKAY to get back into Ott's office after Raksen, the ID tech, had finished. Ott had been in this office since he left college a quarter of a century ago. The walls here had to be a fingerprint archive of the Berkeley left. When he walked in here, Raksen would be in heaven. He would dust every surface; left unleashed, he would turn the office and its contents black.

But print dust was the least of Ott's problems. I made my way out into the hallway, through a knot of off-duty officers. The garden-variety murder scene is no great draw, but one in the office of the biggest pain-in-the-ass private eye in town is box-office magic. I had just hit the street when I spotted Jason Figueroa leaping from the door of a press van. It said a lot that he had beaten print reporters, particularly the undergraduate from the *Daily Californian* who probably lived in a dorm a couple of blocks away. I moved on before Figueroa spotted me.

In an hour a medical examiner would have eyeballed Hemming and given Inspector Doyle a rough estimate of the time of death. Ott's stuffy office, in a building in which the heat had been turned off for the summer in 1954, provided as controlled conditions you're likely to find outside. The medical examiner would have no trouble giving us the murderer's window of opportunity. And when he did, I needed to know if Ott had still been here in Berkeley to look through it. Or if he'd clambered into that dark sedan before then.

I needed Charles Edward Kidd to be a lot more specific than he'd been before. I headed to Ott's car again; perhaps Kidd figured that having found him there once, I would cross it off my list. But, alas, he wasn't that naive. I called in to the university police with a description of Kidd. The campus, with its hillocks and knolls, stream banks and undersides of bridges, its outside stairwells and protected spaces between shrubs and building walls, provided a myriad of lurking spots. I drove on around People's Park, the focus of decades of demonstrations. It was empty now; the nocturnal curfew prevailed, and it would take a more savvy lurker than Kidd to hide in there. I tried the familiar spots, behind shops, apartments, churches. No Kidd.

I tried to see through his eyes. I think better in proximity to liquid. The shower's best, but on the go, a latte's a close second. I got the latte from the Med and stood outside, with the wind fingering my short hair, the fog slipping its icy mitten around my neck. Kidd was bright; he prided himself on originality. He was brash, impatient; he'd make enemies. No wonder he wasn't in the normal hiding places. He'd already chosen one unusual sleeping spot tonight, found because of his insider knowledge of Ott. What else, where else—

I gulped another mouthful of coffee, put a lid on the latte, swung back into the car, and beelined up

Telegraph to the street below Ott's building. If you can't drive with a full cup of hot coffee, you've got no business being a cop. I pulled up, took another swallow, and called the dispatcher.

"This is Adam sixteen. My ten-twenty's Channing below Tele. I'm headed into the alley behind the Tele buildings."

"Ten-four."

"Ten-four."

In the thirty yards between Telegraph and the alley I spotted two guys scrunched up in dim doorways; one who might have been eighteen looked, in sleep, as if he should have a teddy bear in the curl of his arm. By the alley a man sat against the building, a damp paper cup ever ready for spare change, his foot moving slowly to the beat of that different drummer who still tapped out the drug beat of decades gone by.

A pedestrian would have dismissed the alley altogether, assuming it was no more than a path to the garbage cans. I would have overlooked it myself if I hadn't chased more than one suspect down its narrow path.

I pulled out my flashlight, a hefty metal cylinder fourteen inches long. At least one officer had defended himself with one—and got suspended for a month without pay for improper use of equipment.

I recalled Leonard's assessment of the alley: "Getting through here's like crawling through someone's intestines." Had he been talking sudden sharp turns or garbage? If I'd asked, the answer would have been: Both. I aimed my light down and watched for rats. And tried to close my nose against the stink of urine. Twenty feet in I passed two nameless, numberless metal doors—business back doors, sealed tightly against break-ins. The scrapes on them indicated there had been some serious tries. Rats.

Another ten feet, and the alley angled left. The corner was thick with garbage, a compost of garlic, tomato sauce, and urine. A dash of stomach acid, and it could indeed have been an intestine.

The alley turned again, revealing a third metal door with a yellow sign above it, and once more till it ended abruptly at a brick wall. Instinctively I stepped back and flashed the light down. The stench here was less intense, the garbage had been swept away, and huddled in the corner of this poor man's cul-de-sac was Charles Edward Kidd.

He looked up, his face knotted in annoyance. Not anger, or the fear we often see, but the look of a smart guy who's lost a game he thought he'd won.

"Oh, it's you," he said, brushing off his serape as he eased to his feet. "How'd you find me?"

I looked up at the windows two floors above us. "I've been in Ott's office too." But if I hadn't been a police officer, I'd never have bothered looking out Ott's dirt-mottled windows. I had, of course, and noted that the hole outside appeared to be an air shaft. Kidd had gone to some effort to discover otherwise. A good little observer, he.

"I need to talk to you." I added, "I'll take you to the station." His step was jauntier than mine as I followed him out of the alley. He didn't mind sleeping in garbage, he seemed to be saying. But *I* minded for him. I cringed at the thought of his taking this misstep into the quicksand of street life, so easy to sink into, so very hard to yank himself out of. I knew the odds, but still, I didn't want to believe that the open road led to this.

The first thing Kidd spotted in the squad room was the box of bagels left over from a class. "Those bagels over there . . . bribe me."

"I'm hoping you'll give me more information than a stale bagel will buy. But help yourself."

I seated him by the table where he would see officers rushing through, hear the copy machine's hum, smell the coffee brewing—the reminders of the normal life that could once again be his. I had run Kidd's name and birth date through files earlier and been surprised to find no mention of him. Very surprised. Now I poured a cup of coffee for him and one for myself and sat around the end of the table with him. "You saw Herman Ott getting into a dark car last night. What time was that?"

"Almost dusk." He opened his mouth like a baby bird and stuffed a prodigious portion of bagel inside. *Almost* dusk? Was that different from the *dusk* he'd indicated earlier? "But at what time?"

He shook his head in answer to my question.

"Think. What time?"

Still chewing, he pointed to his empty wrist. Finally he swallowed and said, "I don't do hours and minutes."

I gave up. "Well, we'll start from go, then. I know you want to help Herman Ott. Maybe you know more than you realize. How long were you working for him?"

He sipped at the weak coffee, scowled, and put the cup down. It made me think better of him. Hands still clasped on the cup like a crystal ball, he said, " 'Bout three weeks with Herman. But it was hardly full-time. He'd spot me on the street and say there was some errand he wanted me to run."

"Where did he send you?"

"Out for food. To pick up the *Daily Cal*, and the *Express*, and once *The New York Times*. The post office a buncha times. Sounds like nothing, but lemme tell you, you can kill a lot of time in line in the PO. It's not like they put on an extra clerk if it's busy."

"Did you notice the names on Ott's letters or packages?"

"Computer companies mostly. Herman's thinking of going on-line. He's not a man to go into a venture unprepared. When those catalogs start coming in, he'll have to move out his desk to make room."

I was amazed by this revelation about Ott. I'd known Herman Ott for nearly a decade, and the only piece of electronic equipment in his office was an answering machine. He used that, presumably, so he'd know what calls he was not going to bother to answer. As for computers, Ott was a computer network unto himself. No apartment was burgled near Telegraph without Ott's hearing, no corpse cold before he knew. I waited till Kidd sawed through the remainder of the bagel and asked, "Did he send anything to an individual or organization?"

"You mean like the International Kidnap Club?"

"Exactly. Or Harry Houdini the Third."

"Nah. And don't think I didn't look all that time I was in the PO line. Old Herman's no fool. I coulda promised I wouldn't peek, but it wouldn't've mattered. No way I wasn't going to see where those envelopes were going."

"Why didn't he just have you drop them in the box?"

"Probably would've. But he was sending me for stamps."

"Every time?" Ott's business may have been marginal, but he'd been there for a quarter century. He should have had the confidence to buy more than one book of stamps at a time.

"He wouldn't use the flags. Didn't like the flowers. Wouldn't paste a memorial for any general or admiral on his letters. Animals were okay. There was a bird commemorative he went crazy over. State stamps he had to think about. Like Minnesota was fine, and Massachusetts. North Carolina he considered because of all the artists and writers, but he couldn't bring himself to use it. Jesse Helms's state, you know."

I laughed. "And people think it's easy to be an old rad. Did he have any other state preferences?"

"Like the 'Hideout State'? No. The post office only puts out commemorative ones now and then." He leaned back, a share-me smirk on his mouth—as if he were ready to offer a bit more free advice. Or keep it to himself.

"Did you go to the library for him?"

"No."

"Call the newspaper morgues?"

"No."

"Did you get any information on mines or mining?"

"No."

"Was he getting any computer printouts from other sources? Newspaper articles from the Internet?"

"Not that I know of."

"Did he have any clients in the office while you were there?"

"Nope." He pulled the edge of the serape in front of him till the fabric was taut and sat staring at it as if the pattern of colors would reveal the truth. At the far end of the table one of the guys from evening watch settled in to write up a report. Behind their double window one of the swing shift sergeants sat talking on the phone; the other perched atop his desk, back to us, reports in hand, ear cocked automatically toward his shoulder radio. Kidd released the red cotton. "Well, Ott may have had one or two clients come in. I was hardly there all the time. You can't exactly tell who's a client and who's just wandered into the building to get warm. But I never saw an ashtray or a scarf or anything around that Herman wouldn't have himself. His clients, you know they're more likely to stroll in late. I mean, Herman's there all the time. He sleeps late. I mean, I lost my last job because I was late so often, and with Herman I woke *him* up a couple times."

"So are you saying he scheduled meetings in the middle of the night?" As soon as the words were out, I felt foolish. *Schedule* was such a formal word for Ott's operation.

"Well, actually, yeah. This one guy goes to some group that chants at four A.M. Herman saw him on his way there."

"Do you know what he came for?"

"Wanted Herman to check out his incense importer. He was worried he was breathing in unholy pesticides." Kidd's smirk widened into a grin. "If you're poisoned from burning sandalwood and malathion, do you get a free ride into the next life? Or just the assurance your corpse will be free from Mediterranean fruit flies? I asked Herman but . . ."

"I know. He hates the idea of pesticides. Besides, he doesn't have a sense of humor."

"Particularly about his clients. He almost fired me over that."

"Because you laughed?"

"No. Because I talked about the client, even to him."

I nodded. "Did anyone else stop by? Friends, relatives?"

"Does Ott have relatives?"

It was an odd concept. I couldn't really picture him with friends, much less relatives. What would he do with them if he had them? I could hardly imagine Ott taking a couple of nephews to the A's game. "So no one came by?"

"Right."

"What about Brother Cyril? You know who he is, don't you? Did you see Ott with him or his followers?"

"Ott? You're kidding, right?"

"He had a little tin cross not an inch long. Bottom comes to a point, like a sword. Did he ever show it to you?"

"Ott? A cross? You gotta be kidding."

Exactly what I would have said if I hadn't asked the question. Still, I wondered . . . "How about on the street? Who did he meet there?"

Kid thrust back in his chair. "You want me to tell you everyone Herman Ott talked to on the street? We'll be here till next month. Or would if I knew folks here well enough to remember one from the other. I can tell you there's not a guy sitting on the sidewalk he doesn't know."

"Did any contact strike you as unusual?"

He peered at the serape threads again. Finally he looked up, his dark eyes narrowed in concern. "I've thought about that: Was there something I should have spotted? But there's no way to say. Herman didn't stop and talk to everyone on the Avenue, but it was like he could have if he'd wanted to."

"What about Serenity Kaetz? She sells jewelry on the street."

"Maybe. I don't know."

"Did you see him with a big clean-cut guy in his thirties, with brown hair?"

"No."

"Are you sure?"

"No. That's what I'm telling you. I can't be sure. But clean-cut . . . I doubt it."

"Does the name Bryant Hemming ring a bell?"

"No." For the first time his shoulders stiffened.

"Are you sure? Give it a little thought."

"Why? Why is this guy so important?"

I watched Kidd's face as I said, "Because he's dead. Because his corpse was in Herman Ott's office." Then I added, "But you knew that, didn't you?" By now everyone on Telegraph would know.

He plunged the last piece of bagel into his mouth.

"Is that a yes?"

He nodded.

"So, Mr. Kidd, you said you saw Herman Ott get into a van or station wagon or RV last night. And then what?"

He was still chewing, a whole lot more slowly than on previous bites.

"Here's what I'm guessing you did. You went up to Ott's office to—"

"No!"

"Why not? Why wouldn't you do that? It's a whole lot better than sleeping in the car."

"Ott would've killed me if he found out I've got a—"

"A key?"

"Yeah, well . . ."

If he thought Ott hadn't figured that out, he didn't know Ott as well as I'd assumed he did. Ott knew his gofers kept keys; when he started out as an assistant to the elderly detective he eventually replaced, he'd been profligate with keys. He'd told me that himself once. He knew keys to his office floated around the Avenue; he knew his lock could be picked. That's the reason he used his dead bolt.

And the reason it would be left off by someone who had only his door key. I don't know if Kidd came to that conclusion too, but he said, "Listen, you don't think that I . . . I mean, I didn't even know the guy who bought it. I mean, listen, I had a place to crash last night; there was no reason for me to go to Ott's anyway."

I let a moment pass before I said, "I've just asked you to come here as a witness. You're free to go anytime. I'm not accusing you of anything now." All that was true, but the last word hung in the air between us.

I waited another moment, leaned both elbows on the desk, and looked straight at Charles Kidd. "Ott's in a bind here. I don't think he killed Bryant Hemming either. But every moment he's missing he looks more suspicious. You're his friend. Help me find him. Think. Did Brother Cyril call Ott? Did Bryant Hemming call him? Did Ott mention either of them? Did anyone else talk about him?"

He stared at the serape, his hand knotted around the fabric. Finally he shook his head. "I don't remember those names, but that doesn't mean Ott didn't know the guys. Why don't you ask them?"

I tried coming in from a different angle. "What did you do in the office? File things?"

"No."

"Did you make any calls for him?"

"Nope."

"Is there anything else you can think of?" When he shook his head, I said, "Weren't you ever in the office alone? Didn't the man even go to the bathroom?"

"Well, yeah, but it's not like I rooted through his files."

I didn't say, "But you did copy his key."

"Wait. I did answer the phone a couple times."

"Do you remember—"

"Oh, yeah. AT and T offered Herman airline miles. You know Herman hates to fly. Then MCI—"

I almost laughed. I could just picture the old rads around town, a couple of inmates in Santa Rita, the guys in the transient hotels sauntering down the hall to the phone and hearing, "Herman Ott has listed you among his family and friends for a phone discount." "No personal calls?"

He concentrated on weaving his fingers through the serape fringe, ignoring the fact that the threads were too short to house digits. "Once I came in when he was on the phone with some guy named Bill Loon."

"Who's he?"

"Dunno."

"How do you spell the last name? Lewin? Louwen? Or Loon, like the bird?"

The serape flew out of his hands; he guffawed.

"Do you really know Ott or are you shitting me? I walk in on that conversation. Ott glares at me like I'm a fcd cavesdropping. I back out into the hall so fast I just about trip over the doorsill. Do you think I came back in and asked for a spelling? But look, there was one other call." A grin crept onto Kidd's face. I'd seen Howard with that same "gotcha" expression. "Personal. From the blush on Ott's face, I'd guess it was damned personal."

"Really?" I said, amazed. "Did you get a name?"

"Oh, yeah. And I remember it because it didn't fit the voice. The woman had one of those gravelly voices, like maybe she'd smoked years back or maybe she'd just *lived* years back. Like she was old, I mean." He grinned. "You want this a lot, don't you? How much? I mean all advice isn't free."

My hands curled into fists. I shoved them under the desk.

His grin widened. "Okay. The old lady was named Daisy. Daisy Culligan."

The name meant nothing to me. But it was unusual enough to run through files without a date of birth. No Daisy Culligan had been arrested in Alameda County, had an outstanding warrant in California or the rest of the nation, or had contacted our department to report a theft or complain about a neighbor's stereo. Nothing.

But there in the phone book was CULLIGAN D. And the address listed was in the Berkeley hills, hardly one I would have expected for an inamorata of Herman Ott's.

CHAPTER 10

IT WAS LATE TO BE calling an "old lady"—close to midnight—but Daisy Culligan didn't sound sleepy, and she didn't sound antiquated. She seemed delighted with the prospect of a visit and more delighted yet that it was to be from a police officer.

"Leave your red and blue lights on. I do like to intrigue the neighbors."

"I'll be by in a few minutes, but I can't promise flashing decorations."

I dropped Kidd up at Telegraph, near one of the shelters I knew he wouldn't use, and popped into Ott's office to give Doyle an update and check when the scene would be clear.

I took the crowd outside by surprise when I raced into the building. Leaving it was like walking into a wall. Jason Figueroa and his cameraman were at the front of a pack of new people. I didn't stop to note faces, but Figueroa knew mine. The camera light glazed my face. "Officer Smith, what can you tell us about Bryant Hemming's murder?"

"Ask the press officer."

"Execution style?"

It wasn't, but I didn't stop to illuminate him on that.

"Hemming was all set to go to Washington and mediate between powerful forces who could have a lot to lose, right?"

I kept moving, the camera operator polkaing alongside. Figueroa popped in front of me. "Officer, this is an important story. Bay Area viewers are very distressed about Bryant Hemming's murder. They're anxious to know what's being done to find the man . . . or *men* . . . who slew him. What leads are you pursuing?"

"Gosh, isn't that what the Channel Five guys asked an hour ago?" I said straight-faced. The camera light left my face mid-sentence, and as I loped into the dark sidewalk beyond, I could hear Figueroa talking in news cadence about breaking in with the latest developments.

Had Bryant Hemming still been alive, he would have delighted in reminding Figueroa that the average viewer hates having his program commandeered by a teaser for the next newscast. But alas, Hemming wasn't alive, and Figueroa had too much invested in Hemming to let go.

I couldn't park outside Daisy Culligan's house, with my lights flashing or not. Daisy Culligan's address was not on a street but on one of Berkeley's paths that bisect the long blocks of north Berkeley.

There are paths all over town and staircases cutting from street to street in the hills, but north Berkeley is the only section in which the paths actually were part of the street plan when the development was built after the San Francisco earthquake of 1906. Then the selling point was that the new homeowner could leave his car for the little woman and stroll down the paths to the Alameda, catch the streetcar to the ferry, and on to the office in San Francisco.

The streetcars are long gone, the ferry resurrected only briefly after the Bay Bridge collapsed in the Loma Prieta earthquake, and the paths are used not by harried commuters but by hill dwellers on their way to Peet's, or on their way home caffè latte cup in hand.

When I realized which path was Daisy Culligan's, I considered calling Inspector Doyle and removing my-self from Ott Patrol. I thought I knew the man, his ples, the circles in which he traveled. If Daisy an, the lovebird of his lustful hopes, the woman raised a blush to his sallow cheeks, could afford ve *here*, then the real Herman Ott had eluded me these years.

The houses on either side of the path were as close Berkeley comes to mansions—old, rambling places vith big windows, huge trees, and sloping, landscaped lawns dotted with boulders. Howard and I had walked over here a week ago on our day off, lattes in one hand, sesame bagels in the other. We had made our way up the large stones that served as steps, discussing what we'd save if we tripped—coffee, bagel, or butt. Even in daylight the speculation hadn't been entirely frivolous, and now, illumined only by the lawn lan-terns and my flashlight, the weaving path was treach-erous.

I was halfway up when I spotted a plump gray-haired woman in sweatshirt and jeans. "Over here. Watch your step. Right in here," she said, leading me to an open door with her flashlight.

I smiled with relief. Ott's friend Daisy Culligan

was no matron of the moneyed establishment. The house could have had six bedrooms, a study, an au pair suite, but the space that Daisy Culligan occupied must have been the maid's quarters. A nine-by-twelve rug would nearly have covered the floor here if she had had one, but she didn't. No rug, nor much else. It was a room consciously intended to be bare. But as is the case with small living spaces, intentions had been shoved out by the clutter of necessity. Daisy Culligan had papers stacked on each step of the circular staircase as if it were an ascending file drawer. The white futon chairs in front of the fireplace held mail, days of it. Next to one old *New Yorker* magazines were stacked as high as the seat. The little teak table between the chairs, which must have been meant to hold a cup or two, sported one of those sandbox miniatures of Japanese Zen gardens given so the person who has everything can pretend to deal with nothingness.

"A gift," she said. "From a friend here in town. So it'll be a while before I can pack it off to the Goodwill." She scooped up the mail, deposited it on the *New Yorker*s. "Sit."

I shifted my flashlight hanging from the back of my belt and sat on the chair. "Herman Ott blushed when someone walked in on your call," I said, feeling a pang of betrayal of Ott.

"Did he now?" She plopped onto the other chair, pulled her round legs up to cross under her. She was not quite fat, but all comfortable circles—round eyes, ruddy cheeks, long, wiry gray curls, substantial breasts, and a gentle mound of stomach. She smiled like the Mona Lisa. "Herman Ott?"

"I've never seen Ott blush."

"And you're wondering why he'd get all worked up over an old broad like me, huh? Is there fire under the snow and all that crap?" She was watching me, ready to judge my reaction, still smiling.

It wasn't Daisy, it was Ott I couldn't imagine in the sack. But there was no professionally acceptable way to say that. I matched her smile. "Why did you call him?"

"Why are you asking?"

"Because he's missing. And his office door was unlocked." Or so Charles Kidd contended.

Her smile vanished, and I could tell from her expression she understood how dire a picture I'd painted. "I've known Herm since college; he was an undergraduate—"

"He was an undergraduate for a decade."

"I see you do know him. Yeah, Herm avoided graduation longer than cholesterol's been a villain. I was a teaching assistant around the time he realized that a degree in poli sci and philosophy wasn't going to lead to the kind of work that interested him."

"Which department were you in? Poli sci or Philosophy?"

She laughed. "Social work. It's gotten me where I am today."

I cocked an eyebrow.

"Self-employed, thank God." She picked up the tiny Japanese rake that belonged to the Zen garden and dragged it across the box, leaving deep gouges in the sand. "The welfare department destroys you. Occasionally you help someone, but mostly you fill out forms to justify your job, your superiors' jobs, and—" She'd caught the rake on the box edge. The whole thing clattered to the floor, spraying our feet with sand. "Shit. So much for the calming effect of that little gift. Well, I guess time hasn't cooled my passions enough."

I could see why Ott liked her. "So what was your connection to Ott?"

The smile returned to her round face. "We watched the soaps together. I should have known what it meant about us then. I loved to see all those problems that I didn't have to do anything about. And Herman, he liked to guess the deep, dark secrets. Every Friday after the show we'd go to Larry Blake's on the Avenue, have a burger, and Herman would make a guess at the cliffhanger. Who was the father of Tiffany's baby? Why was Lance hospitalized with no visitors allowed? A dread disease or a sex change? Mondays we'd see how he did. Tuesday we'd switch to a different soap, so I'd have new problems to not deal with, and the trends of the show wouldn't become too obvious for Herman."

I laughed, joining her. A bourgeois indulgence from the past, was that the cause of Ott's blush? "Is that all?"

"Surely it isn't material to your investigation now whether I slept with Herman a quarter century ago."

Probably it wasn't. I certainly couldn't make a case for pressing her. But, dammit, this was like not coming back for the Monday soap. I let the silence sit like a demanding pet. Daisy Culligan merely smiled; as a social worker she must have played this game too. Finally I asked, "Have you kept in touch all along?"

"No. Herman disappeared for a few years."

"Disappeared? When?"

"Right after he left college."

Ott had never bothered to graduate. He'd just dwindled away. "Where'd he go?"

"No one knows. No one, believe me. I tried to find out when he came back. If he'd had a secret like that in our soap days, I could have teased it out of him. But whatever he did those three years changed him. Or maybe he just got older. Whatever, he wasn't a cute little waif of a guy anymore. He was in the beginning stages of what he is now."

I picked up the fallen rake and fingered the tongs. "Where do you *think* he went?"

"That question intrigued me for years. I didn't meet with Herman, but you know how Berkeley is; you've always got more than one path of connection to a person. So I heard about him. Sometimes he was mentioned in the papers. A few people remembered him from before. But no one knows about that absence. I've done the sensible thing; I've given up. If you're smart, you will too."

"Sorry, I can't make that kind of promise. But tell me what other connection you have to Ott."

She opened and shut her lips, little fish pouts. Then she bounced up and headed up the circular stairs.

I took it as an invitation to follow. The room upstairs was half the size of the first, its floor covered with abandoned bedclothes and street clothes. Herman Ott could have been hidden under the mounds. "I see you and Herman have the same theory of housekeeping."

She shrugged awkwardly as people do when admitting a failing.

"When did you last see Ott's office?" I pressed.

She turned toward me. "Okay, okay. So maybe I

did have a little thing with Herman. It was years ago, and it was no big thing then."

"Did he give you a key?"

"What! Look, that was over twenty years ago. What possible difference—"

"I'm not here to cause you problems, Ms. Culligan. I just need to find Herman. And to get an idea how many copies of his keys are floating around. Three or three hundred?"

She moved around me and down the stairs and stood waiting at the bottom, hands on rounded hips. "He gave me a key, but what's the big deal? Herman Ott's well-being is hardly a top police priority. Yet it's after midnight, and here you are sniffing out his past." She moved toward the chairs, then changed her mind and stood looking out the window into the dark. "What's going on with Herman? Is he suspected of some crime?"

I considered my options and went with my read of her: She really wanted to help Herman. I motioned her back to the chairs and, when we'd both sat, said, "I have to ask you not to talk about this interview until we find Herman." When she nodded, I went on. "A man's body was found in Herman Ott's office."

"Really?" She was on the edge of her chair, waiting for the cliffhanger.

"I know Herman Ott. I respect him. I wouldn't say this to his face, but I care about him."

She smiled knowingly.

"But when there's a dead body in your office and you've disappeared, neither option is good. I don't see Herman Ott killing a man and walking away from his life here." But apparently he had disappeared before. I could tell from Daisy Culligan's face she was thinking the same thing. "A much more likely scenario is: He walked in on the killer, and the killer forced him into a vehicle and "

"And killed him."

"We don't know," I said, looking her in the eye. My chest was tight, my voice constricted; it was no act I was giving her. I swallowed hard. "Help me."

She sat pulling her stubby fingers over the back of her other hand. Her nails were clipped short, washed clean. She was swaying a bit and behind her, her shadowy reflection in the dark window wove side to side. "I didn't see him for years. Then early one Sunday morning a few years ago, I ran into him at Bolinas."

"On the beach?"

"The garage in town. His car—you know that old Studebaker—had broken down. So I gave him a lift back. After that every six months or so we'd go to Bolinas."

"What did you do together there?"

"Nothing *together*. I'd walk on the beach. Herman hated the ocean. Too harsh, too absolute. For him it was the marshes. He just liked walking there. I think it was because it was so utterly different from the rest of his life—no sidewalks, no crime, no political issues, just grass and birds, and, well, marsh. Afterward we'd meet at the garage and drive back. That's it."

"Did he talk about it?"

"No."

I could tell from the way she said it that the marsh was one of Ott's "denied" subjects. "Did you have the sense he was meeting someone?"

"No."

"Did he bring anything with him he didn't have

when he went home, or vice versa?" It was a long shot. If Ott had been after anything in the marsh, most likely it was information. If he'd paid for it, his wallet wouldn't be so much thinner as to garner notice.

She shook her head.

"How were these events arranged? Did you call him or he you?"

"He called, always. That does sound suspicious, doesn't it? And now that I think about it, there was a certain urgency when we drove out there. He always had to get there before sunrise or before dusk. And"—she reached out as if to hold my attention—"most times when we drove back, he was quiet, relaxed, tired, like he'd been up all night."

Knowing Ott, he probably had been.

"But a couple of times he was elated."

"Do you have any idea why?"

"None." She seemed to sink. The cushion, balanced over the edge of the one underneath, sagged. Daisy shifted back on the chair and refolded her legs. "I'd forgotten all that. There may be more I know. Ask me more. Tell me about the murder. Who's dead?"

"Okay, first tell me about the key. Do you still have it?"

"I don't know. Maybe packed away somewhere with everything else from 1970."

"When Herman gave it to you, did it seem like something special—"

"You mean, like 'I'll break my rule and make a copy just for you?' Hardly. It was more like we did with cars back then, like 'Sure, take my car; just make sure you put gas in it before you bring it back.

Here're the keys.' Romance wasn't . . . well, it wasn't Herm."

I nodded. I couldn't imagine otherwise.

"The murder," she prodded. "Come on, I'm dying to know who was killed."

"Bryant Hemming, the man who—"

"Oh, my God! Bryant?"

"You know him?"

"He's my ex-husband."

CHAPTER 11

THERE WAS BRANDY IN THE teak credenza. I poured it for her, and Daisy Culligan sat holding the glass, lifting it to her mouth but not drinking, as if she were too stunned to remember how to move her lips. Her eager round face seemed to have fallen, and her skin looked looser, older, pale. Tears rolled from the corners of her eyes. Instead of wiping them away, she lifted the glass with both her hands as if it were an offering to her grief, and sipped in a slow, steady rite, pausing only for that first burning swallow, till the brandy was half gone. "Bryant and I were together for nine years. I can't believe this. Why would anyone kill him? It's not fair. He'd come into the perfect job for him; he was doing important work, making a difference. . . . Dead?" She lifted the glass to her mouth again but barely swallowed.

"Bryant was on to something big," she continued. "He was all caught up in it." Her voice grew steadier as she spoke. " 'Look at these guys,' he'd say, 'these bombers and the ones who stalk into an office building with an AK forty-seven; they don't care about the people they kill. What got them started years ago was a post office line that's out the front door. It's the pervasive sense of getting the short end of the stick and looking over to see who snatched the big end and finding that face shielded behind layers of bureaucracy. No one's responsible; no one cares. Instead of apologizing all over the place, they're snotty. If I could just get in there in the beginning . . .' Bryant would say."

I could hear Bryant Hemming saying that; it was essentially what he'd said Sunday night. "When did he tell you all that?"

"Pretty much every time I've seen him since he settled in at ACC and hired an assistant. We've been divorced for five years, but we don't hate each other." A big tear rolled down her cheek, around her mouth, off her chin, and into the brandy glass. She lifted the glass, stared into it, shrugged, and finished the brandy. "Bryant was so caught up in it that it was easier not to try to cut him off. I practiced the age-old feminine technique: smiled and nodded—you can do that quite well from rhythm of the monologue—and planned menus." Now she did let out a laugh, a small one, cut short.

I smiled too. "Let the boys talk about themselves," I remembered my mother used to say. "They like that." By Bryant Hemming's definition of his mediation client—the perpetually ignored—it was surprising we girls from that era hadn't blown up every building in town. I said, "Why don't I make you some tea and we'll talk about him?"

She shifted off the chair. "I'll do that. It would ruin my credibility to let a civilian make me tea."

"A civilian?" I said lightly.

"No way you'd know. I'm not a big deal. But I *am* a cook. At the moment a low-fat cook. I used to be a low-cholesterol cook while that was in vogue." She'd walked by me, ducked behind the circular staircase and into the kitchen alcove, a white ash and enamel affair with pans hanging, spoons and spatulas poking out of thick ceramic holders, and electric gizmos on a shelf above the counter. And three shelves of cookbooks.

There's always a surreal quality to these postshock conversations when I am nudging the witness to talk, to ramble, to keep the channels open. Often nothing notable is said, but there have been times when the gray of the emotion-stripped rambling or purple histrionics has produced a case breaker.

"You have twice as many cookbooks as I do," I offered. Daisy Culligan of course would have no idea what a bizarre statement that was. Mine filled two boxes in the second bedroom at Howard's house. Gifts, all of them; every gift screaming a hope. That I would be a better wife than Nat Smith's aunts figured he was getting; that I would grow up and eat better than my mother had any reason to assume; that Deidre and Jeff would get a better meal the next time they ate at our house. I was delighted with each gift; Howard and I love cookbooks, the more exotic the better. We sit on the sofa, eating pizza or Thai takeout, reading the recipes aloud and making up alternate descriptions for scallops persillade, vegetable pansotti, or, Howard's favorite when he was in Vice, chanterelle tartlets.

But Daisy's books were grease-marked and lumpy-paged from use. Beneath them now she measured leaves or bark or twigs into a tea strainer. As I had hoped, she picked up the conversational thread. "I'm the ultimate home delivery kitchen. Gourmet dishes five days a week, prepared for the individual need and palate."

"How many clients do you have?"

"At the moment, seven. Two couples and three singles. Intense jobs, irregular schedules."

"And you create seven different dinners each night?" I asked in amazement.

"No, no. I don't make the meals to suit individuals; I find individuals to suit my meals. I've winnowed down the people till I've got seven with the same requirements." She poured the boiling water into a white pot. "They all *think* I'm planning just for them. They think they're getting a great deal. And in fact they are, but just not quite so special as they suppose." I felt sure another time she would have caught my eye and grinned; now her lips just widened momentarily. "Probably they wouldn't care; the snob value wouldn't matter at all."

But I could tell she didn't believe that. And, I suspected, her little deception amused her as much as the yuppie cachet appealed to her clients.

"The great thing is I set my own hours, deliver at my convenience, and days go by when I don't have to see a soul." She pulled a tray from beside a cabinet, put the tea equipment on it, and walked back into the living room.

The tea tray fitted the little table exactly. From our futon chairs we were just close enough to put our cups on the table without awkward turns of arm yet far enough to talk without the sense of sitting in each other's lap. For Daisy Culligan, I didn't imagine there were many of those days without a soul. I added milk and sugar to my tea, took a sip, and smiled approval.

I wanted to see Bryant Hemming through her eyes

and to see the coloring of those eyes I was looking through. Even then I wouldn't perceive the truth, just a slant on it. One thing you learn in police work is that there is no truth, just opinions. You aim to round up enough of those opinions, put them in their proper places, and see where they point. I let the silence expand as I plotted logistics.

"I know what you're thinking." Her voice was higher, tight, as if it had squeezed out through a fear-constricted neck. "How come a good-looking, successful guy married a woman so much older than he was, that's what you're thinking, isn't it?"

It wasn't. "Bryant was thirty-six, and you are?"

"Forty-eight." She lifted her chin challenging me. "It wasn't the age thing that caused our divorce. His life just changed."

I liked Daisy Culligan, liked her ability to be comfortable in two small rooms, her delight in the prospect of startling her neighbors with the police car. Why had she accepted the ad copy of youth? If a woman like her, in the city of the Gray Panthers, capitulated so totally . . . I could picture her and Bryant the day they married ten or so years ago. She would have been in her late thirties, strikingly lively with long, curly red hair, the spray of lines around those eager brown eyes tentative, and succulent rounds of breast and hip. And Bryant I pictured still searching for his adult form. "Age doesn't matter," they must have assured everyone. But they had been wrong. "His life changed. How so?"

"He came into the job he was born for. At ACC—the Arts and Creativity Council. ACC does two things: They've got a money fund, and they do mediation. Bryant started out mostly managing the money.

He was lucky with that. He didn't know much about money, and the truth is he didn't care. But he made a couple of environmentally sound investments that panned out, and all of a sudden he was a genius. A modest genius, but enough to get himself called a savvy money manager. A savvy money fish in a very small Berkeley pond."

"Like the biggest sailboat in the Berkeley lagoon, the kind that would be scuttled halfway across the bay?"

" 'Fraid so. But before he got into rough water, he started mediating, and he hit his stride. He was a natural. He could always see both sides. Life was a series of terrifying choices—door number one, door number two—and the one he rejected might have held the grand prize. So suddenly he's a real genius. He knows the mechanics of decision making intimately. He can explain a client's position better than the client can. And do the same for his adversary. Now there are no closed door ones and door twos. Both doors are open—"

"Daisy, people never give you the whole story—"

She almost smiled. "Bryant knew that. He said he'd sabotaged himself enough by ignoring issues in his own decisions. It's more complicated than that. But the point is, mediating freed him from indecision. It was as perfect a match as if my room here were on the cover of *Clutter* magazine." She smiled weakly.

I sipped at my tea. "So, how is it that his new job undermined your marriage?"

"Once he got on TV he was hooked. Public access should lead to cable, should lead to network. He needed to dress better, drive a new car, be seen in public as the public Bryant Hemming. He probably spent more on two new suits than he had on clothes for the entirety of our marriage. How could he remain the husband of the *Clutter* cover girl?"

"And so he left you?"

For the first time Daisy laughed. "No, no, I saw what was happening, and my choice was to keep him forever balanced between my world and the TV world or let him go on and do something important."

Oh, barf! I thought. Or, more graciously, *You insult me!* "Look, I've been through a divorce," I said. "Nobility doesn't enter into it. Things get worse and worse, but there's a last straw."

She fingered her cup, considering.

"Daisy, it's not a case of being disloyal to Bryant. He's dead. Murdered. Shot through the heart by someone who was as close to him as I am to you. I have to know what he was really like."

There was only half an inch of tea in her cup, but she drew out the swallowing of it for half a minute, deciding where her loyalty lay: with his image or the truth. "Okay. This was a couple of years ago. We'd been divorced for three years. He already was the 'mediator.' I was in the process of choosing between two restaurants; I'd do the take-out menus, set up the department, run it. Both deals included my investing in the restaurant—a lot of money for someone in my circumstances." She glanced over at me, and I nodded.

"One of Bryant's private mediations—before he started on TV—was between one of those restaurants, Milledge's, and a woman who had worked there setting up an operation a lot like mine. Some of her dishes were different from the menu fare, some the

same. The restaurant chefs wouldn't part with ingredients they thought they might need; if she brought
stuff in and they ran out, they'd nab hers for their in-
house dishes. Or they'd make entrées for the take-out
orders without all the ingredients, often *key* ingredients, like leaving the saffron out of the saffron rice.
Well, you know, customers may miss a lot, but they
don't mistake white for yellow. Actually she was lucky
there; where they really screwed her were the dishes
with less obvious omissions. Those the customers just
figured weren't very good because she wasn't a very
good cook. She came in pot au feu; she went out
leftovers in canned gravy. The mediation was about
her investment, the reputation she'd never get back.
Bryant didn't tell me about it."

"Are you sure Bryant knew you were considering
Milledge's? Did he know you'd be investing a lot of
money? That you could lose your reputation and your
career—"

"And end up doing take-out meals from my own
kitchen? I'd told him when I was still in the considering stages with Milledge's. And afterward, when we
had it out, he did what he always does when con-
fronted, he threw up a smoke screen, tried to divert
me, went into this big riff about his work and how
vital it was and all and how he just couldn't have revealed a client's confidence." She shook her head,
clearly still disbelieving. "At some level he really believed in magic: Blow enough smoke, and the problem will disappear behind it. But you know, all he'd
have had to do was say the restaurant was involved in
mediation, not even how. . . . But he couldn't, because he was the 'Mediator.' " She glanced at the pot

of tea, then, as if deciding the lukewarm liquid wouldn't make any difference, put down her empty cup. "That's when I realized I had ceased to be a part of his life. And the thing with Bryant was, the past is past."

"And the divorce settlement?"

"That was over and done with by then. Did I grab everything south of his balls? No. I took the car, a nice new Explorer; I could live in it if things got bad. And—oh, shit!"

"What!"

"I made the 'logical' decision. He was twelve years younger. So instead of emptying the coffers now, I took a percentage of his income and his retirement. Double shit! I really will have to live in the car." She grabbed the pot, refilled her cup, drank. "Look, I don't mean to sound—I mean, I cared about him; I'm devastated he's dead. But my own impending poverty isn't making it any better."

Was she saying, "His death has done me out of his retirement money, so of course *I* didn't kill him," or was the truth "I didn't consider the consequences before I killed him"?

I didn't want to think she had murdered Bryant. That made me assess her all the more sharply. Vengeance is a relentless motive; it can explain irrationality. She had the key to Ott's office. If she'd got Ott out of there without him using the dead bolt . . . She could have done that, I realized, seduced him away. Rare as the offer of passion was in Ott's life, if it came suddenly—passion *and* surprise—it could push mundane thoughts like locked doors out of Ott's mind. Then all Daisy had to do was call Bryant.

"What was Bryant doing in Herman Ott's office?" I asked, hoping for some shock value of my own.

But Daisy wasn't shocked. "Oh, that one's easy. He wanted to know what Herman Ott had found out about him."

CHAPTER 12

"How do you know Herman Ott was investigating Bryant?" I asked. "Did Bryant tell you?"

"Hardly. Herman's not that obvious." Daisy set her cup down with a clack. "Well, maybe he is. He called Roger Macalester, Bryant's assistant."

"And assumed he wouldn't tell Bryant?" Now there was a pregnant assumption.

"He could have. Roger's an old lefty. Herm could have pressured him, or guilted him, or had something on him from fifteen years ago. You know Herm."

I nodded. If Roger Macalester had been on the leftist scene, Ott would know his secrets and feel morally impelled to use them for his own investigation. Its subject could have been Bryant Hemming. Peering at the underbelly of the establishment guy: Now that screamed Ott.

Where would he get his data? That too was an easy one. Bryant Hemming may have been an Oxford cloth and jeans with pressed seams kind of guy, but the people he mediated between were not. Serenity Kaetz wouldn't get near an iron if her life depended on it, and if Brother Cyril saw an iron, he'd mistake it for a doorstop. Or a weapon.

But right here in front of me sat the crème de la

crème of detectives' sources, the subject's ex-wife, the disgruntled employee of the marital world. And she was Ott's old friend. "Let's see if this will help us find Herman. Who was he investigating Bryant for?" I asked as Daisy Culligan refilled our teacups.

"You know Herman," she said, tossing off my question, "he'd die before he'd reveal a client's name."

"Right, but you know Herman too." I sipped the tea. "And I'll bet you'd be curious, and you'd make it your business to find out." I took another sip. "Do I overestimate you?"

Daisy laughed. "You got me dead center. Here's what happened: Herman stopped by. Odd enough in itself. He hadn't called about Bolinas in almost a year. Other than that I never heard from him. Oh, I'd pass him on Telegraph now and then, once every few months, but it wasn't like we ran into each other at fund-raisers or 'did lunch.' I saw Roger Macalester at Chez Panisse last week, and I thought the world had come to an end, but if I'd seen Ott at someplace like that . . ." Her expression brought up the ludicrous picture of Herman Ott wearing one of his yellow polyester shirts, ordering the vegetables feuilleté with nasturtium butter at Chez Panisse. And the idea of Ott at a fund-raiser was unthinkable. I knew Ott as well as anyone, and I had no idea what cause would elicit his money, much less his presence, or even what he did with his free time.

"But then," Daisy went on, "he up and calls and invites himself over. Sits right in that chair where you are. Drinks tea. Complains that the Darjeeling Fancy I offered him wasn't Darjeeling Extra Fancy Se-limbong. Then he asks what I've been doing since we last saw each other." She put down her tea cup and leaned forward. "Now, I am not a fool. And in all that time analyzing the soaps with him, I learned how Herman's mind worked. (A) He wouldn't care what I'd been up to, and (B) he'd already know. 'So, Herm,' I say, 'you're investigating Bryant, right?' Well, you'd think I'd poked him in the stomach."

I could picture Ott flapping around as if he'd been pushed off his perch. The humiliation. I wished I could have been there to see it. "Blindsided," he had said smugly and more than once, "is what happens to sloppy detectives." "What did he do?"

The rougy tint of glee vanished from Daisy's face, and the skin around her eyes quivered as if unsure what expression to settle in. "He was so stunned he just sat there, like an animal caught in the headlights. Then he walked out."

Just as he had with me at the Claremont. "And you let him! How could you do that! Before you knew what he was looking for? Before you'd asked him why?" *What kind of woman are you?*

"That's the price of 'going with your feelings' and all that garbage. Afterward, of course, I got to where you are now. Then I scurried around trying to find out why Herm would be after Bryant. I called Margo Roehner—she's on the ACC board—she hadn't heard anything. Roger, at the office, was useless. I even tried the newspaper morgue." She shook her head. *"Nada."*

"You could have called Ott back." It was an accusation. I forced a smile.

"No, I couldn't. I'd stopped going with my feelings, but I couldn't bring myself to go against them, not that much. It would have galled me."

"So you called Bryant?"

"Before the restaurant perfidy I would have. But I thought: Fine, let Herman Ott stir up the dust around him. A little fuss wouldn't hurt Bryant. I figured I'd call Roger in a week, find out what'd happened, and we'd have a good laugh."

"And?"

"The week won't be up for another day."

I asked about Bill "Lewin." But Daisy just looked at me as if I were a loon. "Daisy, do you have any idea where Ott could have gone? Of his own volition or not? He got into a vehicle with someone Sunday night."

"Well, my van's out front. You can check it." Slowly she shook her head. "I can't imagine Herm leaving Berkeley. Where would he go? What would he do if he couldn't work?"

She'd hit that on the mark. If Herman Ott was free, he was still on the case. He'd know Bryant Hemming was dead and he'd be after him all the more. Assuming of course, that Daisy had been straight with me and Bryant's assistant had been straight with her, and Ott had been investigating Bryant.

I walked down to the patrol car, pausing to flash my light in the Dining with Daisy van. Then I called Inspector Doyle to find out who had interviewed Bryant Hemming's assistant and where I could find Macalester now.

Who was this guy who had got Ott to reveal himself and, having done that, alerted not his boss but his boss's ex-wife?

CHAPTER 13

Aʟ "ᴇɢɢs" ᴇɢɢᴇɴʙᴜʀɢᴇʀ, ꜰʀᴏᴍ ʜᴏᴍɪᴄɪᴅᴇ, had already interviewed Roger Macalester. He'd found him at Bryant Hemming's Arts and Creativity Council offices, and now at 9:00 ᴘ.ᴍ. Macalester was still there, busily ignoring the ringing phone.

The Delaware Street Historical District was an odd place for the Arts and Creativity Council. The block of post–Civil War cottages and storefronts was odd in general. Painted and landscaped and set behind wooden sidewalks and numbered parking slots, it was chained off at night from the low-income area around it. People lived in the houses, businesses and nonprofits occupied the storefronts, but the street had none of the chumminess of a neighborhood or the browsability of tony Fourth Street a mere block away. Had the charming block been up by the Gourmet Ghetto, it would have been prized, but down here it sat like a movie set waiting for shooting to begin.

The oddest of the buildings on Delaware Street was the one that housed the Arts and Creativity Council. Behind a mini manicured park a plain old wood water tower twenty feet square loomed at the edge of the light post's range. *Distressed wood* would be a euphemism here. No street access, no water, just two slant-walled rooms atop each other. On three sides houses were ten feet away. Maybe the development had been built around it.

The top half of the Dutch door opened before I could knock. A short, bespectacled man in his mid-thirties eyed my uniform with a look of weary annoyance that suggested I was on a par with the nagging phone. "You already sent someone, a Detective Eggenburger."

"I'd like to ask you about something different. I did try to call first."

"Yeah, well," he said as if that explained everything, and glared at the phone as it went silent, then started ringing anew. "Our members."

"Calling in condolences?"

"Calling to see if their money's gonna be tied up. Talk to the bank, I told the first couple of them. But if you know Bryant's dead, I could have added, the bank'll know it by morning and the account's in Bryant's name, so it'll be frozen harder than the stones in StoneWash Denims, one of our new members." A compression of cheek that could have been a grin or a grimace passed over his face. Perhaps he was embarrassed to be associated with the ecologically objectionable stonewashing.

"Okay if I come in?" I asked.

He gave that shrug that translated to "What choice do I have?" and stood squeezing a small, squishy yellow ball in one hand, all the time looking not at the ball or at me but beyond me at the sky as if expecting a celestial explanation for why Bryant's death was plaguing him.

"You're here late, Mr. Macalester."

"I just came down here to do a search on the Net.

The Internet," he said, glancing inside. "Then your buddy showed up. Then the phone started. I shoulda stayed gone." In another city I would have said that a guy in torn overalls and a Grateful Dead T-shirt had been pulled away from his leisure time, but here it was an even guess that this was what he wore to the city council when ACC was angling for support. He had the look of one of those guys who have spent their wiry youths downing deep-fry and beer and were just beginning to see the result above their belts. His hairline had receded, and a little curly pigtail trailed in back as if his hair had seeped down from his crown and he'd barely caught it before it fell off his head entirely. The little-boy hairdo suited his elfin face, and my guess was that he was a social grumbler whose preferred response to complaint was the offer of a beer.

"Does anyone else work here, Mr. Macalester?"

He glanced back at the tiny structure. "If they did, we'd have trampled them by now. It's all Bryant and I could do to be here together. I'm only part-time. But even so, if he was pitching a project downstairs, I was a prisoner in the tower." As if he realized for the first time he was blocking the doorway, he jolted back and nodded me inside.

Papers were strewn haphazardly, mixed with manila folders, computer diskettes, compact disks, pens, pencils, a cordless phone, and more squishy balls in primary colors. The slanted rough wood walls were hung with watercolors and prints. A clear plastic desk had been custom-made; it fitted against all four walls, barely leaving room for entry and the second-floor stairs. With the window on each side the effect was of entering a fast-food kiosk.

I wished now I'd changed out of uniform and faced Macalester in less threatening garb. What did Ott ask you about? I wanted to say, but I knew better than to charge head-on with that. With a guy like Macalester, I needed to give him time to see me as a person rather than a uniform. "What are the balls for?" I asked, picking up a purple number.

"Digital motility. Or at least that's the rationale. Bryant wanted to protect against carpal tunnel syndrome and the rest of those wrist things. The balls also give clients something to do with their hands."

And watching those actions would have given Bryant Hemming a good read on his clients' levels of anxiety. I wondered if he'd thrown Brother Cyril a ball before he decided he could safely mediate him off Telegraph.

Macalester lobbed the ball against a bare wall. "But this's the real therapy. How do you think Bryant kept his calm dealing with some of the assholes calling about their investments? On the phone, I mean. He didn't toss them off while they were sitting here."

"Investments? I know Bryant and ACC are involved in mediating, but what is this investment part, and why are your people so anxious about their money?" The phone had stopped for now, and it occurred to me I had only Roger's assumption for who was calling.

"When Bryant founded it, the Arts and Creativity Council could have been called the Starving Artists' Bitch and Beer Society. He did some classes on promotion, arts and the law, and the artist and the big buck. That's the one that clicked. So he formed the artists' fund, an investment group for small—very small—investors. He invested only in socially responsible funds approved by our board, and if you don't think those meetings need a mediator, between, say, Edgar, the candlemaker, who refuses to support electricity because of the danger of power lines, and . . . Well, we don't invest in cattle or alfalfa because they're water-intensive, nothing in Japan, whale abuse; Norway, baby seals; France, nuclear tests; Asia, child labor; Central America . . ." He shook his head. "Finally Margo Roehner decreed nothing outside the country, not that that's stopped the arguments."

"Margo Roehner?" Daisy Culligan had mentioned her as a board member, but it wasn't till now that she struck me as an odd choice. "Is she an artist?"

"Was before she got into her medical thing. But she is a Roehner; her family had money once, long enough for her to learn to tell a stock from a bond, which makes her the Adam Smith of our board. The rest of us on the board are more like the Addams Family." He squeezed the little yellow ball till it gave what sounded like a screech. He grinned. "Maybe I've been left alone here too long."

"Be careful your yellow friend there doesn't organize his fellows and beat you silly." I leaned back against the counter. This strange, ratty water tower was to the nattily refurbished Victorians around it as Roger Macalester was to Bryant Hemming. I couldn't imagine Bryant Hemming sitting in here, much less choosing the place. Or Macalester, for that matter. Herman Ott was the only one who would slide right in. I wanted to ask about Ott, but again I forced myself to wait as Macalester was forcing himself not to call my hand. I needed a clear picture of Macalester before I could judge his relationship to Ott. "How long have you been with ACC?"

"Not quite three years. I tried mediating on my own, but I, well, it's hard to take seriously a guy who looks worse than you do." He shrugged. "I knew mediating the day-to-day abuses would make all the difference, tried to establish it for years, but you've got to have a certain *je ne sais quoi* to mediate, and I, alas, am *quoi*-less. I was in despair—just south of Reno. Just kidding." His voice had risen half an octave. "Well, you can see why I didn't make it as a mediator. Doesn't do . . . to laugh . . . at . . ." He turned away and covered his face, trying to control his face, trying hard to swallow his emotion. "Sorry," he kept saying from behind his hands. "Sorry. I just can't believe he's dead. Sorry. Shot. Murdered? How? He could have made the mediation work. He was a natural. He could have taken my idea and run with it, made it important. Like Jimmy Carter."

"*Your* idea?"

"Yeah, I was sort of the Cassandra of the mediation world. I could foresee clients' disasters and the solutions, but nobody cared until Bryant."

And the concept made Bryant famous. Famous enough to move on to Washington and take Roger's idea with him. When you let another guy fly away with your baby, you want to believe he's taking it to a better home. "You trusted Bryant that much?"

Slowly he let his hands down. His face was blotchy but already fading back to its pale norm. He turned toward me, as if to show me his bared face. It didn't look elfin now, still too subdued, but there was something so likable about him I almost missed his hand squeezing a yellow ball so hard it shook. "Bryant was a genius at presentation. He took the idea and ran. And when he went on TV, suddenly everything dazzled. We got new investors, even conservatives—a brouhaha*ha* over that one—but the board finally agreed if the guys on the right put their money where *our* mouth is, all the better. Now businesses see ACC as a way to ingratiate themselves with the community and make a buck at the same time." His lips twitched, and this time a definite elfin grin flashed. "They're the ones who grabbed the phone as soon as they saw the news. Our original members won't connect Bryant's death with their money until they need it. They're used to waiting; they'd have to be after dealing with Bryant."

"Did Bryant withhold their money?"

"Oh, no, I don't mean that. He was just, well, focused on other things, and he'd forget about stuff that didn't interest him, like the classes ACC used to have. He dropped those to concentrate on the mediation. He would have dropped the money fund too, but he couldn't do that. So he let it limp along. People got their money, but sometimes they had to call him a couple of times. They understood that. It's the new guys who expected more."

"Is that what Herman Ott was asking about?"

"Ott? No."

I could tell from his expression I hadn't slid that question in quite as smoothly as I'd hoped. "Mr. Macalester, Herman Ott was investigating Bryant. What did he ask you about him?"

"I didn't—"

"Daisy told me you did."

He sailed the ball against the wall, a swooping arc of defeat. "Yeah, okay. Ott called me. I know Ott, respect the guy, but sheesh, Bryant's my boss; I can't be inviting Ott over to peruse the office."

"What specifically was he after?"

Macalester pushed himself up on the desk. "You want to know what I think? He was fishing."

"But why?"

He shrugged.

"Look, I'm going to be straight with you," I said. "Ott's missing. I can't picture him shooting Bryant. It worries me that he's been gone for over twenty-four hours. You say you know Ott; then you know how strange that is. I need to find him, and I'll tell you, I have not a clue. Except that he was investigating Bryant. Now if I knew what his focus—"

"I . . . don't . . . know. Ott didn't favor me with his purpose. Maybe if he hadn't been so condescending—like whatever he thought Bryant had done, he figured I was up to my eyeballs too—maybe I'd have helped him. I told him to go screw himself." He paused and stared me in the eye. "Maybe that's what he's gone and done."

Herman Ott, the equal opportunity irritant. It amused me that he'd infuriated Macalester as much as he had any cop. But finding him was like hunting for a skunk; no one cared where he went, just that he went. "You know Ott, right? Then you know he wouldn't politely accept refusal and walk away. Is there anyone else he'd have asked?"

"Friends, you mean? Bryant was too busy for a social life."

"Any business associates?"

"Me."

"Could Ott have gotten in here without you knowing?"

His mouth twitched. "I wouldn't know, would I?"

Touché. "But signs? Things out of place?"

"No."

"Is there anywhere else he would have checked?"

"Bryant's apartment maybe. He could have tried the storage locker, but he'd only have found junk and not much of that."

"Where is the unit?"

"Storit Urself, down on—"

"I know the place."

"Yeah, it's good. The third-floor units are like cheap—very cheap—apartments, no outside door, so spur-of-the-moment thieves don't notice they're there."

"What"—I was holding my breath—"is the unit number?" And I nearly whistled when he said, "Three-oh-seven."

I had been standing right beneath 307 this afternoon. Margo Roehner's locker was 207.

CHAPTER 14

COINCIDENCES HAPPEN, BUT THEY'RE NOT highly thought of in police work.

I headed up the station stairs, through the squad room—almost empty at this time of night—through the old records room to the inspector's office. During the day his clerk guarded Doyle's peace of mind the way Raksen did his crime scenes. But now I strolled through the empty outer office and tapped on his glass right above the INSPECTOR FRANCIS DOYLE sign.

Doyle wasn't asleep; he just looked that way, head back on the headrest of the faux leather director's chair Mrs. Doyle had given him in celebration of his fifth cancer-free year. For her that milestone had been the day the lights came back on. He, a pessimist in the finest Hibernian tradition, had looked me in the eye and said, "You think those cells wear calendar watches?" He hadn't said that to her, though, or that the expensive chair embarrassed him. That day was the first time he had said the word *cancer* aloud.

As he recognized me now, his blue eyes widened momentarily in anticipation, then narrowed as if to block the disappointment before he could see it. "So, Smith, you nosed out Ott?"

"If he were that easy to find, he'd have been dead

years ago." I perched on the edge of a padded metal chair and rested an arm on his desk, careful to avoid the three ceramic rhinoceroses that'd made it to this side of his IN box.

When the inspector was hospitalized, it was rumored he liked rhinos. In lieu of yet more flowers or the no longer acceptable candy, relieved visitors arrived with rhinos. Now the herd in Doyle's office outnumbered those in most African countries. It covered the top of his metal bookcase, spread onto his windowsill, trailed across the ledge of his interior windows, and, when not carefully supervised, made beachheads on his desk. I never did discover whether the original rumor was true.

I plucked a blue rhino off IN box patrol and massaged its midsection as I relayed Ott's interest in the mysterious Bill Lewin and Daisy Culligan's pronouncement about Ott's investigating Bryant. "Roger Macalester confirmed it, grudgingly. But Daisy was too caught up in pique and Roger in principle to find out why."

"Berkeley," Doyle muttered.

"But here's the interesting thing. Bryant Hemming's organization ACC has a storage locker right above Margo Roehner's, and Roehner's was burglarized today. And, Inspector, Roehner is on the ACC board."

"The reward she gets for service, huh? We'll"—he glanced at a list on the desk—"*I'll* get to her."

"Any word from the ME's office? Time of death?"

He emitted something between a hoot and a laugh. "Sunday night, after he left the television studio, before you found him."

"Bullet?"

"Nine-millimeter."

"What about Ott's office? What did the search turn up?"

"You've seen that rat's nest." He shook his head, sending carroty strands onto his forehead. "Jesus, Mary, and Joseph, the man could have a litter of piglets living in there, and no one'd notice. I'm surprised the place doesn't smell."

I laughed. "Maybe it's anaerobic. What about the neighbors in Ott's building? They must have heard the shot."

"You'd think, wouldn't you? Anywhere other than Telegraph, any place but that catchall building Ott's in. First two families didn't speak English, and we had to wake up Clifton to figure out what language they were speaking. We've got a Hmong interpreter scheduled for the morning. Next batch of tenants was so busy flushing we were on the verge of going for a warrant. When they said they didn't see anyone odd in the halls, they're probably telling the truth; *they* probably haven't seen *anything* for months. And God knows what would be odd to them. Other units appeared to be empty. Maybe some of those offices really are used just for business again. Anyway, Smith, the upshot is that we know not a da—blessed thing."

"What about his files? Not the ones with no names in his desk, the records in the file cabinets—"

"All six of those manila folders? The rest of the file drawers are crammed with books. Taxes, penal codes. Guy's got a whole room of bookcases, you'd think—"

"Those six files, did they—"

"Code."

"What?"

"They're all in some kind of code. Gibberish. I

know you like Ott, and I don't think the better of you for it, but he's got to be fodder for the bin. Code! You know it's not like he's got a computer in that rat's nest of his to do the encoding. He had to do it by hand, letter by letter. Has the man nothing at all to do with his time?"

I'd wondered what Ott's hobbies were. I'd wondered what had moved him to look into computers. "There's got to be a key."

"Well, he's your friend. Maybe you can find out. I suppose we could send the files to the feds for decoding, but Smith, you know it's only going to make us a laughingstock."

"Give me a couple days to find Ott—"

"A couple days! Tight as manpower is, if you don't have Ott in here by this time tomorrow, you'll be back on patrol."

"Tracking down Ott in Berkeley is like playing against the game master. One day isn't—"

"Out of my hands, Smith."

There are two times to keep your mouth shut, the old joke goes: when you're angry and when you're swimming. And there's a third: when you're facing a done deal. I got Doyle's okay to check out Ott's office and left. Another time I might have stopped to change out of my clunky uniform. Now I paused only long enough to call Howard at home and say I'd be late, real late. I didn't have time to tell him more. I was racing not only against the murder case clock that ticks away the value of evidence and heat of leads but against the threat of the FBI. Ott had cooperated with me on a number of cases. I had given him slack. I'd taken chances for him. I had kept secrets for him, the

kinds of secrets an FBI operative would never understand.

Ott knew how to cover his ass. It would be like him
to document my cooperation in the files he was sure
were safe. If I planned to survive in the department,
and have Ott survive, I needed to find him, and fast.

CHAPTER 15

CARY KOVACH WAS ALONE, GUARDING the scene, at Ott's office. The rest of the building's units were dark. Here a dead body was clearly nothing to lose sleep over. From the look of Kovach, slouched on a hard chair, he felt the same. But he could hardly complain. He was warm, indoors, and on dog watch losing sleep was his job.

"I'm Smith, here to check out the scene."

He wriggled to straighten his ursine form in the chair. Like all of Ott's furniture, it looked inadequate to its task. "Inspector had five guys going over the place. Plus Raksen. Raksen got called to another scene or he'd still be here."

"He'd be here till the Second Coming if he could."

Kovach grinned. "Yeah, I got that feeling. Anyway, if there's anything left, you're welcome to it."

"Thanks," I said with a sarcastic laugh, and started past him.

"Smith?"

"Yes?"

"You okay here alone for five minutes?"

I patted my holster. "I'm not afraid of the dark."

Kovach pushed himself up.

Guarding the scene and surveillance: They've got

the same drawback. "Use the john at the university, Kovach; it'll be worth the extra ten minutes. I speak from experience." When you're on patrol for eight to ten hours, bathrooms are a big issue. Clean is good, and ones where you won't be caught with your pants down (and your gun belt hanging out of reach on the door) are better. The hospitals, the UC patrol station are the best. A minute or two of banter with the UC guys would break up Kovach's long, isolated night.

Ott's rooms had been aired while the crime scene team picked and packed, and the smell of death clung only in cracks and corners. I closed and locked the door, and the little breeze treated me to a whiff of urine and decay.

As Kovach intimated, anything worth finding in Ott's office would already be gone. The files I had noted earlier—the flowerpot case in the folders with no name, for one—was at the station with Ott's coded case notes. I made fast work of the desk and file drawers, looked under and around the furniture. I'd been here often enough, perched on that desk to demand, to goad, to beg, that anything out of the ordinary now would have struck me. It didn't. I moved on to the bedroom.

In crime scenes, housekeeping standards are rarely improved by police searches. Herman Ott's bedroom was the exception. The room normally looked as if it had just been tossed; now it merely might have been the apartment of someone about to skip town. No longer was the floor awash with homogeneous clutter; when planning to cross to the window now, I didn't think of it as fording. Ott's belongings now were in individual piles: bedclothes here, clothing there, newspapers by the outside wall, magazines piled precariously against the hall door, miscellaneous items in a cardboard box next to his chair.

Never before had I seen his once-overstuffed chair uncovered. It was akin to running across an aging floozy the morning after, when her eyes were puffy, her corset discarded, her skin sagging in unseemly places, and her sunflower print bathrobe threadbare and with two springs poking out. When Daisy Culligan admitted she'd slept with Ott, I'd wondered why. Now my question was how. Or more to the point, where?

Gingerly I sat on the edge of the chair and surveyed Ott's jutting bookcase. Shelves of political periodicals, books on Berkeley, a few volumes on organic farming, and two on pesticides. Had Ott nurtured a secret garden? Perhaps the crop of choice in Northern California? I brushed that thought away. A plot of marijuana was far too dangerous for a man in his position, particularly when supply was so easy to come by. Perhaps he'd been one of the flower growers in the fleeting era when locals tried to cultivate People's Park. But I couldn't picture Herman Ott with a spade in hand. He was hardly an early bird. Or a bird of the wild. No, Herman Ott was meant to perch right in here and merely look awry at the methods of California's biggest industry, agriculture. The one time I had shown up here with an apple, Ott had sneered: "We're so cocky insisting on toxic standards for our fruit and vegetables. And then come winter, what do we think we're eating? Artichokes from Argentina, peaches from Peru, and who knows what from Mexico, where they dump their shit in the rivers."

I had of course responded by biting into the apple, but it wasn't the tastiest snack I'd ever had.

On the bottom shelf, under what looked to be another haphazard pile of newspapers, I found the last thing I would have expected, a sturdy gift box from Wanamaker's department store. Wanamaker's? Those stores had been only on the East Coast, and they'd been closed for years. Not that Ott was one to throw out a box merely for age.

The box was ordinary compared with what was inside. It held a small picture album—one shot per page, black paper, corner keepers for the black-and-white photos. An album of pictures a mother culled from the family book, made especially for a child.

It had never occurred to me that Ott had a mother. It was hard to imagine him ever having lived with a family or in anything other than these two rooms. At best I could see him sitting by an inadequate hearth, reading the picture book version of *Political Injustice for the Young Reader*.

The album held twenty pages, two sides each, but there were only three pictures. There were holders for others, holders as crisp and unmarred as the day they had been pasted in. Ott must have pulled the photos out. A wave of sadness came over me, not so much for the memories torn out of his life as for those he couldn't bring himself to part with. So easy to destroy in fury, but to halt angry hands before the righteous pleasure of shredding, to wall off part of your heart from your principles . . . And then to sit in this shabby room, not moving lest the chair springs poke into your butt, and break into that wall for just a peek . . .

Just a peek, because if you open too big a hole, your whole heart will fall out . . . and the world will tramp on it. I turned away as if I'd come in on him naked.

The first shot, on the first page, was of a plain blond woman of about twenty, in a skirted bathing suit, sitting next to a hamper under a beach umbrella. It could have been taken on any East Coast beach to which families carted more than their ancestors had loaded on to the *Niña*, *Pinta*, or *Santa María*. Ott's mother, I had to guess. It pleased me that she wasn't a pretty woman, one who would have been distressed at the sight of the round, sallow child Ott must have been.

I turned the page, and then about ten more to get to a shot of what must have been Ott's extended family. Blonds of all ages. It took me several minutes squinting over the picture to find Ott himself. I checked all the other boys twice again before admitting that the eight-year-old on the left had to be Herman. If so, Mrs. Ott could have been beautiful and things would have been all right. The boy with Ott's eyes, and that familiar little smirk on his lips, was a knockout. Eyes that I had seen only narrowed in anger were open wide in pleasure. A smile stretched his mouth wider than I could have imagined it going. His hair had been full and wavy and glowed in the sun like white gold. And most surprising, he had his arms around the shoulders of the two children next to him, and theirs encircled his back.

The last photo was wider than the others, a professional job, and near the back of the book. It was the most stunning of all. If I'd had to guess which club Herman Ott had headed in high school, it would have been the Nerds' Club, by whatever name it was known in that era. Wrong again, Smith. There, in black and white, was Herman Ott, squatting in the second row of boys in football uniforms, behind a banner: GO MONGEESE!

The Herman Ott I knew was not even as tall as I, with shoulders so stooped that only a shrug made him look near normal. His cheeks were rounded; his chin receded. His were arms that never lifted more than a pen, his legs were toothpicks, and when he was sitting, he looked as if he were holding a volleyball on his lap.

I stared at the handsome little boy in pads. Already he was shorter than average. He'd have played running back, one of those little guys who size up their slower-thinking opposition, fake to the right, and squirt left through the line. He'd have been a hero. Herman Ott, the all-American kid.

What had happened to him? I sat down between the sprung springs of his chair, smelling the remnants of death from the doorway, the cold of the unheated office chilling me through my thermal shirt. Ott had had everything and had chosen this. What, indeed, had happened to him?

There's a theory that floats around in the esoterica above Berkeley about walk-ons. When someone is depressed, becomes ill unto death, or perhaps attempts suicide and is resuscitated at the last moment, the theory is that the initial tenant of the body really did give up on life and, in that moment before reviving, ceded the body to another soul anxious to enter life midstream. The body regains health. Friends and relatives are astounded, delighted, not only at the victim's recovery but at his wonderful change of spirit. If they note there is something just a bit different about him at base, they're willing to overlook it. They probably didn't like that aspect of him to begin with. The maudlin devil you know is hardly preferable to a chipper one you don't know.

If Ott was a walk-on, he'd gotten the sequence backward.

Still, where better to hide out than with his old buddies and his own family? I squinted at the photo, peering closer until I could make out the word above *Mongeese*. Monongahela Mongeese.

Anyone who has watched the Raiders is all too familiar with the fearsome Steelers in Three Rivers Stadium. Three Rivers: the Ohio, Allegheny, and the Monongahela. Ott was from Pittsburgh! Or thereabouts.

I could have called the dispatcher, but you can never be sure who is listening to the police scanner, and I was too impatient to talk in code. Instead I pulled out my cell phone and dialed information. It was still late evening here, but in Pittsburgh it was after midnight. I punched in the number, flicked off the light, and settled on the edge of the chair as Ott himself must have done many times.

"Sergeant Laura Goldman, please. Is she on duty now?"

"I'll ring."

"Goldman."

"Laura! Jill Smith." We'd been roommates at the National Women's Police Officers' Association convention the previous spring, placed together to share the joy of not smoking. "Still snoring?"

"I'm working up a storm for you next year. You still emptying hotel minibars? You gave me the worst moment of the convention, coming back to that empty—"

"Just the chocolate, Goldman. I left you plenty of those little liquor bottles. You could have drowned your grief in bourbon, vodka, and Grand Marnier. Yeah, four ounces each."

"Ugh."

"Listen, Laura, I've got a missing suspect who grew up in Pittsburgh. Could be he's back there. Not dangerous. But we did find a murder victim in his office—"

"Bet that victim found him dangerous. And you'd like to have him back, huh? Shoot."

"All I've got is a football picture from a high school team called the Monongahela Mongeese. That mean anything to you?"

"Nooo. But there's a Monongahela High School here in town. And I'll bet the Monongahela High School alumni woke up one morning and changed that team name back to Lions or Tigers like it should be. 'Can't call our little lads furry snake eaters!' "

I laughed. *Snake eater* suited Ott.

"You got a name and DOB for the suspect, Smith?"

"Right. Plus, I've got a photo that looks like an old family gathering, but it could have been taken anywhere. So I don't know if there was much of my guy's family in Pittsburgh at all. He's been out here since the sixties. But anything you can find on him, I'll appreciate. And if there's nothing—" I shrugged. Not that Laura could see it. "His name is Herman Ott—"

"Ott?"

"Right."

Laura Goldman was laughing. "Smith, I think I can help you out. Ott, huh?"

"What were they, the town crooks? Or the drunks? Or the old lefties at every factory gate?"

Goldman laughed harder. Finally she spit out, "Coal."

"They were coal miners?"

"No, Smith, the Otts didn't dig the coal. The Otts owned the mine. Now which Ott did you say you're after?"

"Herman Ott."

"Which Herman Ott? They're all Herman Otts. John Herman Ott. Richard Herman Ott. Robert Herman Ott. The mother was a Herman. You've heard of Herman Steel, haven't you?"

I hadn't, but Goldman wasn't waiting for that admission.

"Herman Steel and Ott Mining. That marriage made the papers for months. My grandmother still talks about it. She was a housemaid at the Hermans' before she married my grandfather. That wedding was far and away the biggest event of her life, way more important than her own marriage. The only glamorous thing she was ever involved in. She kept hoping her daughters and then her granddaughters would go into fashion or theater or at least be airline stewardesses. We've been disappointments, Smith."

I laughed. "And if you don't get back to my Herman Ott, you'll be one again."

"But you say you don't know which one he is."

"He's forty-six years old."

"Oh, okay, he'd be the oldest. Of course. The one who disappeared. Sure, that makes sense."

"Why, Goldman? Why did he disappear?"

Goldman laughed again, but a different kind of laugh, with the merriment replaced by bitter knowledge. "No one knows. Believe me, finding out would have made a reporter's career. But a family like that doesn't go on *Oprah* with its secrets. Your guy, Alexander, graduated from high school and was never mentioned again. People knew better than to ask, or presumably they learned after the first time."

"Do you have any idea?"

"No. But I'll tell you this, Smith, whatever it was, it cut to the core. His mother died fifteen, twenty years ago, and he didn't show up at the funeral; there was talk about that, believe me. Nana carried on so long we had to threaten her with 'the home.' I can't imagine anything in the world that would bring Alexander back to Pittsburgh."

"Rats. I really hoped . . ." Ott's outside door rattled. Kovach hadn't dawdled at Cal. Automatically I lowered my voice. "Check around for me, Goldman, just in case."

"Goes without saying. I'll go through our files and the news morgue and fax you what I uncover. Cheer up, Smith, you still have this year's convention to look forward to. Another couple of great nights with me."

"I can handle that. They've got this plastic staple that clamps between your nostrils to keep you from snoring."

She laughed. "You sure it works?"

"Not positive. But if it doesn't, I'll tie a string to it and tether you outside the door." The door rattled again.

It was a rattle, not a knock.

"I have to go." I turned off the phone, moved behind the bookcase, eased my gun from the holster, and waited.

CHAPTER 16

I<small>T WASN'T KOVACH AT OTT'S</small> door.

I turned off the volume on my radio and tightened my grip on my semiautomatic.

"Hello? Ott?" A question, not a demand. I didn't move, barely breathed. The voice wasn't familiar. Male, not young, not old, a middling voice with a squeaky core. He knew Ott wasn't here. No surprise. All of Ott's cronies on the Avenue would have heard about the crime scene. But this guy knew Ott's entry routine: Never let on you're in here till you're sure who's out there, and even then never open the door till the third demand.

Carefully lifting, silently setting down my feet, I moved to where I could see the door to the corridor. A celluloid strip waggled between it and the molding. It moved slowly. The guy wasn't worried. He must have missed me coming, just seen Kovach leave, and figured all that was protecting the scene was the locked door.

I eased back into the darkness of Ott's bedroom.

The plastic strip hit against metal, then slapped the wood as the guy snapped it out to try again. Loiding a lock isn't as easy as people think.

I moved back a couple of steps along the bookcase.

I'd always wondered why Ott had chosen to have this large, flimsy piece of furniture poking out into the room he slept in. Not wise in earthquake country. The smartest people don't have bookcases at all in bedrooms. The rest of us have them bolted to the walls. The end of Ott's bookcase was eight inches away from the wall, so the whole thing was standing free. There was no back to steady it. In a tembler it would shimmy once or twice, toss its six shelves of books and clutter, like Parmesan cheese sprinkled thickly over an everything pizza. And over Ott. Why not screw the thing to the wall?

But now I understood why. And the import of it made me feel sorrier for Ott than I'd ever imagined I could.

For the first time I realized why the newspapers and magazines and crumpled paper cups were mixed in with the books he cared about.

I was standing hidden in the narrow aisle between the bookcase and the window. This was where Ott slept. He may have considered the danger of burial under books, but if so, it had been overridden by a more pressing threat. From any position, standing, squatting, sitting on the floor, even lying down on his side, Ott could peer between the bookshelves and see through the doorway into his office. Ott must never have gone to sleep without the thought that he might be woken up by a burglar, a pissed-off client, an irate subject he was investigating, or just some wacko from the Avenue looking for drug money. How could the man live like this? And why? Why, when he seemed to have an ideal life in Pittsburgh?

The door burst open.

I stood against the wall, in the darkest corner.

The burglar was nearly as tall as Howard. And about half Howard's weight. He looked as if he'd been on meth so long he'd forgotten what food was. Everything about him was long and bony and sickly pale. Greasy brown hair hung over his forehead and hooked behind one ear. Black leather jacket and black jeans had that loose hang that screams "sick." I'd seen him on the Avenue, skulking along the sidewalk, never stopping to chat with the street artists, never patronizing the sushi wagon or the strawberry smoothie stand. I'd had no reason to stop him; he hadn't broken laws when I was on beat here, nor had he been connected with anyone who did. He was an alien on this strip of macadam much of the country viewed as home to the politically deranged, drugged out, or just strange. An alien aloof from aliens. His name, what was it?

He loomed over the room. He was so much taller than Herman Ott his presence seemed to change the dimensions of the room, an eagle pushed into the canary's cage. As he pulled open Ott's file cabinet, I had a good look at his talonlike hands. He wasn't shaking, and his movements had none of the jerkiness of the crack addict's. And he knew just what he was looking for in here.

Or he thought he did. "Goddamn fucking fuck!" He slammed a file drawer shut. The metal shrieked under the thrust of books hitting metal. He yanked open another drawer, looked inside, and slammed it shut. And a third.

The files of course were at the station. I wondered how many fileless drawers he would have to see before he realized they all were like that. *Hurry up!*

Show me if you're just looking for a file or something more.

Give me a lead.

He was out of my range of vision now, attacking the near file cabinet next to the office window. More drawers slammed.

My head was nearly through the bookcase, my chin propped on a precarious stack of newspapers. I pulled back, stood up, and moved against the wall. Any minute Kovach would stroll in, and I'd lose this lead forever.

The burglar froze, then slowly looked around him, eyes squinting as he peered into the dark bedroom. I could almost see his thought: *I should have checked in there.*

He started toward the bedroom, reached in through the doorway, flipped the door back against the wall. The crack of wood on plaster surprised him. He hesitated, hand still on the door.

As he pulled his hand back, I saw the jagged black lines bisecting his thumb and forefinger. Now I remembered his name. Griffon. No first name, just Griffon.

With his other hand he grabbed on to the molding near the light switch.

Come on! Something tapped. Footsteps on the stairs? Kovach's?

Griffon didn't turn on the light. He glanced around the room, then down at the floor, his brow wrinkled in suspicion just as mine would have done in his place. He moved slowly, feeling with his feet as if Ott's normal clutter might pop up and grab his ankles. He passed the end of the bookcase. I slid around the other end, as Ott had prepared for.

Definitely feet coming up the stairs. How could Griffon not hear that?

Griffon stopped in front of the window, staring out through the sooty pane into the dark of the air shaft, peering down. He hesitated, weighing options, then lifted Ott's mugs from the windowsill to the low bookcase next to the window. Then the sugar jar and a bottle, maybe vitamins.

The hall door opened. "Smith, I brought you—"

Griffon spun around, raced past Kovach and into the hall.

Kovach dropped his paper bag, grabbed for the doorway, pushed off, and ran.

I called the dispatcher. "Adam sixteen, Control. Got a suspect headed out of Herman Ott's building. Kovach giving chase. I—"

"Adam seven. I see 'im."

"Roger, Seven," the dispatcher said. "Headed which direction?"

"South on Tele."

Adam 6 reported in; he was two blocks away. Griffon would never go that far. I knew where he'd head. He would keep.

But what he was after outside the window wouldn't. I shone my flashlight out the dirty window, along the sill.

Screwed into the sill was a metal cup holder. And in it was a handgun. A nine-millimeter.

CHAPTER 17

"You have reached the homicide Detail of the Berkeley Police Department. . . ."

"If you've found a body, press one," I muttered over the recording.

Inspector Doyle wouldn't have gone home already —thank God. When I was in Homicide, I'd woken him so often his wife referred to me as the other woman. I called the dispatcher to tell Doyle to answer his phone, waited a minute, and called him again.

"Why didn't you just come through the dispatcher, Smith?" Doyle grumbled.

"This isn't a public announcement. I'm at Ott's office. Been here half an hour. One break-in and one hidden weapon, a nine-millimeter."

"Where is it?"

"Out the window. But the interesting thing, Inspector, is that the burglar knew to look there."

"Okay, Smith, I'm lifting out of my chair."

Exactly seven minutes later Inspector Doyle walked in. And almost on his heels came Wisniewski from beat 1 and Crowe from 8.

I pointed out the gun.

Doyle and contingent strode to the window. Doyle yanked it up. At six inches it stopped. He tried again, getting no movement at all, and was set for a third assault when Crowe moved in next to him. "Let me try. All my years in the weight room should be worth something to the department."

Through Crowe's shirt I could see the outline of muscles that must have looked sexier in his mirror than to 95 percent of the female population. Crowe squatted, straightened back, and lifted.

Another two inches.

With a volcanic exhale he resumed his squat.

"Inspector," I interrupted. "It doesn't matter how high Crowe can bench-press this window. We're talking Herman Ott here. Ott's arms could pass for Crowe's fingers. He's had *me* open his peanut butter jar. You got this window up half a foot on the first try; you can believe Ott never raised it farther."

Crowe backed away as if he'd been pulled off the mat in the middle of the match, and Doyle shone his light out the window. "Jesus, Mary, and Joseph, Smith, you know what he's got the gun in out here? A flagpole support. Jeez, isn't it just like the guy? Musta tore him up that he couldn't figure how to desecrate the flag while he did it."

He challenged me with a glance and, when I didn't respond, said, "Crowe, get Raksen back here. Camera, print kit, the works. Herman Ott's got a lot of explaining to do."

"We don't know it's his gun," I said.

"Right, Smith. Maybe he rents out this holder outside his window like a garage for his neighbors' guns."

"Is it registered to Ott?" Kovach asked.

Doyle laughed. "You been on this beat how long, Kovach?"

"Six months."

"So maybe you can picture Herman Ott standing in line at the department, waiting for us to fingerprint him, so he can register his weapon with us."

Pigs may fly, but they'd be taking transatlantic passengers before Ott would give us that much control. I couldn't put my finger on why, but this out-the-window arrangement didn't ring true. "Inspector, Ott wouldn't have a gun out there."

"Why not? You think he flew a flag there? In the alley?"

"The holder's rusted. It must have been there forever." As soon as the words were out, I readied for the natural rejoinder, which came at once.

"Ott's been in this office forever, Smith," Doyle pointed out. "Give me another good reason why that window opens just six inches."

It amazed me it opened at all. I wondered how recently Ott had wrenched it up and how long that process had taken him. Whatever, you don't put a flag in what's essentially an air shaft where there's no one to see it—or at least no one but Charles Edward Kidd. But I wasn't about to wander into that byway. "Inspector, I don't believe Ott would have a gun, period."

Doyle made a show of surveying Ott's insecure rooms, letting his eyes rest on the wooden panel nailed over the broken glass pane in the door. I didn't mention Ott's sleeping arrangement or the "secret passage" behind the bookcase, which to me screamed, "Flight rather than fight." To anyone else it would merely giggle "loony."

"Inspector, Ott's a realist. He wouldn't have a gun, because"—I knew I was right, but I had to grope for the reason—"because what he loves about being a private eye is the puzzle. His treasure is his contacts and his knowledge. He prides himself on using his mind; you don't have a body like his otherwise. He doesn't need a gun, and more to the point, he knows any kid on the street could snatch it out of his hand and shoot him." Ott had been in shape to play football. If he had cared about physical protection, he'd have stayed in shape. His decline was a political statement.

Doyle shook his head. "Smith, when you find a corpse in a room, shot with the same kind of gun that's stashed out the window, and the tenant is missing . . . But he's not going to be missing long. We are going to pull out all stops. We'll get his picture in every paper." Doyle paused, smiling. "It's not a face you'd forget."

"And where are you going to get that photo, Inspector? From the Chamber of Commerce annual picnic picture? It'll be easier to find Ott than a picture of him."

"Okay, we'll use the sketch artist. With all of us who've seen Ott, it'll be the easiest drawing in ID history."

"Right, and every one of Ott's supporters will feel it's their civic duty to mislead us. They'll have us running in more directions than we knew existed."

In the next room Crowe was calling the dispatcher. Wisniewski had planted himself by the outside door, a safe distance from which to observe the interchange between Doyle and me.

"So," Doyle said, as if he were continuing his train of thought, rather than shifting subject, "what have you got on this burglar, Smith?"

"Name's Griffon. Operates the Chartreuse Cara-cara."

Doyle sighed. "Chartreuse, indeed. And what in the name of Berkeley is caracara? It sounds like something you wouldn't want to eat."

"Close. Something you don't want eating *you*. The caracara is a tropical American vulture."

"And what is it Griffon is running under this charming name, a café?"

"A tattoo shop. It's under a yellow sign in the alley that leads back here right below Ott's window."

CHAPTER 18

THE CHARTREUSE CARACARA WAS HALF a block off Telegraph behind one of the metal doors in the alley I'd sloshed through only two hours ago. There was no alley name posted at the street, no looming likeness of a caracara with an arrow pointing potential customers back to the tattoo parlor. But Griffon was the silent, mysterious kind of man who draws attention the way, well, carrion draws caracaras.

Two hours ago the alley was dark, slimy, and fetid. Now it was merely dim, slimy, and fetid, the heightened illumination coming from the kind of wrought-iron outside light that might have graced a tract house in the suburbs. Here it shone on the Chartreuse Caracara sign above. Chartreuse is a color of many possibilities. I had never seen a caracara. But the puke yellow vulture on the sign didn't speak well of either. On the other hand, it suited the setting.

I'd been in these alley rooms before, on 911 calls to check out doors that hadn't opened in days, buddies friends were so worried about they were willing to call the police. I'd come with a crowbar, into airless rooms with filthy, grate-covered windows that allowed neither light nor escape.

Now I knocked, covered the essentials, and walked inside. Kovach was waiting with Griffon.

Griffon's place was bigger than most—an eight-by-twenty-foot room, kitchen/bath at one end. And it was like something out of a different world. Clean, to begin with. The beige linoleum shone, and the smell was not the familiar eau de body fluids of the alley but Clorox. The place reeked of it. It was almost more offensive than the smells outside. The room was a shoe box, long enough to accommodate a Formica table between two kitchen chairs and a sleeping bag. Beyond the archway were toilet, sink, and hot plate, and between them a drawing board. Presumably the toilet seat doubled in purpose as the artist's chair.

But it was the walls that stopped me dead. Every inch was adorned with plastic-covered sheets of tattoo sketches. Hearts: round happy hearts, hearts bearing bannered names, hearts broken as if by lightning, and, filling two entire sheets, Jesus and his sacred heart. Skulls, snakes, wolf claws, bear claws, bird claws. And dragons, mythical, Chinese restaurant varieties, and purple polka dots. There were photos of single scenes spanning men's entire backs, women's breasts, scenes that covered the wearers like a T-shirt (some short-sleeved, some long). The tattooed models were posing; they were strolling; they were standing as if waiting for a bus. As if their engraved epidermises were not colored skin but clothes. I wondered if the ink had seeped into their brains and colored their perceptions till they no longer recalled the reason for clothing. It's one thing to have sag and flab under sweatsuits, quite another to display the result of too many desserts beneath the Last Supper. Particularly when the table shape has stretched from rectangular to oval.

But if Griffon saw any oddity in the displays, he gave no indication. Griffon had to be a business name chosen to accompany the vulturous shop name, but it suited his predatory appearance. Dressed all in white now, he looked like a vulture in crane's clothing. Hair tousled, stuffing the hem of a long-sleeved white turtleneck into his jeans, he glowered down the length of his long, beaked nose. He had the tight mouth of one who'd never stretched it in laughter. Even his hands were talonlike, I noticed as I sat in one of the kitchen chairs, tacitly forcing him to take the other and rest an arm on the Formica table. The veins were marked with the black lines I'd spotted in Ott's office. I decided against asking him to remove the drills and bits on the table. With the bottle of tongue depressors on the table, the whole setup could have belonged to a disbarred dentist.

He lifted a white-clad arm and tapped one nail on the table.

"So what do you want to know about ol' Herman? He's no killer, man, you can believe that. You here for a character ref? From a member of the Chamber of Commerce?" he said in a gravelly voice.

Good try. "You break and enter into a murder scene; then you flee the scene and try to avoid arrest" —I glanced at Kovach, and he nodded that he already had covered this ground—"the only question you should be asking now is, 'How can I help you, Officer?' Your one hope is me; you got that?"

He nodded quickly, unconditionally. It made me suspicious.

"Your real name?"

"Griffon. It's legal." He pulled out his driver's license.

I copied down his birth date and the street address here. "What were you looking for in Herman Ott's office an hour ago?"

"Herman asked me to take a look."

"Puh-lease."

"No, really, he called. Said he was worried about you cops and all, and he needed to know if the place was a shambles."

Shambles was the place's natural state. Now I wondered if Griffon had ever been in Ott's office before tonight. "Go on," I said, but I could tell by the way he sucked in his already sunken cheeks that he knew we both understood he was spouting fiction.

Still, he gave it one more try. "Herman needed a report on his files and his books and all."

"And about his gun?"

Griffon's face didn't move. He just sat, his arm taut on the table between us, fingers snaking around a tube of Vaseline. "That's it. I'm not answering any more questions."

He was within his rights. If I planned to arrest him, I'd have to Mirandize him. But arrest leaves no room for maneuvering, for the suspect or for us. I wanted to forestall that every bit as much as Griffon did. "You broke into a crime scene. I was there; I saw you. The easiest thing for me to do is arrest you . . . unless . . . you give me some reason not to. You understand? But if you don't want to talk, we can go on down to the station and the jailer can book you."

Griffon didn't move. Behind him Kovach shifted his feet, scraping one sole across the linoleum.

"So, Griffon?"

"Okay, okay. What do you want?"

"Where is Ott?"

"If you're going to ask the impossible, there's no point. Ott and I aren't close."

"Yet inside his office you walked right over to the murder weapon."

"What? Murder? Hey, man, I wouldn't—"

I held up a hand.

He stared at the wall behind me, perhaps asking guidance from a purple wizard or strength from a snarling red tiger, perhaps just staring. When he spoke, I couldn't tell if he was giving up or just trying out a new riff. "Okay, why don't you tell me what you need to know."

"When did you talk to Ott last?" I asked, hoping it had been after Kidd had seen him hauling ass into the mysterious car.

But he said, "Last Thursday."

Too early. "What about?"

"This and that."

"Griffon!"

"Okay, he needed some background for an investigation he was doing."

"On?"

"The Tele scene."

"Enough!" I stood up. "You can play your game in a holding cell." Ott had been on Telegraph forever; *he* was the authority.

"No, honestly. Shocked me too." Griffon hadn't budged from his chair, but his talons were wrapped tightly around the edge of the Formica table, as if he'd known his story was unbelievable and expected Kovach and me to drag him out.

So unbelievable suddenly I believed it. "*Why?* What exactly did Ott ask?"

"Background on Serenity Kaetz, Brother Cyril, anyone else who had over five hundred dollars in the ACC money fund."

"But, Griffon, why did Ott ask *you*?"

"Because," he said, exasperated, "I've got more money sense than the local 'artistes.' If they spent the time they bellyache learning their *business* . . . But then they wouldn't be starving artists, would they? When I heard Bryant was starting a money fund for artists, I was the first investor."

"Griffon, you're not tight with the artists, are you?"

He could hardly dispute that now.

"Then why would Ott think you'd know anything about Serenity Kaetz beyond the fact that she invested?"

He shrugged.

I watched him, wondering if his condescension toward the artists was not so much world-weariness as the result of their scorn of his "art." My gaze drifted from his long, bony face to the wall behind him, to the swords, and harpies in black and brown, blue and red, green and yellow, on pictured backs. The roses, the crucifixes, the angels blowing angry trumpets. "If you aren't thick with the artists, why would they trust your financial judgment?" I glanced around the tiny room. "You can't be making a fortune here."

Now he did jump up. So fast Kovach almost made a grab for him. "Hey, don't let this studio deceive you. I'm doing just fine. Clients come to me from Los Angeles, from Reno, from as far away as Tulsa."

"Oh, really?" I hadn't moved.

"Really. They see my work, they've got to have it. No matter if they've got to travel, no matter what it costs them. They've got to have it."

"And what, Griffon, makes your work so special?"

"Look!" He pointed to a magazine photo of a man's back. A tree trunk grew out of the crack of his buttocks, wove toward his right ribs, back past his spine, and ended in a branch running just below his shoulder and down his arm. On the shoulder a black panther crouched. I glanced from it to the photo next to it, a similar scene on a similar body. Artistically Griffon's treatment wasn't much different —but his composition seemed alive. The panther glowed.

"How do you do that?"

"Trade secret."

"Griffon."

"You can toss me in the can for a century, but I'm not giving up my secret. That's my career, my life, man."

That I'd keep for leverage. "Okay, fair enough. So you're making good money, and clearly you're not spending it on overhead here. Where is it? In the ACC fund?"

It was a moment before he admitted, "Yeah."

"How much?"

"A couple thou."

"Exactly?"

"Thirteen thousand two hundred forty-three dollars and some cents."

"Whew!" Kovach couldn't resist.

"Why have ACC start a fund?"

He stared down the length of his bony nose, eyeing me as if I were offal not even a vulture would take. "Liquidity, of course."

"You invested the money in the natural place that would suit a group of artists committed to personal freedom, to artistic expression, commerce, and the sudden urge to get their money and move fast—ACC. And then I find you breaking into the office where the head of ACC was murdered. How do you explain that?"

A wise vulture would have shut his beak, abandoned his carrion. Demanded a lawyer. But Griffon said, "I wanted to get Bryant's case file."

I couldn't keep a small smile from settling on my face. So Daisy Culligan had been right; Ott was investigating Bryant Hemming. "Why'd you assume Ott was interested in Bryant?"

"Why else would he be asking me about the ACC investors?"

"And what did you want to find in his file?"

"What Hemming was up to with the ACC fund."

"You think he was siphoning it off for his own use?"

"Oh, no, not yet."

"So why were you concerned?"

"I know people. I could read Bryant Hemming, and the book on him is he's lost his focus. It's like these guys who come in for a full back job here. I spend days customizing the design, choosing the symbols that resonate with them, creating balance in the sketch, harmony in the colors, picking the accent shape and that one color that's just enough out of harmony to make the whole thing come alive. Half the time guys don't even know what their own backs look like. Some skinny kid comes in here demanding a mural. Hell, a mural would wrap around his back and stomach three times. Or a fat guy wants a panda perched in bamboo. Well, that's a champagne glass shape. So what you got is this delicate design coming up from his waist and spreading out over his shoulders. And to the sides of that, untouched, you got all the fat hanging off his ribs. Not a pretty sight."

I laughed, or as close to a laugh as I could come by this hour.

But Griffon was absorbed in his diatribe. "And a whole back, even using a tattoo machine, you don't do a whole back in an hour. It's a long, long process. Days. By the end we're both wiped out. And then what does the guy do? Does he go home and apply Neosporin like I tell him? Does he stay out of the sun so the colors won't fade? No way. He brats out of here like school's out for the summer. He shows his work at every pool in town. And then when it fades, he bitches."

"And Bryant?" I said, pulling him back to his original point.

"Oh, right. Well, investments take maintenance too. You just can't go to the beach and forget about them. They bleach out too."

"Or get involved in mediation and forget them?"

He ran one of those talon fingers across the back of his other hand. Considering. Weighing.

In the silence I stared beyond him at his design on the wall, the shining black panther that looked so alive I expected him to hop off the host's back and attack.

" 'Forget' wasn't it," Griffon said. "Bryant got co-opted by the mediation. It took over everything, and then it sucked him dry."

"And he *forgot* the rest?" I prompted.

"It didn't matter." Griffon leaned forward, tapping one of his talons on the edge of the table. "A decade ago people—not *you*, pillars-of-the-community types —assumed the only misfits who come in here were bikers. Now they figure it's bikers, and their own teenage daughters after discreet hearts on their tits or butterflies on their butts. Truth is I could do you a full-blown psychological survey of society without ever leaving this room. Like the skinny guy after the mural. I talk them out of it, design them a panther over the shoulder. Panther's poised on a wall of full rounded rocks. Now the guy looks in the three-way mirror and he doesn't see his skinny ribs anymore. He's looking at mighty rocks. He gets to thinking of himself as Rocky. He starts strutting down alleys, baiting bikers—"

"And Bryant Hemming?"

"The Mediator Who Could Solve Anything? A mediator's supposed to be behind the scenes, *facilitating*, right? When he starts making himself the star, he's out of control."

"Is that what you told Ott?" I asked on a hunch.

"Yeah."

"What did Ott say?"

He laughed. It was a quick, unpleasant sound of contempt and of triumph.

I raised an eyebrow and waited.

This time he didn't need time to think. "This is what you're after, right? Okay, I'll make you a deal."

I waited some more.

"It matters to me to stay out of jail. Leave me be, and I'll tell you something you won't find out from anyone but me."

"How do I know that?"

"You'll know when I tell you."

I leaned back as if I were pondering his offer. I kept myself from grinning. This was just the offer I'd been planning to make myself. It was clear he knew more than he was telling me; I'd been biding my time to get enough of a handle on him to know what to deal for. "Okay, Griffon, but here are the parameters. Show me what you've got, and you don't make any calls, don't give any warnings. That clear?"

He shrugged off the warning so easily I was sure that the idea of protecting anyone else hadn't crossed his mind. "Ott asked me about Bryant and Cyril. I told him he'd got a pair there."

"Pair of what?"

"The two of them, they wrapped their causes around them like full body murals. The causes are the ink, see, seeps under their skin, but the skin's still their skin. The cause is underneath, you got it? Instead of them being the canvas to advertise the cause, the cause becomes just subcutaneous color for the all-important them."

And that blindness, I thought with a shiver, is what makes them truly dangerous. "Why was Ott asking that?"

"Ott didn't say."

"Did he ask anything else about Bryant?"

Griffon's thin lips pulled up into an eerie parody of a smile. "I ought to charge you extra for this."

"Extra? What is more than freedom?"

He gave me one of those looks that reminds me that sarcasm and philosophical inquiry are unsuitable to police interviews. "What else did Ott ask about Bryant?"

"If his trips to Mexico were just for pleasure."

"And you told him?"

"Far as I knew."

"How far is that?"

He laughed. "I can spit farther. But Ott didn't ask that. Because . . . see, Ott's not the same kind of inside-out fool as Cyril or Bryant. Not quite. Ott's just too damned smug. He figures he can outsmart anyone. He forgets when it gets down to fists, he's just one more skinny little guy."

"Suppose Ott got into a car with Brother Cyril?"

"Then Ott figured he could outwit him. But I'll tell you, Cyril's shrewd. Mix that with unholy ambition, a God-given certainty you are right, and a pack of bullies, and it'll take a lot more than one paunchy little PI to topple him."

A cold shiver shot down my back. Griffon was dead right about Ott, about what he'd do. Ott survived on Telegraph because of his connections and because people feared and respected him. Cyril would do neither.

"And now, Griffon, the question you keep avoiding: You made your way through Ott's office right to the gun. How did you know it was there?"

"I didn't."

"You were just moseying over to take in the view of the air shaft?"

"Hell, no. I was after whatever Ott had found. There was nothing in his office, was there? You saw me go through there, didn't you? So whatever it was had to be in his emergency hideout, where he puts stuff when it's not safe inside the office."

His talonlike fingers were not tapping decisively as they had before but making nervous little circles. He was lying, of course, but I couldn't figure just why or about what. For anyone else the idea of hanging valuables out his window would have been ludicrous, but I wouldn't rule it out for Ott. Then what was Griffon adding, subtracting, substituting, subverting?

CHAPTER 19

At 12:30 A.M. I SAT in front of the typewriter off the squad room pondering Griffon's lie. A sin of commission, or more likely omission. Everyone's got something he or she doesn't want us to know. Mostly the desperate silence is more a sign of self-centeredness than unrevealed clues. Griffon was well enough endowed in the ego department to assume that I'd not only want to know his secrets but would broadcast them to the waiting world. He was also sly enough to withhold a valuable lead, and shifty enough to be involved.

I swayed to the siren song of Ott's asking the purpose of Bryant Hemming's trips to Mexico, Bryant Hemming going there to score contraband for a big Berkeley sale and Ott hot on the trail. But what would Ott expect to find in Mexico beyond the fact that he couldn't speak Spanish? Ott's kryptonite was his knowledge of Berkeley. Outside the city he was no Superman. If he needed information from Mexico, he'd step into a phone booth and call a Mexican counterpart. And if we suspected Bryant Hemming had tanned himself in Acapulco waiting for contraband, we'd go through our own channels.

I took my pasty white face to the typewriter and

started on my reports from the day. I was desperate enough to plunk coins into the wretched coffee machine and drink the brown water without white powder and hope that it had, this once, more caffeine than a No-Doz.

"My office, Smith," Inspector Doyle snapped.

I picked up my little stack of reports and headed through the half-lit records room with its empty desks and brown metal files that screamed "fiscal restraint." In Berkeley not funding the police is seen as keeping the playing field level.

I rounded the corner and headed into the inspector's outer office. Jackson and Eggs were in the inner sanctum, behind the rhinoceroses grazing along the interior windowsill. They were settled in chairs, Homicide detectives as I had once been, sitting in the Homicide inspector's office waiting to deal with the outsider. I wasn't quite that, but I could tell from the polite nods they offered that I wasn't one of them anymore either.

Doyle braced himself beside his chair. "Smith, Griffon breaks into Ott's office and goes straight for the gun and you leave him on the street?"

"It was a judgment call." I claimed the doorway.

Jackson whistled. Eggs said nothing. I had worked homicides with each of them. I'd taught Clayton Jackson's son to dive in the pool, and Jackson had brought me cups of Peet's coffee to get me through Detectives' Too-Early-in-the-Morning Meetings. He'd given me the black man's view, and I'd swapped him the woman's take. He and Eggs—Al Eggenburger— were the perfect partners. With the exception of sex they were in every way opposites. Jackson was burly, Eggs pencil thin. I'd virtually never seen the top of

Jackson's desk under the papers; Eggs's was waxed. Jackson's wall was covered in family pictures; Eggs went home to a fish tank. Yet they'd come to know and trust each other in a way that's hard when your subconscious assumptions are so different. For a decade Eggs had ribbed Jackson as Clay mourned his football Raiders lost to L.A. In his hands Jackson's prayers for the miracle of his team's return to Oakland had become a department standard. "Right, Friedman," Eggs would say, "you'll close that case. And Jackson's Raiders will come home to Oakland." Eventually any dead-end case was classified as a JR.

And when, after negotiations had piqued hopes, then failed year after year, suddenly the beloved Raiders did come back to Oakland, Jackson said not a thing. He waited.

Eggs filled their office with silver and black balloons.

Jackson said nothing.

Eggs sent singing caterers to Jackson's tailgate party.

Jackson said nothing.

Jackson was waiting.

Like Jackson, who had mourned in frustration over the years, Eggs realized there was nothing he could do.

Eggs was waiting too. He knew Jackson would choose the perfect moment to— So Eggs was watching his tail. And the rest of us were watching, waiting, eagerly. Warily.

Occasionally Eggs had pushed Jackson too hard in spots he never expected to be tender. Once or twice Jackson had pierced Eggs, mistaken his icy restraint for indifference and weeks later wondered why he was

being cold-shouldered. Then they'd been glad to have
me in Homicide to tell them where their knives had
stuck and how to pull them out without cutting
deeper. They watched out for me, translating Inspector Doyle's grumbles, warning me when he was waving his shillelagh.

That was why Jackson's critical whistle now sent a
cold wind down my spine. Was he keeping his distance because of his disdain for Ott? Or had something happened in this case I didn't know about?

"The judgment call I made," I said, "was that
Griffon is of more use to us while he's afraid of being
arrested. The guy really doesn't want to go to jail."

"Why? A tattooer like him, jail'd be like hitting a
trade fair." Jackson laughed.

I shook my head. "Don't know his secret. But he
might as well have affixed a pump handle to his
mouth. We can go back to the well again and again, as
long as he's on the street. Here's the tasty drop
pumped out tonight: He says Ott asked him whether
Bryant Hemming's trips to Mexico were just vaca-
tions."

"Mediation, ACC investing, and now smuggling?
Our Bryant was a diversified lad," Eggs said. "While
we're talking Hemming and money, here's Macalester's droplet. He thinks maybe—he's not sure—
he doesn't want to be quoted—"

"Say he hemmed and hawed enough to be a Hemming himself?" Jackson asked.

"Yeah, Clay. But I'm a patient man. And patience
got me this: He thinks Hemming was paying off none
other than Brother Cyril."

"Whew! And proof?"

"Not a whit, Smith. Nothing in the ACC books, or

so he says. But you don't document your bribes for any accountant to see."

Doyle leaned back in his chair, eyes half closed, looking for the thread that wove through this case. His loose skin was gray, and every hour of the long night seemed to have made its mark. To come up with the base thread, he'd have to have been in better shape than I was by now. Ott was investigating Bryant. Bryant was paying off Cyril.

I picked up an amber rhino and held it out in front of me like a talisman. Or a guard. I'd have given a lot to avoid saying, "I saw Ott Sunday afternoon."

"So that's where you went off to." Emotions battled in Jackson's voice. I'd left him—my guest—I'd left the Raiders game, in favor of Ott. He sounded appalled at my lack of taste rather than hurt the way Howard had been.

Eggs's expression didn't change. He was a master of the mask, but I could read the taut tendons in his neck required to hold his mask in place and the shock, disgust, even suspicion beneath it. Doyle didn't bother with masks.

I hurried on. "Ott shucked me. He insisted he had to see me then, at the Claremont, for something vital, and when I got there, he'd changed his mind. But a little cross fell out of Ott's pocket. It could have nothing to do with Brother Cyril, of course, but—"

"Shorter than an inch?" Jackson demanded. "Did it come to the point at the bottom, like a sword?"

"Uh-huh. Why?"

"That's Brother Cyril's all right. Gives them to the holy."

"That lets out Ott," Eggs put in automatically, but his eager expression discounted his own witticism.

"What you're saying is either Ott's fooled Cyril into awarding him the cross, or he swiped it."

My throat tightened as I recalled Griffon's assessment of Ott smugly striding into the lion's den.

"What'd Ott say about it?"

"What do you think, Jackson?"

Jackson shut his mouth against that thought.

"I gave him till five to get back to me. He didn't." I didn't recount that as an offering, but as I glanced at Eggs and Jackson and Doyle, I knew it wouldn't have been enough. My meeting with Ott was on my own time. But I hadn't mentioned it to them; I had separated it, and myself, from them. Now their faces said they didn't know if they considered me one of them.

I had one of those flashes then, when the insight comes too fast and deep and it's only later that you translate it into words so you can remember it. I knew two things: that I could have reinstated myself by regaling them with a ribald account of Herman Ott hanging his valuables out the window over the alley for safekeeping and that I couldn't do it. Not because of them, my friends and colleagues, but because of Ott or maybe me. When I did mention it, matter-of-factly, offering no camaraderie, the only response was a groan from Jackson and a formal question from Doyle on whether I believed Griffon.

I replaced the amber rhino on the desk, away from the herd. Protecting me was beyond its ability now.

"Griffon's holding back; I just don't know what. But I'm beginning to view that alley not as a dead end but as a thoroughfare to eye Ott's window."

Doyle shook his head. Out the corner of my vision I spotted Jackson eyeing Eggs. Doyle cleared his throat. "We got zilch from the neighbors."

"Company Ott keeps, no right-minded person would open the door if he was squeaking 'Help!' in the hallway either," Eggs said.

Jackson nodded in agreement. "Way I hear it, only the blind were on the Avenue last night."

I glanced from Jackson to Eggs, waiting for another line of banter, but they offered nothing more, nothing they wouldn't want repeated outside the room.

"What about Kidd?" Doyle asked.

"He could know more than he let on, but what, I can't guess," I said. "Still, he's smart enough not to kill Hemming in Ott's office, then dream about it in Ott's car. I'm buying his story of Ott getting into a dark car on the Avenue Sunday night."

Doyle gave a snort. "Eggenburger, what'd you get from Hemming's assistant, Macalester?"

"He had no idea why his boss would be in Ott's office. He appeared appalled. He said he was baffled, although he did want me to understand that Hemming mediated for all segments of society. The implication seemed to be that Ott was a step beneath all those segments."

"What about Brother Cyril? Anything on him?"

"Cyril Bernauer. Two assaults. Felonies. Three and five years ago. Nothing since. He's known to Monterey, but only for helping out society by hiring ex-cons."

"Local address?" Doyle asked.

"Zip. We know he's got a place big enough for two dozen guys somewhere around here. *Where* is the big Q."

Doyle nodded at Jackson to keep on it. "Eggs, you're still backgrounding Hemming and ACC?"

"Right."

Doyle nodded. Neither of them looked at me.

Jackson pushed himself up. He had seemed as worn out as Doyle, but now there was no sag in his dark brown cheeks. "I am prepared for the good brother when I track him down. Ain't no passage or verse I can't answer."

"So you can go head to head with Cyril and his Scripture on Jesus in the temple obliterating the money changers and their pigeons."

Jackson shook his head. "We're not talking Kentucky Fried here. Smith, where did you spend your Sabbath mornings?" He glanced at Doyle and Eggs, but clearly whatever I had missed had passed them too. "Mark eleven: fifteen: 'and Jesus went into the temple, and began to cast out them that sold and bought in the temple, and overthrew the tables of the moneychangers, and the seats of them that sold doves.'"

"Doves?"

"Doves, pigeons, same bird, different translations. Point is, Smith, Jesus was after the people, not their birds."

"But Cyril said—"

"Right, and he's not the first preacher to rewrite the Scripture in his own image."

I felt a cold stab of fear. "So killing the birds is his own idea?" Was Ott in Cyril's cage? Was he, as Howard said, a bird held for sacrifice?

"That and who knows how much more. I've seen more phony men of the cloth than this boy's got years. Hauling his ass out of bed's going to be like a good cup of coffee." He nodded to Inspector Doyle and headed for the hall.

I followed him into the hallway.

He was a big guy, but his gait was closer to a glide than a walk. Now the slide had been preempted by the heavy steps of finality. He stopped and for the first time tonight stared me in the eye. "I'm keeping my mind open, and my eyes." He didn't ask, *"What about you?"* He took a step back toward me and lowered his voice. "The system can set you up and send you up. No one knows that better than a black man. Yet and still, you got a guy dead in his office, killed by a nine-millimeter like Ott's got out his window, and Ott on the lam. We don't look for him number one, we might as well boogie on home and pull up the covers."

I stared him back. "Hemming controlled people's money. He's got an ex-wife he screwed. There could be girlfriends he was leaving behind and disgruntled mediation clients all over town. We know squat about the man, and you're writing off everyone but Ott!" I wasn't shouting, but I had to choke back the urge.

"Smith, the dude sidled into a car and drove off into the sunset. The same night as Hemming was shot in his office."

"Right, he left, Jackson. Ott was *gone*. But we go charging after him because he's the outsider."

"Smith—"

"Don't big-brother me."

He stared, clearly as shocked by my fury as I was, then shook his head and left.

I stood watching till he disappeared behind the reception door, till my shaking stopped and I'd tightened my face into a mask worthy of Eggs. Then I turned back to the office. Doyle was examining a yellow jade rhino with the care of a trophy hunter redecorating his den. I didn't know how much Doyle had heard, probably all of it. Didn't matter. Nothing I could do.

Doyle replaced the animal and leaned forward over the pile of papers on his desk. "Smith, I never thought I'd have to say this to one of my officers." He inhaled, swallowed. I watched his Adam's apple flutter and descend. "Maybe I should take you off this case."

"No!" burst out through my tightly pressed lips. But that was just my first reaction. I forced myself to stop, think. Doyle was giving me a way to maintain my bond with Ott and not undercut the investigation and my career. Taken off the case, I could go back to Ott later, if he was found innocent enough to be on the street again, and still be his least undesirable cop. Among the sworn officers there would be questions, gossip about my reassignment, but that would die down; I'd go on riding patrol; nothing would change much. Doyle was offering me an out; all I had to do was take it. I looked at Doyle, leaning back in his too fine desk chair, eyes half closed, giving the illusion he was resting behind the lids instead of watching between the lashes. Again I wondered: Is there something more going on here? I said, "I don't think Ott is a killer."

"Smith—"

I held up my palm. "But if he is, Inspector, he'll have duped me and duped me good, and you can believe I will be pissed enough to make him crawl in here."

Doyle fingered the rhino. Slowly, equivocally he said, "All right."

I stood up. "You've got an APB out on Ott, right? You've got everyone on patrol hunting for moving yellow. They're not going to find him. Ott's got a thousand places he could go to ground in this city. Don't hope for a snitch. Ott's too savvy to stay put long enough to be turned in. Odds are a hundred to one we'll never find him. But, Inspector, if you care about that 'one,' you're going to have to go with me. And trust me."

The yellow rhino was in his hand, belly up. "I'm trusting you, Smith," he said in a skeptical tone. "I've already talked to half the media in the Bay Area and had two calls from L.A. I've got a press conference scheduled in the morning. By noon we'll be news in D.C. We're under the microscope, Smith, and the rest of the country's going to be looking through the other end. Looking to see how ridiculous Berkeley can make itself." He laid the rhino on its side, as if it had been gored. "Man shot. Office tenant disappears. Tattooed vulture breaks in; cop lets him walk. The loonies are running the institution, they'll be saying. And, Smith, they'll be right."

CHAPTER 20

I CONSIDERED CHANGING OUT OF uniform. I could make the rounds of Ott's associates in jeans and turtleneck in my own VW bug. But the only difference between that and arriving in full gear at People's Park would be the increased danger to me. My first beat had been by the park; it would be a decade or two before I could pass for a civilian there. I signed out a patrol car and headed back to the Avenue.

Set behind a row of shops on Telegraph, People's Park is safer than it used to be in daytime. At night the curfew is strict, but still only the ignorant, foolhardy, or greedy walk through alone. Any other time I could have stopped at the far end and found an "informal campsite" of homeless men, bundled in drab, dirt-sweated coats, asleep next to their Safeway carts, amid the bottles and needles that cause and ease their plights. I could have given my spiel about Ott once and known it would make the rounds before I got home. But now there's a curfew, and for the time being sleepers have dispersed to alleys, to doorways, under bridges and bushes, plus the university campus, and miles and miles of state park bordering Berkeley on the east.

I spotted Wesley, a guy in his thirties who had

blown in from Texas and got caught on a laid-back branch. He had staked out a spot leeward of a restaurant Dumpster. The café was a breakfast and lunch place. It spoke well of Wesley to have chosen this Dumpster, which wasn't touched after dusk. He was curled around a covey of plastic bags, his nose almost on the macadam.

"Wesley."

His eyes shot open before I got to the second syllable. He was on his feet in an instant. "Hey, man, I didn't—"

"No problem. I'm looking for Herman Ott."

"Don't know the dude." He checked over his shoulder. If anyone else was in the alley, he wasn't moving.

"You do know me. Jill Smith."

"Smith? Oh, yeah."

"Ott's in danger. Big time. He needs to call me."

"Don't know the dude."

"And Brother Cyril. I've got to find him. I'm looking for where he stays in Berkeley."

"Don't know."

"Thanks."

I repeated variations of the conversation with six other guys, one in a doorway, a couple of dealers, three old rads, putting the word on the World Wide Web of the dispossessed. It would reach Ott if he was reachable.

I rolled west to the station, signed the car in, unpacked myself from uniform, and headed to my VW. Those first steps without twenty-five pounds of equipment hanging off my hips, and the bullet-resistant vest corseting each breath, were like flying free.

Then the weight of the day, all sixteen hours of it, fell like sandbags onto my shoulders.

It was nearly 2:00 A.M. when I trudged in the door at Howard's house. The lights were on—a bad sign. Frequently one or another of the tenants was in the living room with friends or a lover. Low lights meant compromising positions for them and a quick pass through for me. But brighter lights warned of an eager, chatty group or one anxious to argue the politics of my being "the man." Or worse yet, one of the lovelorn needing to talk. I could put them off, but not without cost. Right now the most diplomatic response I'd be able to muster was silence.

I summoned my last spark of energy and opened the door.

In front of the big stone hearth Howard stood looking like an oversize Christmas ornament with his long red-tufted legs jutting from the hem of the green terry-cloth robe I'd gotten him from the Eddie Bauer catalog.

"I'm cooking."

"Cooking?" I said. "No one has cooked here since the Berlin Wall fell. Alex"—the tenant in the back room—"keeps his thesis notes in the oven. Are you baking 'Ecological Disaster Subsequent to Excessive Timber Exports and Land Fill Implementation'?"

Howard straightened to his full six-six. "I've got yesterday's satay waiting for the magic finger. Follow and behold Chef Seth nuke to point of perfection."

He strode through the half-lit living room, his bare feet splatting like flippers on the bottom of the pool. It was no wonder the man came in ten yards ahead of me when we swam laps. He pressed the start panel on the microwave, and in a minute the kitchen was filled with the spicy smell of peanuts and hot peppers and I realized how startlingly hungry I was. "You've been home for hours and didn't eat it? Is there a love greater than that?" I wrapped my arms around him from the back and wriggled a hand between the sides of his robe, sliding my fingers along his warm furry stomach.

The microwave beeped. Howard gave my arms a quick squeeze with his elbows, extricated himself and the satay container. Extricated himself a mite quickly. I stepped back and looked more carefully at him. His hair was not mussed from sleep. His hands weren't stained by Spackle. There was no sheen of sweat from a nocturnal run or pseudorun in the Y. "What have you been up to all evening?"

"Doing you a favor." He stared at the satay bowl, and for a wild moment I played with the idea of what were desirable gifts to porcelain bowl or peanut sauce.

Howard swallowed. Once when he was a child, he had told me, he'd stared at a glass of castor oil and orange juice for two hours before forcing it down. How hard to swallow was what he couldn't quite bring himself to say now?

"You were doing me a favor?" I forced out.

"Keeping my ears open—for you. Went to dinner . . . with a couple of the guys. . . . Came back to . . . finish up some paperwork." He swallowed again, deliberately this time, and looked directly at me. "You want to hear what the word is around the station?"

"I just left Doyle's office. I already know." Balancing rice carton, spoon, bowl, and chopsticks in my arms, I headed for the coffee table.

"You sure?" He plunked the satay carton on the

Chronicle. "Is this what you know? You don't find Herman Ott, you're either incompetent or sleeping with the enemy."

"They said that to you?"

Howard nodded.

My throat constricted. It wasn't so much the comment that frightened me as the realization that my fellow officers—my friends—viewed me as so suspect they felt free to damn me to my own lover. "And you said?" I choked out.

Howard sat and spooned broccoli over prawns over zucchini in the already mixed satay.

I pulled my arms closer against the chill. I knew what was coming. I just couldn't believe it was really happening.

"Jill—" His voice caught. "Jill, on the force trust is all we've got. You know it. When we're out there alone on patrol, we've got to be able to count on each other one hundred percent—"

"Are you saying my fellow officers can't count on me?"

"Of course not. But if they aren't sure they can, it's the same thing."

I could hear my voice hardening as I repeated my question, "And you said to them?"

He kept stirring the satay.

"It's going to be cold," I snapped.

"I *said*, Jill, that you knew Ott, you'd find him."

"But not that they could count on me."

It was a moment before he answered. "That wasn't the question."

I yanked his arm around. His chopsticks shot onto the floor. "It wasn't *not* the question."

He pulled his arm free. "Hey, don't yell at me. I'm the one who's trying to help."

"I didn't ask you to help. You can just mind your own damned—"

His voice was so muted I couldn't hear it over the pounding in my ears.

"What?"

"It is my business." He corralled the chopsticks off the floor. "It's my business because I love you."

Oh, God, how could I do this to him? I sank back into the emaciated cushion, onto the overstretched supports. Another half foot and I'd be seated on the floor. Howard should have replaced this hand-me-down years ago. Like he should have me. "Look, if you can't trust—"

"God damn it, Jill, I'm the all-time expert on broken trust."

I stared up unbelieving. A protest was almost out of my mouth before I realized that he was of course referring to his mother. To their sudden departures from one town after another throughout his childhood, to her disappearance after he had gone to college. His freshman year she had called him four times, his sophomore year twice. And when summer came, he had a job on campus as part of his work-study. He waited to hear from her. But her call didn't come till over a year later. That was the time he suspected she had been institutionalized. He didn't know for sure. Didn't want to know. Couldn't bear to think of her floating spirit caged. Or to wonder if she had been normal at his age.

I knew how important was the security of this house, his job, his friends. The house made up for apartment after apartment in which they ate off packing cartons under pictures left by previous tenants. It was the place his mother could always reach him should the spirit move her. He cherished his friends, made excuses for their failings, luxuriated in shared memories as if they were pictures in a family album, the kinds of pictures Herman Ott had torn out of his album in the Wanamaker's box. Howard's job protected it all and gave him entry into the family of police that no outsider could hope for.

And his friends were constant reminders that he was normal, that he would never be sucked off into the terrifying ether, as his mother apparently had been. The open road that beckoned me was to him the path to nothingness.

He was still standing over me fear-stiff. I longed to pull him down to me, to hold him so tight there was no room between us for emptiness or terror. To make the problem go away.

But the problem was me.

I struggled to sound uncompromising, to keep my voice from breaking. "Howard, stay out of it. There's enough swirling around me; I can't deal with dragging you into it too."

"No choice." He eased down next to me. "Jill, you've got to—"

"I've got to find Ott. And that probably means tracking down Brother Cyril and maybe Bryant Hemming's killer."

"Jesus, have you heard anything I said? Hunt the killer, and you're going to be tramping on toes. The toes of everyone in the department, if there are any you haven't already trampled."

On the table the peanuty smell of satay mocked us, too sweet, too oily. Howard spooned rice onto plates, satay over the top. It was cold, of course, the way the room was cold, the way I was cold, down to my marrow. I longed to shift a couple of inches closer to Howard and feel his warmth, but I couldn't move.

He waited another moment, shook his head slowly, and forked a shrimp. "So, Jill, you've got the word out on the Avenue?" It was the kind of question, shoptalk, that had gotten us through tension and crisis year after year. No one dived into a case like Howard, tossing out strategies, catching twists, loving the game of it. The question was one he would have asked anytime, but now there was no life to it, as if he had been called into a game he knew was already lost.

But I grabbed it. "Hardly. If Ott's hiding out, no one's going to convince him he would be better off in a cell. If he's shackled and chained, it's not like I'm offering a reward." I fingered my chopsticks. "And if he shot Bryant—right, I can't rule out the possibility —it's the same difference. No one's going to lead me to Ott. I'm going to have to figure him out like an acrostic puzzle and just hope I don't have to substitute every letter in the alphabet before I find the answer."

Howard trapped a pile of rice between his chopsticks. "I've given this a bit of thought." He lifted the sauce-coated mass to his mouth and chewed. "Why were you at Ott's office today? It's not on your beat. So why were you there to find Hemming's body at all?"

"Because," I said, "Kidd was sleeping in Ott's Studebaker."

"And why did you discover him? I'm ignoring the fact that you skirted your superior officer to do it," he said, brushing off what would normally have been a serious issue between us.

"I checked the car because Ott hadn't called me back Sunday afternoon, like he swore he would—"

"—when he called you to his command performance Sunday afternoon. So, what did he want then?"

Slowly I bit down on a prawn, through the taut skin into the yielding, defenseless flesh. I was remembering that brief, infuriating confrontation with Ott Sunday afternoon. "No clue. He told me zip. Only thing I can be sure of is he was on to—or after—something important enough that he was willing to bargain with me."

"But between the time Ott called you and you got to him, something happened to make him decide—"

"—he could do without me." I plucked another prawn from the sauce and poised it an inch from my mouth. "It wasn't that he was threatened; then he wouldn't have shown up at all. But he was there, on time, in costume. He wasn't going to give, but—"

"Yeah, Jill, he wasn't burning his bridge with you either. In case he needed to make use of you later."

"So graciously put. Ott wasn't swept into someone else's game; he was on to something. A lead. Something so explosive he didn't need me. What, dammit?"

We both continued to eat, pretending to ignore the wall of difference that pushed between us like an overbearing guest. We took swallows of beer. Howard moved the serving bowls to the floor, slid his white-socked feet on the coffee table like two great sails on an outrigger canoe, and said, "Let's try a different angle—Hemming himself. You always like this one, Jill: What did the man do to bring this heinous crime upon himself?"

I forced a tepid smile. Howard did know me. I acknowledged random shootings, houses broken into for no better reason than beer, coke, or dare, but with each case the stupidity struck me afresh. I clutched to the tenet of cause and effect, as if each victory over chaos was an affirmation that life was ultimately controllable. As if a woman whose husband had meticulously planned her shooting were less dead than if she'd been hit by a ricochet. It almost pleased me to find the victim had taunted, slighted, cheated her eventual killer, that all the strands curled back into the center of the ball. "What," I mused, "was so vital to Hemming that he would stop at Ott's office on his way to the airport? To see Ott, he'd have been assuming. What was there that Ott had discovered or Hemming thought Ott had discovered or might be on the way to discovering?" Our plates empty, we just sat.

It was Howard who said, "Hemming's a big event guy. Do you remember what bounced him into mediating big time to begin with?"

I shook my head.

"The post office! Hemming's in the main branch. He takes a number; he's standing against the wall, balancing a boxed urn on its way to Pacific Beach. He's worrying if he'll get to the window before his meter expires when all of a sudden the clerk calls number seventy-seven and Harold Mackey walks up to the window with a ticking package he says is a bomb. Bryant drops the urn, and while everyone's staring openmouthed, he asks Mackey what he wants, like it's an everyday question. Mackey, not the sharpest knife in the drawer, hasn't thought that far. He's pissed; what he wants is trouble. It may be a bomb that's ticking. There's no time for negotiating back and forth. Bryant gets the postmaster down and says to Mackey, 'You're the guy who pays the postage, and you want to be treated with respect, right? With all these people in line here the postal service can hire an extra clerk to staff the window; if they keep you waiting, they can pay your parking ticket.' Then he eyes the postmaster. What's the guy to do in the face of a bomb and a roomful of citizens, all in Mackey's corner?"

"Surely that deal didn't hold?"

"Not the parking tickets. They'd have to charge a buck a stamp to cover that. But they did add an extra clerk. Harold Mackey gave up his package, which turned out to be a real bomb. One of the postal customers was a newspaper columnist. Next edition Bryant Hemming's front-page news. A month later he's on *A Fair Deal*."

I nodded, a silent "That's nice."

"Bryant's first three mediations on *A Fair Deal* were bombs—no pun intended. But that didn't matter. The post office triumph gave him time to get the game right. So now Bryant's heading to the big show in Washington, where the stakes are huge and the pitfalls bottomless. He needs to come riding in off a triumph."

I nodded again, a silent "aha!"

"So the Serenity Kaetz–Brother Cyril deal was vital to Hemming."

"And the reason the deal worked at all," I said slowly, "was that Brother Cyril caved in."

"And how did ol' Bryant convince the godly brother to turn the other cheek? We talking threat or bribe?"

"And if we've figured this out, of course Ott did

too. Of course Bryant would be panicked that Ott would go public. Of course he wouldn't dare ignore a summons supposedly from Ott no matter how inconvenient."

I called Jackson's beeper, waited for him to get back to me, and relayed Howard's theory. I don't know where Jackson was calling from, but it was a place he didn't mind laughing in. "That's one fast blessing for the money, Smith."

Howard was already upstairs when I got off the phone. The shoptalk was done, and the chasm still hung between us. Taking a step into its bottomless black terrified Howard even more than it did me, but he didn't have the generations of avoidance techniques that my family had provided. I could dally a few minutes and he'd be asleep or at least in bed with his eyes shut. I took my time tossing out the satay cartons and washing the few plates—a mere shrug to my family's tradition of scouring pots, scalding china, and polishing silver in a crisis—before I went upstairs, but when I opened the door, Howard was sitting against the headboard. "I'll tell you the oddest thing I came across today," I said before he could speak. "Break-in at a self-storage locker right under ACC's unit. Renter's Margo Roehner." Hoping for a sign of recognition, I glanced at Howard. But I would have been surprised—amazed—if she'd been known to a former Vice and Substance Abuse detective. "She's got this locker filled with medical records and files and stuff even the thief wouldn't touch. And in the back of the locker, what do I find? A backed poster of a flashing pig."

"Flashing, naked?"

"Raincoat open."

"Takes all kinds." He was warming to this safe topic.

"This kind—Margo Roehner—is on the board of ACC."

I walked into the bathroom and shut the door. When I emerged, he was lying on his side, and I couldn't decipher his expression. As I slipped between the sheets, I said, "Bryant Hemming's ex-wife, Daisy Culligan, delivers dinners—"

Howard muttered something. Then he pulled me to him with a desperation of love and fear and helplessness. I clutched him, squeezing him so tightly I could feel each of his ribs, pressing our mouths together until the passion wiped out grief and hope and thought.

We didn't speak again. It wasn't till he was gone the next morning that I remembered those mutterings and realized he had said, "Maybe the pig poster was Daisy's."

CHAPTER 21

I WOKE UP BEFORE THE alarm. It had been one of those nights when I slept like a stone and woke exhausted, as if my inert body had been the gridiron for the Super Bowl. The room was the disheartening fog gray that masks the dawn in Berkeley. Something had happened, something deep-gut bad, but I was still too close to sleep to translate that feeling into language. I nestled against Howard. Automatically he cupped himself around me. I felt the comfortingly familiar ridges of his ribs and hipbones, the warmth of his flesh; I let my eyes shut against the day and curled myself into the sweet sanctuary.

He had the day off, and when the alarm rang, I caught it mid-ring and in fifteen minutes I was in my car on my way to the Y. It wasn't till I was sitting in the sauna, post-swim, an hour later that I recalled the last thing Howard had said the night before: "Maybe the pig poster was Daisy's." Not "Culligan's." "Daisy's." So, he knew Daisy Culligan. Or at least he knew of her.

Professionally?

In Vice and Substance Abuse Detail?

Daisy with a stash wasn't hard to imagine, even doing a line of coke, though it seemed beyond her budget. But if she came to Howard's attention for narcotics, she would have been on the departmental files. Her only listed contact with the department was as a witness to a doctor's tirade when he discovered his car surrounded by a castle wall of cement blocks. The caller, whose driveway he had parked across, returned to find him strewing blocks as far as a tiny ophthalmologist can toss.

As I recalled that, I smiled. The story had made the papers. The doctor demanded we arrest the woman, insisted her alibi—she was in traffic court—was faked, and ended up with orders to stack his blocks neatly on the curb and a ticket for blocking her driveway.

The only odd thing about it, which I had overlooked at the time, was the presence of Daisy Culligan.

I wouldn't bet my life on why Howard was familiar with her. But wager a month's salary? Easy.

I dressed in record time—green turtleneck and slacks, gray tweed jacket—and called Howard on my cell phone before I realized our home phone would still be turned off. I could have driven back to the house, but I was in front of the station, and there was an empty parking spot. I pulled in, telling myself that it was a sign, that I could call Howard later, that he'd stayed up late for me and needed to sleep. I didn't admit that seeing him face-to-face would force both of us to bring up last night or pointedly to ignore it. Besides, I didn't need Howard to enlighten me about Daisy Culligan; she could do that herself.

From the station I dialed Daisy.

"Dining with Daisy! I'm sorry I can't get to the phone right now, but if you'll—"

"Call Officer Jill Smith." I left my number. No

explanation. I was more likely to get answers from her face than her words. I needed surprise on my side.

I checked my mail slot and voice mail, vainly hoping for word from Laura Goldman in Pittsburgh. For the hell of it, I dialed Ott's number.

"Ott. Go 'head." None of this "*So sorry to have missed your call*" for Ott.

I didn't leave a message. Even if Ott had wandered in from the dead or the lam and picked up the phone, he of course wouldn't have given me any answers.

So, who would?

Before I could tackle that question, my pager went off. I picked up the phone and dialed Pittsburgh.

"Goldman?"

"You miss me, Smith?"

"You bet. What've you got?"

"On your Ott?"

"Right."

"You said he's a counterculture guy? A denizen of a scabrous dwelling? A defender of the underdog? A termite-infested pillar of antiestablishment?"

"Right, Goldman. Ott's so antiestablishment I'm surprised he accepts payment in American money, even when it's offered, which isn't often. His clothes come only from secondhand stores. He buys day-old doughnuts on Fridays and eats from the box all week."

A fuzzy sound came from the phone.

"Goldman?"

She was laughing.

"Goldman!"

"Well, Smith, like I told you, your Ott vanished after he graduated from high school. I still don't know why. Officially no one does. And, Smith, no one but Esther Jakobs's granddaughter would have been able to get Sister Joseph Martha, formerly Mary Martha Macray of the Herman housemaid corps, to admit what she heard from her niece, who took her place in the Herman household thirty years ago. My grandmother was her best friend. Nana started there as a young girl right off the boat. It was a scandalous thing for a proper Jewish girl to do, living in the house of Gentiles, but that's another story. I'll tell you about her someday.

"Anyway, here's what Sister Joseph Martha's niece heard. The Hermans and the Otts were both very controlled families. Voices were never raised. Nana said for years she assumed that WASP vocal cords had atrophied over the centuries and just didn't have the range of normal people's. But this one day something threw your Ott's family into a fury. Your Ott—Alexander—and his father screamed at each other. Blows were exchanged. It ended with Alexander shouting that he would never set eyes on his father again. In fact he couldn't stand being in the same country, on the same continent with his father. He stormed out of the house, took nothing with him, and had the chauffeur drive him to the airport. He was last seen at the Iberia Airlines counter."

A righteously angry young Herman Ott stomping off to Spain? I could picture that. A quarter of a century ago escape to Europe would have fitted a young radical. Still, something wasn't right.

It sounded as if Goldman were smothering a chuckle.

"Iberia Airlines? Goldman, did they fly out of Pittsburgh that long ago?"

"Nope." She hooted. "Your Ott was a real silver-spoon radical. He stomped out of the mansion and had the chauffeur drive him to the Iberia gate—at Kennedy!"

I howled. I could hardly wait to tell Howard. In fact the only person who wouldn't be amused by this story would be Herman Ott. Clearly he'd *never* possessed a sense of humor. When I got myself under control, I said, "Do you have any idea what caused the fight?"

"None. But I'm on it, Smith. When I know, you'll know."

"Thanks." After I'd hung up, I was left wondering if I had anything more valuable than an amusing anecdote. If Ott had friends in Spain, or Paris, Amsterdam, Moscow, or Copenhagen, what did that tell me? It only made the net I'd need larger. It told me nothing new about him now. Certainly it shed no light on where Ott might be. He had been gone too long. All my moves were into dead ends. I needed to uncover an entirely new route.

I left a message for Jackson: "Anything on Cyril? Call me with *anything*."

Then I headed to Ott's office. It would amuse him to skirt us and hide out there.

It wasn't till I was pulling up outside on Telegraph that it struck me that it might amuse the killer to deposit another body in Ott's office. Ott's.

CHAPTER 22

TELEGRAPH AVENUE AT 9:00 A.M. on Wednesday was the asphalt and storefront equivalent of the morning after. The pizza plates and bagel bags that ricocheted from curb to curb in the night lay in soggy heaps where puddles ambushed them. Crushed paper bags and abandoned bottles marked dress shop portals; snowy hillocks of paper napkins stood firm by the doors of restaurants serving samosas, lamb kabobs, and vegetable mu shu. Those doors wouldn't be open for nearly two hours. And it would be nearly that long before the sidewalk vendors began setting up. Craftspeople don't choose their trade because they're enamored of the nine to five.

Nothing had changed in Ott's office: no bodies live or dead. I circled Telegraph and environs once, keeping an eye out for Ott's cronies, but the truth was I had been everywhere, talked to everyone who could connect me with him. I wasn't going to find him by charging straight on this way. I wasn't going to find him unless I figured out who had lured him out of his office; that meant tracking down who had killed Bryant Hemming there. Or, as Howard would put it, by stepping on toes.

Serenity Kaetz's address was up nearly to Grizzly

Peak Boulevard at the crest of the Berkeley Hills. Real estate values elevate with the land. But there are enough building eccentricities in Berkeley that Serenity Kaetz's address didn't surprise me. She might be renting a tiny room in a 1920s stone and stucco mansion, much like Daisy Culligan. She could be staying in a cliff-hanger whose pylons hadn't been driven deeply enough into the steep ground to reach bedrock, renting cheaply from the owners unable to face the unpalatable alternatives of living there: death or financial destruction. Serenity might own a pastel stucco box that sat above its element. She could have bought a wooden craftsman's bungalow twenty years ago, before property costs rose higher than the hills themselves. Or she could be hanging out in a tree.

In fact she had moved into the garage of what appeared to be a small, woodsy cottage but that ran two more levels down the hillside in the back, creating one of those bleacher-seat houses in which every room has a view of redwoods, live oaks, the Bay and Bay Bridge, or San Francisco beyond. It was her heavily mortgaged house. Rented out, she told me, to pay for her art. And it was her garage.

"I gave myself three years," she said, turning off a soldering iron and pushing an irregular sheet of metal back from the edge of her workbench. The unconverted garage was just that. Stucco walls, pull-up door in front, exit door on the side. Room for one car or a five-foot-five-inch woman in caramel denim overalls over maroon sweatshirt, a sleeping bag rolled in one corner, canvas camp bed frame folded next to it, two suitcases under the workbench, and Peg-Boards displaying delicate copper crane necklaces, intricately entwined brass cuffs, earrings of silver irises, multimetal lotuses, and flowers and birds I couldn't have named. The peacock ear cuffs with brass feathers that wound upward to reach to the top of the ears would be perfect with my short hair. I had to restrain myself from asking their price. Maybe *after* the case was closed.

She shoved a clump of her wild brown curls behind her shoulder, where there was no chance it would stay, then pulled one stool up to the workbench and motioned me to the other, the one with a back. "Sit. You want tea? I've got an immersion heater," she said in just the same Bronx voice, with the same "I should come back from the deli with half the bag empty?" tone, my great-uncle's Mrs. Bronfmann had had.

"I'm fine. But how do *you* eat here?"

"Well, when I rented, I chose stockbrokers. The West Coast market opens at six A.M., to coincide with Wall Street. So Don and Betty are on their way to San Francisco at five-fifteen. Then I've got all day to use the kitchen and bathroom. They know that, it's part of the agreement, but I make a point of leaving things just—and I mean exactly—as I found them, so Don and Betty can forget I'm ever there."

"What about weekends?"

"They ski; they sail; they've got time-shares at Tahoe and Bodega. They're money people; their pleasures are money sports." She put out a hand to stop the protest that hadn't quite formed in my mind. "I don't mean to put them down. They work like crazy. When they drag in here at four, they need the hot tub. Me, I merely love it, but them, they need it. On their weekends they need to go fast and hard and sweat out all that stress." A grin crept onto her dark cherub face, rouging her cheeks and making her brown eyes sparkle. "What about the weekends they're home, you're going to ask, right? If I know beforehand, I cook beforehand. I've got an ice chest. On the Avenue I can get a deal on the fruit that hasn't moved at the end of the day. If not, it's take-out, but I'll tell you, Jill—that's your name, right, Jill?—it gnaws at me to blow money like that. Like I'm eating a sheet of copper, or an extra day and a half I could give myself here, before I have to go crawling to the house door and ask if there are any flunky jobs at the stock exchange. Those weeks I don't get a decent number in the lottery and I can't even get a space to sell my jewelry, I work for one of the out-of-town vendors, but it doesn't pay shit. I'd be better off back here pounding the metal or cruising the galleries seeing what I can do when I get the cash for stones and fine tools. Where I can sell when I get a name. I'm an artist, but like I always say, that doesn't mean I'm not a businesswoman. You don't pay attention to business, you end up making jewelry for the unemployment line."

I liked this take-a-chance life of hers. She was older than I, probably forty-five or so, and she could still afford to blow a few years? Of course she didn't have nearly ten years invested in a pension. . . . My throat tightened. "Invested in a pension" had been my father's condemnation for my friends' fathers in the towns we moved in and out of when I was a child. I envied those girls their continuity of friends, but I despised their fathers chained like front yard dogs. When I was a high school senior, Dad gave up on the pot of gold at the end of the leprechaun's rainbow and got a government job. He's still at it. I've never asked him to tell me exactly what he does; I cared too much to hear the roteness of it; and he's never mentioned pension. By the time I am his age I could be living well off my pension. I've made the smart choice. He never mentioned that; I think he cared too much.

Serenity Kaetz had given up that chance and gambled everything on her craft. If that didn't pan out . . . In three years she'd be nearly fifty, too late to start dropping pennies in the pension pig. She could keep her hillside house, but she'd never be able to live in it. "You've got money invested with Bryant Hemming, right?"

"My savings, such as it is. I could put it in the ice chest, but I feel like I should show some responsibility."

"How'd you choose to go with Bryant?"

"Griffon."

"Do you trust Griffon?"

She grinned. "Oh, yeah. I figure if his money's there, the fund's safe. He's the one who told me I'd never make it selling off a table in the middle of the street. I need to get into shops around town, then catalogs, then department stores. Griffon should know, hooked as he is on opening a shop on Union Square."

"Are you serious?" I asked, amazed. "A tattoo parlor in downtown San Francisco by Lord and Taylor and the St. Francis Hotel?"

"You got it. And Griffon was on to that plan before tattooing became fashionable. Year or two you'll be seeing discreet dragons breathing fire out of a cotillion décolletage. Griffon might just have the cash to do it by then. Or get the backing. He's hot in the world of flash—tattoo design. His flash is inspired, and on the skin it shines like foil on a book jacket."

I watched for signs she shared my incredulity, but if she found Griffon's plan at all bizarre, she covered her reaction the way you do when describing a friend's overblown dream to a stranger. Griffon and Serenity, counterculture burgomeisters and two people with futures tied up in the ACC fund. "Do you know Margo Roehner from the ACC fund board?"

Serenity nodded, and it was a moment before she motivated herself to say, "Not well." The hesitation said: And not likely to.

That's the tone I like to hear when asking for an opinion. "You're used to assessing people, Serenity; give me your take on Margo."

She considered for a moment, balancing the dry comfort of discretion against the creamy delight of dissing. "Committed, utterly. I mean Patient Defenders is a worthwhile project. She's told me that, every time I've met her; the woman talks about nothing else. And if you're not dumbstruck horrified about the haphazard care people get, Margo acts like you're Marie Antoinette."

"Do you have health insurance?" I couldn't resist asking.

"Yeah. I'm still on my ex's policy, I think. But I'm in good shape; I never need it except for the dental."

And if she were struck sick, Serenity would be exactly the person Margo Roehner would charge in to save, a lamb who figures she's too smart for the slaughter. I leaned back against the workbench. "So you wouldn't say Margo Roehner had a great sense of humor."

Serenity laughed openmouthed. Her long, curly hair shook in reaction. "In her book laughter is a waste of time. Making a joke just shows you don't understand the seriousness of the problem."

"What would you say if I told you she had a poster of a flashing pig—"

"Like naked flashing?" She was laughing so hard now I feared she'd rock off her stool.

"Right. And right in her storage unit."

"Well, I'd say either you need glasses bad, or Margo's letting someone else store in her storage."

"Someone like Daisy Culligan?"

"Daisy?" She bobbed her head amid her shaking laughing. "Yeah, *if* she knew Daisy."

Serenity knew Margo through Bryant's organization, ACC. Daisy knew Margo because of Bryant Hemming himself. "Serenity, how is it you know Daisy?"

The laughter stopped as if someone had turned off the sound. Her lips pursed; her brows lowered. Anger, fear, pensiveness, I couldn't decide. But for the first time Serenity Kaetz was not the chatty "friend" in the garage but the adversary I'd seen on *A Fair Deal.*

"It's not just through ACC, right?"

"I do know her from there."

"And?" I gave her time to offer another possible innocent connection; Daisy might have delivered dinners to fast-living Don and Betty Davis in the main house. When Serenity didn't respond, I moved on to my real suspicion. "Daisy's into pranks, right? Practical jokes? Just the type of thing to use a poster of a naked pig. Isn't that right, Serenity?"

Her stool jiggled. She grabbed the edge of the workbench to save herself and then fussed, resettling her feet on the rung, shifting her butt, her shoulders, rearranging her hands. Giving herself time.

"Just tell me the truth, Serenity. I'm not out to get Daisy. I like her. But you're carrying on like she's involved in something illegal."

"She's not breaking any laws! She's just—" Serenity did a double take realizing she'd committed herself and Daisy. She pushed her hair back off her face where it had fallen in her flurry of distraction attempts. "You won't use this against her?" It was more of a plea than a question.

"My job is to find Herman Ott. Ott was a friend of hers." I hadn't answered her question, but she chose to take it as the assurance she needed.

"Okay, here's the thing. Daisy's got one of those senses of humor with a zinger. When you've been had and you're pissed, Daisy can always think of what to do. I mean, I've heard enough stories. I've never used her myself— No, really. I don't mean I'm above a little recreational getting even, I'm just too busy now."

"So how do you know—"

"Let me tell you about a friend of mine. Sara. She doesn't even live in town anymore, so it's not like I'm incriminating her or anything. But she was still here last year, and she needed a new hairdresser. You know what a pain that can be, calling everyone you know who looks halfway decent and getting recommendations and then weeding out the friends who are willing to spend more than you are and others whose hair would look shitty on you."

Of course I knew; every woman knows.

"Finally Sara takes the recommendation of a friend who'd been to a wedding and asked the bride, 'Who does the minister's hair?' So, Sara makes an appointment with a guy named Damon, who does the hair of the Episcopal minister who she's never seen. She makes two appointments, one for a cut and one a week later for a color job, both at ten on Tuesday mornings. The first Tuesday she goes swimming and gets back at eight-thirty to find a message from Damon saying he's real sorry but he's at the dentist having an emergency root canal and has to cancel. Can she reschedule? So she calls the shop at ten and reschedules for two weeks later, same time.

"The next week, at nine, there's another call from Damon. He's sorry, but he lives in San Francisco and he's had car trouble. This time she doesn't reschedule. She's pissed, but she's not certain about him. After all, Tuesday is the Monday of a hairdresser's week, and she can remember her first job out of college and calling in sick after a hard weekend or a good weekend that hadn't quite ended. So she waits for the next Tuesday, hardly able to believe a guy in business would cancel a third time. But he does. He leaves a message saying he has to go to the hospital for medical tests. Now she's torn; she's sure the guy's lying. Well, almost sure. But she can't dismiss the thought: Suppose the guy really was sick, sick enough to go to the hospital for tests. . . .

"Well, you can see her dilemma. Is she heartless or just a patsy? She wants to call the salon and let loose, but suppose she is the reason a sick man is canned? He'd lose his job, his health coverage, any hope. . . . The guilt! She agonizes; meanwhile she's got to find another hairdresser. Then, suddenly, she runs into a friend whose hairdresser used to work with Damon and says, 'He's famous for canceling appointments.'

Well, then she's really furious, first for the inconvenience and doubly for the grief she's wasted feeling sorry for the asshole."

"So?"

"Calling him at the salon isn't enough now. Neither is calling the manager."

"So?"

"She gets on the horn to Daisy." Serenity smiled. "It took Daisy about twenty seconds to come up with the right scheme. She told Sara she'd get three friends who had never been to that shop, have each one make an appointment with Damon for a cut and color, or a perm—things that take three hours and are a big part of the beautician's income—and make them for the middle of Saturday afternoons, the busiest time of week. Then not show. Brilliant, huh? And the best part was that Sara got an appointment with someone else in the same shop the third Saturday so she could watch him wait and sputter and wonder why life was abusing him."

I laughed. It was perfect. It fitted Daisy; it told me what Howard would have said if I'd shaken him awake last night. No wonder he had grinned at the mention of Daisy's name. Like him, she was a pillar of the posse of pranksters, an amorphous group that never met but knew of one another and delighted in their stings. It made me like Daisy even more.

It also made me wonder just what perfect revenge she had concocted for an ex-husband too self-absorbed to warn her about the restaurant debacle.

Howard would never let a slap like that go unanswered. Maybe Daisy was a "better" person than Howard, but I doubted it. I tapped my finger on the workbench. "Serenity, the last time I saw you was on

A Fair Deal. I have to say I would never have guessed the mediation would turn out so well." *For you.*

"Yeah, Bryant was a genius, wasn't he? I figured the best I'd get would be that asshole Cyril wouldn't be able to storm-troop down the Avenue chasing off customers like a bad smell. I figured Bryant'd get him into the lottery for an Avenue space like the rest of us, and I'd have him preaching from a booth on the next block, which would still be one big pain in the ass."

"But he's banished to People's Park, so far off the Avenue no one has to deal with him at all."

"Yeah, I couldn't believe it. I mean, the guy's aim is not to save souls but to be in your face."

"Serenity," I said slowly, "you must have put up with a lot from him before you contacted *A Fair Deal.* In all that time did you find out where he stays in Berkeley?"

"No. Guy's slippery. That was the infuriating thing; he could always pounce where I was, but I could never find him till he burst onto the Avenue. Best I can tell you is it's not a church here."

"How do you—"

"One of his boys laughed when I suggested it. He said, 'Yeah, like I told the little man, he stays at Grace Cathedral.' "

"Which 'little man' did he tell?"

Serenity shrugged.

"Bryant?"

"No. The kid already admitted that Cyril ordered them not to talk to Bryant."

"Herman Ott?"

"Look, I just don't know."

I nodded. It didn't have to be Ott. Cyril was the type who would have a lot of guys after him. But it could easily have been Ott—the little man. If Ott had been looking for him and got that close . . . If he'd been hot on the trail, he would never have stopped to call me. If he had found the kid between the time he called me Sunday and when he saw me, of course he'd blow me off.

I pushed that possibility back for later consideration and returned to the issue of the mediation. "Brother Cyril didn't argue with Bryant. Why not?"

"That's Bryant for you. You saw him. The man was such a charmer. It was like you were the only person in his world. He hung on your every word. He never had that glazed look, you know, the 'I'm waiting to talk about myself' look. It was like he gave his all to figure out what you really wanted and how he could help you get it. It was, like my niece says, awesome. I don't think that's happened to me more than once or twice in my whole life. I can see how Bryant seduced Cyril."

"How, yes. But why? He gave you an eighty-twenty deal. Why?"

"Because it was right," she insisted. But she didn't meet my gaze.

"And what else? Let's talk practicality."

"Got me. Whatever the reason, I'll take it. Cyril's gone half the time. He's got 'congregations' in Monterey and in the valley, if you can believe that. But I guess they grow suckers like they do strawberries in Monterey and vegetables in the valley. I'm hoping that the next time he takes a trip he'll forget to come back."

I jotted a few lines in my notebook. When I looked up, Serenity Kaetz was holding a copper lily, eyeing where the etching should go. Now there *was* a certain serenity in her, a sense that she was mistress of what she created, that she had settled into the life niche she had mastered, the one that she loved. Once again she reminded me of Mrs. Bronfmann, her skin glowing rosy from her walk, the keeper of the lives in one building on the Grand Concourse, handing Uncle Jack a box of soda crackers, two cans of ginger ale, a package of onion soup mix he would savor but wouldn't have asked for if he'd been without food for a fortnight.

Mrs. Bronfmann had been the epitome of Bronx domesticity. And then she'd run off with the exchange student. "About Bryant Hemming," I said, "I know what you mean about that burning light of attention. But attention's not forever. Sooner or later the light shines on someone else."

Slowly Serenity shook her head. "No, it's not light; it's like helium. It pumps you up till you're floating. Then suddenly he looses the cinch, and you sputter out of control. You make humiliating noises; you feel like you have no control over where you're going. When you hit the ground, you've got nothing left.

"And the next time he comes by with the helium, you know better, and you step right up to the pump anyway. Then, when you sputter down, you're not only humiliated but aware the whole time that you've got no one but yourself to blame." She stared down at the metal lily, her breasts and shoulders quivering, her face unreadable. "You can see why one-shot mediating—the quick in and out—was perfect for him. No one was around long enough to realize the gas had gone out."

But Serenity had. And I could understand how one of those emptied balloons of a person would do anything to snatch back Bryant's attention and, that failing, go to whatever length necessary to kill him.

CHAPTER 23

I RACED TO THE STATION, around the gang in the squad room, through the records room to the Homicide office. Neither Jackson nor Eggs was there. I tried Doyle's office—empty—and ended up leaving callback messages for all three. Serenity Kaetz had opened an intriguing new path of inquiry with her statement that Bryant Hemming in his way had seduced Brother Cyril and her.

Serenity Kaetz had barely mentioned Ott, but now I was more worried about him than ever. If he strode into Brother Cyril's lair armed only with wits and wile, after Bryant Hemming had just played Cyril for a patsy, I hated to guess how Cyril would react. Ott could drive a saint to murder. I hurried back to the squad room. Surely someone on patrol had some hint, some clue, some sighting of Cyril's boys.

The place was Vladivostok on vacation. At 10:00 A.M. shoulder radios were silent. No one was bitching about dead batteries yet. The copy machine wasn't punching out memos too urgent to wait. Team 6 seemed as placid as the off-white walls. They ambled around the room, waiting for their meeting to get under way. Wednesday was the first day of their week, the only time they worked daylight hours. To a one they looked as eager to get back to the beat as Damon, the hairdresser, must have been to clip and color. They hadn't called in sick, but they were eager to ward off the inevitable with questions. "Hey, Smith, what're you doing in here on your day off? Can't tear yourself away?" Jabbar asked.

"No, man, she's not off duty; she's just off patrol. Well, our patrol. She's on Ott Patrol," White said.

"Yeah," Wilkins put in, "she's the Ott Hound."

"You hunting him down?" White asked. "Well, lady, you best get yourself a pair of hip boots for the amount of shit you're going to be going through."

" 'Course now, she gets on with Ott. His favorite cop, right, Smith?"

"His *least-despised* cop," I snapped. "Get your terms right, Wilkins."

Wilkins stared, jolted.

"Ott may be with Brother Cyril. Any lead on where Cyril stays?"

"Smith, you have really gone over the edge," Wilkins said. "But we'll be keeping our baby blues peeled today. You can count on us."

"Yeah, Smith, we'll be there to rescue your friend."

Eggs, who had been standing back by the mailboxes in the hall, stepped into the group. "And if by some chance, it was Ott who thought to use the gun he kept out of sight out his window to kill the man in his office?"

"Then I better buy hip boots that go up to my throat." I said it lightly, and White, Wilkins, and the others laughed. Eggs flexed his lips, what passed for reaction to comments he felt unworthy of a real laugh. He started to speak, checked himself, seemed to reconsider in a process so long that the room had grown silent. "Macalester," he said, and headed out of the room.

I followed, wondering if his hesitation was from ambivalence about sharing data with me. Was this suspicion—his and mine—how it was going to be from now on? I shoved the deadening thought to the back of my mind and focused on Roger Macalester. Spotlighting him suddenly made me realize how central he was. He was the genesis of the Bryant-paying-off-Cyril rumor. He knew Daisy Culligan, and Margo Roehner, and Serenity Kaetz, and Griffon, and—I plopped on Jackson's chair and duck-walked it across the floor to Eggs's desk—Ott. And he had Bryant's records. "Eggs, Bryant must have had an address for Brother Cyril."

"Right, same one we have. Monterey."

"Or so Macalester says."

He leaned forward, resting his forearms right below the elbow against the edge of his desk. The remarkably uncomfortable position suited Eggs and his awkwardness about this conversation. "What's your take on him?"

"Macalester? He knows his limitations. Mediating between the bureaucracy and the average joe before the joe grabs an assault weapon was Macalester's idea. According to him, Bryant was just the guy to bring it off."

"I had another conversation with Mr. Macalester this morning. By then Hemming was not so untarnished in his eyes. He was more of a pie with shiny crust, covering what might be a murky middle, not that Mr. Macalester wants to believe that, you understand."

"But he does?"

"Well, here's the thing, Smith. Macalester's a lefty, not an active rad, a library lefty."

"Are we talking coffeehouse radical, only quieter?"

"And he doesn't have to nurse a cappuccino till it evaporates."

I smiled, but Eggs didn't see that. He would never deign to check for a reaction. At times his compulsive restraint had driven me crazy; I'd wanted to shake him, kiss him, poke till he showed what was underneath it. Now I was glad it gave me an excuse to pretend nothing had changed between us.

"Macalester is committed in his way. He has a somewhat utopian mediation plan; he's read everything cross-referenced to it; he had Bryant Hemming front it, committed ACC to its success, and what did Hemming do in return?" Eggs eyed me. There was nothing on his desk for him to bend, stab, or rub, not that he would have done so. He sat still, as if he were interviewing a suspect or, I imagined, at dinner with a blind date.

"Spit it out, Eggs. Hemming did?"

He flexed his lips. "Opened the ACC fund to right-wing groups."

I remembered Macalester's alluding to that. "Macalester said if the right wanted to invest in the fund's chosen stocks, ACC was happy to guide their money there."

"Sure, Smith, Macalester *said* it was fine. But a lefty in bed with Family Rights Coalition, how do you think that would fly in the coffeehouse? And what could Macalester do about it? He couldn't get the board to fire Hemming. Hemming was too popular, not to mention successful. In any conflict between the two, Macalester'll be the one to look unreasonable."

I glanced at the windows, as I had when I was a Homicide detective, hashing out a lead, bemoaning a dead end, or just watching Porter, the squirrel, on the ledge eating the organic walnuts that Eggs had shipped in from a farm in Pennsylvania. "Macalester could have made life uncomfortable for Hemming. He could have done it alone or with a little help from his friends."

Eggs nodded. "Here's an interesting point, Smith. Macalester was the ACC manager, and by contract, if Hemming left, Macalester was the one to choose his successor." Now Eggs did smile, but he did it without meeting my eyes.

Still, he did elect to hash this out with me instead of waiting for Jackson or Inspector Doyle. He trusted me that much. I felt a ridiculous rush of warmth for Eggs, the type you need to subdue before you try speaking again. "But why kill Hemming? I mean, Eggs, the guy was leaving. Macalester'd already gotten what he wanted."

"Not quite. He wanted ACC back and his mediation plan intact. What Hemming left is the money fund politically compromised and the mediation plan ethically suspect. What does Macalester need to salvage them? I'll tell you, Smith, he has to pile the blame on Bryant Hemming—"

"Where it belongs."

"So, if Ott was investigating Hemming, who hired him? Who's more likely than our Roger, right?"

"Sounds possible."

Eggs took that for agreement. "And in this investigation of his, who was Ott contacting?"

That was a question only I could answer. No wonder he hadn't waited for Jackson or Doyle. He *had* to deal with me. Eggs would never watch my face *overtly*. I hoped I'd shifted away before he could see my flushed face or my misguided hope. "Ott," I said, "had one of Brother Cyril's little tin crosses. I don't know how he got it, but he did have the cross. Daisy Culligan called Ott; Ott blushed."

"The call must have been unexpected. A man doesn't blush for a return call, not one to discuss a case."

"And Bill Lewin. He called Ott, too, and Ott got all excited when he heard his name. Have you heard that name around town?"

"Spell."

"Overheard. Could be l-e-w-i-n, or l-o-o-n, or some—"

"You sure it was a man?"

"What else, Eggs—Wilhelmina?"

Eggs leaned forward in his chair. "Could Ott be a birder?"

"A bir—" All the tension of our interchange overflowed, and I howled, picturing Herman Ott with his round head, thin blond hair, beaky nose, his narrow shoulders and round belly, his bird-thin legs. And they say dog owners resemble their pets! "You mean bird, like in loon, l-o-o-n."

"Like yellow-billed loon." Eggs's eyes were opened wide. He stared unabashedly at me.

"Is that one of our birds?"

"Hardly. We have a plethora of avian life on the West Coast. Some are breeders here. Others migrate from Canada. So in one sense this is a birders' paradise. But in another it's hell because the possibility of sighting a rare bird is so frequently lost in the cover of our regular birds."

"And a yellow-billed loon?"

"Smith, in the bird world there are breeding birds, the ones that live here, regular visitors that migrate here or through here, and casual visitors, migrants that stray off course. Your common loon and your red-throated loon winter along our coast. Even your arctic loon flies in for the cold months. But the yellow-billed loon summers in northern Canada and even in the dead of winter never flies farther south than the Canadian border."

"So it wouldn't be here then?"

"Normally no. But if an accidental flew south, it'd be a great rare bird alert, and birders who knew would drop everything to get to the spot." He himself was half off his chair.

I sat back down. "Eggs, I assume I'm safe in assuming that you are a birder?"

He nodded.

"And knowing you, I would say you are probably the most well-read, well-prepared birder in the state. So if there's a rare bird alert, how come you haven't dropped this case and headed for a marsh, or estuary, or whatever?"

"I couldn't leave, not with a high-profile case like this just started. I almost don't want to call the rare bird alert. To know that a yellowbill is here and I can't see it and that that spotting will never be on my list . . ." He let out a sigh and looked too depressed to be humiliated about it.

Things were becoming clearer now. "Your birder colleagues wouldn't alert you?"

"A close friend maybe. A guy I see with binoculars hardly, not when he's got his own life list to worry about."

"Life list? You mean you jot down all the kinds of birds you see for your entire life?"

"It's the equivalent of career home runs in baseball or touchdowns in football. The more birds you've actually seen, the more respected you are in the community. And to be the one to see a yellowbill all the way down here and have that verified . . ." His voice trailed off into the swampy realms of a birder's dreams.

"How can we find out about the loon?"

He wrote out a number. "But don't tell me, Smith. I don't want to know if it's here or how many people are eyeing it."

I headed for the door. "Eggs, if it's a life list, you've got time."

It was only partly consideration that prompted me to make my call to the rare bird alert number from another phone, so that Eggs wouldn't hear me asking whether the ranger had seen Ott.

Suppose Ott was a bird-watcher. He could be. Those trips to Bolinas lagoon at dawn and dusk could have been not for nefarious meetings but to bird, if that was the term for what birders did. Did that mean Ott had walked innocently out of his office and someone else had moved in for the kill? Was that too much of a coincidence to believe? Was it the yellow-billed loon of my own life list?

As it turned out, there was no rare bird alert. Might a birder have spotted the yellowbill and not alerted the rare bird alert? I asked the bird observatory manager. Reluctantly the man admitted that it was, alas, possible. Eagerly he gave me a list of the probable sighting spots of the improbable sighting.

Desperately he begged my assurance that I would notify him when I spotted a sighting.

I settled in at the phone and in the next forty minutes talked to department personnel in ten sites around the Bay Area, repeating Ott's description and getting their promises to check if any such unlikely bird had landed in their premises. They insisted I notify them immediately, call them any time, gave me their home numbers, their pagers, the fax numbers of friends who would seek them out in forest or fen.

I put down the phone, amazed. I, who had thought of birds mostly in connection with Thanksgiving, never expected this level of, well, obsession. It seemed in fact at odds with the tranquillity of observing avian flight. More porcine than avian, this drop everything and run—or fly—attitude.

Still, the whole thing seemed like such a long shot. I could much more easily imagine Ott in Pittsburgh, merely avoiding the despised Hermans or Otts.

I called Laura Goldman again and left a message again.

Then I walked back to Eggs's office, stepped in, shook my head before he needed to ask, and said, "If Ott was investigating Bryant Hemming, and if Roger Macalester hired him—two still unprovens—then Macalester must have had some credible suspicion to hook Ott to begin with."

Eggs nodded slowly and kept nodding, thinking, assessing. Finally he spoke. "As we speak, Pereira's over at ACC going through the books."

If it hadn't been for the yellow-billed loon, I knew he wouldn't have confided that.

CHAPTER 24

IN THE BRIGHT YELLOW TRAPEZOID of sunlight coming through the ACC water tower window, Connie Pereira resembled a short-cropped Rapunzel in a squat tower. She didn't look up when I walked in. Across the room Murakawa leaned against a segment of the clear plastic desk that hugged all four walls.

Roger Macalester was resting his rump on a portion of the desk between them. He was fingering a squishy orange ball, but not squeezing. *Color me nonchalant.* "Three police officers for what she said was just a superficial glance at the books? Like the road repair crews: one to work, two to watch? Or is one of you going to hold the flag?"

A little testy. "The investigation seems to be stressful for you, Mr. Macalester," I said smarmily.

"When your colleague's been murdered, it can ruin your whole day."

"What do you think we're going to find in your books?" *A retainer to Ott?*

"Not *my* books, Bryant's books. Bryant founded ACC. He hired me. My contribution was showing him the importance of mediating for individuals. I've got no idea what's in his books."

Pereira stopped still, then leaned into the books like a woman transfixed.

Macalester shook his pony-tailed head. The man looked as if he'd been up all night worrying. His Grateful Dead T-shirt was crumpled around the sides from hours of being pressed into a chair back. The skin on his elfin face sagged. Even his bald spot had lost yesterday's shine. "ACC's dead." His voice was so soft I couldn't tell whether he spoke in anger or grief.

"Because of the right-wing contributors?" I softened the edge to my voice and leaned against the desk near him.

He was still shaking his head. "Nah. Bad move. But Bryant insisted he had to be evenhanded. 'Maintain my image of evenhandedness' was his exact phrase."

"Bryant only started being evenhanded in the last two months," Pereira said without turning around.

"We didn't have the financial credibility before that. No solvent group would have touched us, unless of course it was impressed with what we stood for."

Now it was "we."

"But you're saying that isn't what will kill ACC?"

"It's incidental. Our members may be pissed, but they aren't going to drop out of the fund. They're not in it because it's better than a CD; they're with us because we're their only option. We take peanuts; we give back on demand. So if there's a great shipment of Wyoming picture jaspers or white jade leaving Cheyenne, an artist can reclaim his seven-hundred-dollar investment before the stones cross the California line. With our investors, access to their money is a lot more important than earning another percent or two."

"Another seven to fourteen dollars," Pereira muttered. "Per year."

"But if the fund loses moral credibility," Murakawa said, "what does that say about mediation?"

"Exactly." Macalester gave him a somber nod. "Mediation, the chance to look at the truth, that's what it's all about. For that you've got to have trust. Without trust it's just another sham. Doesn't matter if you settle cases, if you've paid off one of the parties."

"Did Bryant pay off—"

"How the hell else did he get Cyril off Telegraph?" Roger slammed the ball into the window. The glass rattled, and for a moment I thought it would break. "Our members are calling in; he's putting them off. Then Cyril's saying, 'Yes, sir, yes, sir, how far from Telegraph should I go?' "

I waited till the window was silent. "How much did he pay Cyril?"

"I don't know. Bryant didn't take me into his confidence. He was the big man, the dealer. I was—"

"Is that transaction in the books?"

"Listed under 'Business Bribes'?" Pereira demanded. As she returned to her task, a sharp-edged sound escaped her lips, the union of a sneer and chuckle. It was a sound made while she looked down her nose, a sound I'd heard only from Connie Pereira, only when going over sloppy books. "The closest I can come is two entries for unexplained 'Professional Services' last month and one 'Business Entertainment' at Chez Panisse to the tune of a hundred ten dollars last week."

"That's hefty entertaining for a nonprofit." I remembered Daisy Culligan's being surprised about spotting someone from the ACC office at the city's premier restaurant.

Macalester shrugged.

"Do you have any proof that Bryant bribed Cyril? Or are you just making an assumption, Roger?"

Macalester shrugged again, then muttered, "No. No proof."

"Why take the chance of dealing under the table with Brother Cyril? I mean, everyone agrees Bryant was a great mediator. So why not trust himself?"

"Because Bryant couldn't face failure," he said in that soft, soft voice. Again, it blurred the line between anger and remorse. "It's my fault. I liked the guy. I was taken in by his 'most likely to succeed' attitude." He scooped up an orange ball. "But here's the thing. Under that was nothing. He couldn't face that. For him, looking at failure or even the possibility of failure was like giving it life. You know, like the New Age theories of 'We are what our thoughts are.' Allowing a thought of a snarling dog in your mind means getting your ass bitten. Bryant was terrified of the bite. He never faced his mistakes or the danger of them; he just kept moving forward."

"Hoping he could outrun them?" I recalled Serenity's comment about Bryant's inflating you with the intensity of his interest like a helium balloon and, when he moved on, leaving you to sputter to the ground. I wondered when he'd popped Roger Macalester's balloon. How long had this man with the dream sat in the dark watching Bryant destroy it? And with it his reputation? Bryant was dead, but it would be Roger who was pulled into the grave when ACC went down.

I scooped up a purple ball, tossed it up. It made a nice thud back in my hand, and when I squeezed, it resisted only momentarily before bowing to my strength. So satisfying. I tossed again, caught, and repeated my question to Macalester. "Why bribe Brother Cyril?"

"Because Serenity Kaetz wouldn't give in."

"Did Bryant try her?"

The ball didn't move in his hand. It was the first time his fingers had been still. "Don't know."

"But you suspect, don't you?"

He didn't answer. He didn't need to. So Bryant had approached Serenity Kaetz. I was only mildly surprised Serenity hadn't told me that. Bryant had tried and failed. The man who hated failure. How desperate must he have been to be forced to deal with Brother Cyril?

I looked back at Roger's hand in time to see his control dissolve and orange rubber squeezed out between his fingers. He looked at the ball, not at me.

"See, Bryant couldn't avoid that dark hole entirely. So, much as he wanted to believe he was his image through and through, there had to be times when he was alone that he had an inkling that he was fickle, untrustworthy, temporary to any situation."

"How do you know?"

"A couple of things he said, a phrase here or there, after too much booze at the Solstice Party, that type of thing. He didn't let on to anyone else; with them he was always Mr. Charm, Señor Apropriado. But me, I was part of the office, like the desk here. After you've been here awhile, you're not so careful where you put your butt." Macalester stood, then flopped back on the desk.

"But still, Roger, why did he bribe Brother Cyril? If Bryant couldn't be sure of the outcome, why have Brother Cyril on *A Fair Deal* at all?" I expected him to concur with Howard's and my conclusion that Bryant needed a big case, big ratings for his send-off.

Roger shook his head slowly. "He couldn't see the importance of mediation, of creating unity, of diffusing irritation before it turns to fury. Oh, he mouthed the words well, but he never really believed them. And so, Officer, he couldn't trust that the importance of his mission would demand attention, inevitably. He was like a pony pulling a beer wagon, prancing and huffing, dragging, whinnying, sure that he's the only thing that will draw men to the truck."

Put more succinctly: He needed a big case. I pushed myself up and turned to face Macalester head-on. "Roger, save us some time here. You hired Herman Ott, didn't you?"

"Why would I?"

"To find out what Bryant was doing and how bad it was going to be for ACC and for you."

"Are you crazy?"

"We'll find the entry in the books."

"No, you won't."

"Because you paid him out of your own pocket?"

"Look, I couldn't even get Bryant to pay *me*. I haven't had a check in two months. I'm doing well to eat, much less hire a private eye. Even Ott!"

"But you talked to Ott when he came by with questions."

"I told him to go away."

"Did he ask about Brother Cyril?"

His hand relaxed enough to begin working the ball again. "Yeah, he did."

"What specifically?"

"I don't know. If he'd been here in the office, if he'd called, if Bryant had called him. I don't know."

"And you told him?"

"No, no, and I didn't know."

"But you do know, don't you?"

"No!"

I let a moment pass, then said, "Okay. Where can I find Brother Cyril?"

"I don't—"

"Bryant knew. Where did he keep addresses, phone numbers?"

"On his Rolodex." Macalester was smiling. "Don't bother checking; Ott already did when my back was turned to answer the phone."

"Could Ott have pocketed a card from there while your back was turned?"

It was a moment before Macalester said, "Oh, shit."

"Is that a yes or a maybe?"

He looked down at the ball. I'd seen that same expression on Herman Ott's face, the lump in the old rad's throat as he considers helping the police. With Ott the blockage was usually so large he was in danger not of speaking but of choking. Occasionally I eased that lump out, greasing his throat with a portion of the discretionary fund. But Roger Macalester seemed to manage his impediment. "I saw a paper going in his pocket. I called him on it. He pulled out a receipt of some sort. Then he accused me of losing my principles, and he stomped out."

The Ottian inverse of bait and switch. I could picture him stalking out in a huff of righteousness.

And stalking into Cyril's lair. I sighed.

As if in concert with me, Pereira groaned.

"What? Something in the books?"

"I can't tell yet. But . . . I don't know . . . something."

"How soon are you going to know?"

"I don't know." She turned a page and leaned closer. She wasn't groaning anymore. All the semesters and quarters she'd taken classes in economics, stocks, trading strategies, accounting, forensic accounting, all seemed in vain. Her family siphoned her profits; her patrol buddies' eyes glazed at numbers and theories and terms we'd heard but could never define. But here she was like a pig nosing out the best truffle in France. She'd sniff and dig until she'd found it. Nothing was going to deter her. Alas, nothing was going to rush her either.

"I'll check back," I said. And to Macalester: "One last thing. How did you come into your job here?"

He was staring at Pereira's back as if updates of her suspicions and discoveries were being spelled out across the back of her neck like the news in Times Square. "This job? That's easy. Daisy recommended me."

CHAPTER 25

Was that Daisy Culligan's revenge, sending her ex-husband Roger Macalester for an office manager? The concept appealed to me. I yearned to drive across town and ask her about it. But that wasn't going to bring me any closer to finding Herman Ott.

I left a note about it on Inspector Doyle's desk and moved on to the mailboxes. No word from Goldman. But there was a message from a DeLisle Draper at Golden Gate National Seashore. I called.

"Draper."

"Jill Smith, Berkeley Police. You got back to me about Herman Ott"—I checked the message—"fifteen minutes ago."

"Right. You wanted to know if we'd seen the guy who looks like a giant canary, right?"

"Canary in a mustard raincoat."

"Right. Well, here's the thing. I didn't see your guy myself, but one of the other rangers is sure he spotted him Sunday just as he was closing the parking lot at Muir Beach. He noticed your guy because he didn't have a car, and when he told him he was closing the lot, your guy headed toward the lagoon there, and my buddy figured your guy'd sneak back onto the beach. He warned him. He was going to come back and check later, see if he spotted a fire, but he got sidetracked by some kids. . . . But he was doing a double shift, and so the next morning, when he opened the lot, he checked, and there your guy was. Clear he'd been on the beach all night. Looked damp and bedraggled. You know wet birds don't fly at night." A chortle rattled the line.

"True." I'd heard the old joke too, but I couldn't bring myself to laugh now.

"But looks like your bird flew after that. No one's seen him since."

"Was anyone with him?"

"Nope. That's part of why he looked suspicious, lone man in trench coat and all."

"The guy who spotted him, has he been on duty since then?"

"Zeise? Oh, yeah. He went to Mexico for two weeks. He's got to pay back everyone in the station. He'll be doing double shifts till his tan is gone."

"Zeise is sure he didn't see my guy again?"

"Yeah, see, he wasn't about to have him sneaking back on that beach another time. So he checked all the hideouts. You'd be hard pressed to burrow down in a spot we don't know about. Squatters think they're going to drop in here cold and outsmart us. Hardly. We're here forty hours a week. They think they can hoodwink us; it's insulting."

"Ott—my guy—did Zeise notice any scars or bruises on him? Anything to suggest he was banged around and dumped off in Muir Beach?"

"This is Muir Beach, not the Jersey meadowlands. We don't do cement bootees here. And even if we did, you could crawl to a house. Not to mention that the beach is rarely empty, even after hours," he added with a soupçon of pique.

"Gotcha. If my guy shows up there again, let me know, okay?"

"You bet."

"And, Draper, thanks." I restrained myself till I put the receiver down. Then I kicked the waste can into the wall. The squad room was empty, so I didn't have to explain that was the closest I could get to kicking Ott where he'd remember it.

Herman Ott—I smacked the can upright—you are lucky there's an entire bay between us. Or there was when you were last seen, strolling on the beach, alone, in no danger. Did you rent your office out for murder and use the money to hire a driver to the beach? Maybe you had a little left over, huh? Maybe you extended your vacation to Puerto Vallarta?

I took the steps down to the parking lot so fast I was nearly sliding. Sapolu was checking the trunk of his patrol car, but I didn't say hello. I needed to be by myself and think. I drove a couple of blocks and parked.

Ott got in a car on Telegraph Sunday night. No visible gun pointed at him. Still, the driver could have been armed.

Sure! And he had Ott hold the gun on himself while he, the kidnapper, drove? And if Ott tried to escape, would he have shot himself?

And then what? The kidnapper drops Ott off at the beach, figuring he'll be too intimidated to walk a few yards to a house and knock.

What did you really do, Ott? Call a friend, someone who owed you, and ask for a ride out of town?

There are ample people who wouldn't dare mention that trip if you told them not to.

I slammed my fist into the seat. If Ott hadn't been kidnapped, that meant he wasn't potential victim number two. If Ott hadn't been kidnapped, then he had left his office on his own. And I wasn't looking for an endangered hostage but a witness, or an accomplice, or a murderer.

It's hard to make a case that a man's not a killer when a body's dead in his office, shot with a gun stashed outside his window, and he's gone to the beach.

Gone to the beach, hung around overnight, and disappeared. Where was he now? In a safe house with the friend who had taken him to the beach? Or back in Pittsburgh? Cairo? Des Moines? Had he gone to the beach just long enough for his cohort to ready his present hidey-hole?

Herman Ott, murderer.

I guess I'd been seduced by Ott. I just couldn't believe a man who'd governed his life by integrity, who'd given up things monastics and street people consider necessities would kill a man.

In his own office yet.

But it was just a belief—my naive belief about Ott —and every bit of evidence and logic argued against it. Ott had made a chump of me before; he could do it again now, big time.

It all pointed to Ott.

But I couldn't believe it.

Maybe the truth was I couldn't *bring myself* to believe it. Everyone has his price, Leonard had insisted. But if Ott sold his soul . . . Ott *was* the soul of the old sixties ethic here, the undercurrent of individual integrity that ran through Berkeley. That commitment to the integrity of the individual was why we put up with annual protests for People's Park, with being panhandled three times on a block, with the toughest police review commission around. It was why we had a tree ordinance to protect citizens' views, a gourmet ghetto ordinance to protect neighbors from being overrun with restaurants. It was why the city council had risked money and reputation setting aside an acre for transients living in vehicles, forging sister city agreements with cities that needed us more than we them. It was the good still left from the sixties, the assurance that people were more than impediments to downsizing, that on some level every person mattered.

If that ethic was a sham, then so was the city. My city.

I knew then if that were true, I'd have to move on, leave the only place I'd ever belonged.

My hands burned from squeezing the steering wheel. I wrenched them free, pressed my half numb fingers around the keys, and started the car.

Cops work not from hunches but from evidence. What does this show? Can this be used in court? Each bit of evidence I found about Ott was more incriminating.

What about that cross that fell out of his pocket at the Claremont? I would believe he sold his soul and his city before I'd buy his becoming a disciple of Brother Cyril. He *had* to be investigating Cyril. Bryant and Cyril. The question was which came first. Had Bryant sicced him on Cyril and aroused Ott's suspicions himself? Despite his poor-mouthing, Roger might well have thought the cost of getting the goods on Bryant was money well spent. The ACC books had to show that one of them paid him for that investigation. Surely.

I turned on the engine and headed to Delaware Street. When I pulled up in the parking lot, Connie Pereira was smiling.

CHAPTER 26

"DID YOU FIND ANY RECORD of a payment to Ott?" I demanded as Connie Pereira loaded the ACC books into her trunk.

"Macalester gave his permission." She indicated the books. "He thinks that makes him look innocent." Her expression said: More fool he.

"Ott?" I prompted.

"No, Smith, they didn't hire him. Nothing in the books. Nothing on Ott, that is," she said in an ask-me-more tone.

"Did you find a payoff to Brother Cyril?"

"*Nada*, believe me. I've inched through Hemming's books; he's not good enough to hide a bribe. Or a retainer to Ott. Unless there's another set of books, of course."

But if not for a bribe, why had Brother Cyril allowed himself to be mediated off Telegraph? And Ott, what was he after in the ACC books, the connection between Hemming and Cyril? Had he too been expecting to find a bribe? Focusing back on the revelation at hand, I said, "Okay, what's the secret of the books?"

"Pyramid scheme," she whispered.

"ACC? A pyramid? With the little money their people invested?"

"I didn't say they could bury a pharaoh, Smith. It's more like, remember those little metal pyramids people were sticking under or over their pears to keep them from spoiling?"

One of Howard's tenants a few years back had been a devotee of pyramid power. He'd had a glass pyramid over his strawberries, clusters of metal ones under his broccoli, under vases of flowers, and when we found one under his girlfriend's chair, we started to worry. "A sort of molehill of the pyramid world?"

Pereira grinned. "You got it, Smith. Tiny but structured like the big guys." She followed me to my car and climbed in beside me. "The classic pyramid was the New Age Foundation in Philadelphia. There they had a fictitious group of donors, who supposedly would double any investment worthy nonprofit groups left with the foundation for six months. Nonprofits invested, and when it came time to pay off, New Age paid them from the money invested by later groups. The nonprofits told others about their great investment, and soon boards of charities all over the country were begging to be allowed to hand over their cash."

I recalled that, though not in the gleeful detail Pereira did. "Connie, doesn't it occur to the crooks who cook up pyramid schemes that there has to come a point when they can't pay off?"

Pereira shrugged. "These con guys fall into three categories. One, the regulation crooks who figure they'll attract a bundle of cash, clear the coffers, and disappear before the jig is up. Their problem is they forget they're greedy. They're like the Indian monkeys caught in the monkey traps. You know what those are, Smith?"

"The traps?"

"They're nothing more than holes big enough for the monkey to slip his empty paw through and grab the banana inside. Too small for the paw holding the banana to come out. All the monkey has to do is let go of the banana, and he'll be free. Does he? Does the pyramid con man clear out the account when there's a million dollars in it or wait another month for the next million?"

I nodded uncomfortably. The con men were on their own, but I hated to think of the monkeys. Or the moral.

Instructing on economics, or her theories thereof, was Pereira's banana. "The second group is too stupid to see the end. And the third—probably Bryant Hemming's—probably started paying off initial contributors out of capital because he was pressed. He'd have intended to straighten things out as soon as pressures eased up, the next check came in, as soon as he had time to really go over the books: any number of excuses. And when no one noticed what he'd done, chances are he just forgot about it and his plans for making it right."

"And the next time it was easier," I said. "That sounds like Bryant Hemming. He got too busy with *A Fair Deal* to focus on ACC's financial problems. He could hardly tell Roger Macalester to do it when he was skimming the funds."

Pereira shook her head. "The guy wasn't even promising his contributors a gonzo return on their money, just what a decent mutual fund would bring in. Without the new investors whose money came in the last week, ACC was broke. And people let him mediate their problems!"

I laughed. For a murderer Pereira might have compassion; for a financial philanderer, fat chance. "Hemming might have made as innocent a mistake as merely not paying attention. He chose the wrong stocks—"

"You can say that again."

"He didn't keep close enough watch on them—"

"Guy didn't watch at all. When the market goes up fifty points and your stock drops, and you don't at least think—"

"Bryant Hemming should have considered the rule of holes."

"The rule of holes?"

"When you're in one, quit digging."

Pereira laughed and, when she stopped, shook her head in weary disgust.

"What this comes down to," I said, "is Bryant Hemming could have made a careless mistake early on. Then the ACC fund got popular, and it was too late to 'fess up. Do that and he's discredited, and much more publicly than before. No *A Fair Deal*, no big groundbreaking international mediation project, no ACC, or much of anything else for Bryant Hemming."

Pereira was shaking her head again slowly, disgustedly. "ACC. I understand it wasn't the Dreyfus Fund to begin with, but they had trustees. Didn't those people ever look at the books?"

"Supposedly Margo Roehner did?"

Pereira stopped dead and stared at me. "Margo Roehner of the Roehner-Castillo Fund?"

"Could be. It's not a common name."

"And *she* didn't notice the—"

If Ott had gotten a look at the books, he'd have come to the same questions. He'd have known about the Roehner-Castillo Fund, as he knew about everything in Berkeley, and he'd have had the same thought as I did: "Why don't we drop in and ask Margo?"

Pereira called Murakawa to take possession of the ACC books, handed them over three minutes later, and climbed into my patrol car.

I pulled into the street. "What's the scoop on Margo Roehner? In the world of big bucks?" I asked minutes later as we stuttered east on Ashby Street, another of Berkeley's stop-and-go thoroughfares. There used to be a belief that the city council refused road repair because bad surfaces slowed traffic, prevented accidents, reduced the need for police presence, the environmental government's dream. Now congestion did it for them.

"You've heard of the Roehner-Castillo Fund?" Connie asked, pausing only for a breath. The question was of course rhetorical. Not only would I *not* have heard of the Roehner-Castillo Fund, but for years I'd assumed the Dreyfus Fund was a charity set up in the aftermath of the great case. My view of competent money management was having no checks bounce. It was the VW bug style of finance—no frills, no hassle, as long as you don't change gears on a hill. Connie Pereira knew all that; it appalled her. She drove an Audi. "Smith, the fund was set up by her grandfather and Mr. Castillo. It's one of the most respected in the state. Margo Roehner worked in the fund offices when she was in college, so she should know something."

"If she cared. Could be she just worked there from family pressure or lack of ambition to find something else." Though the woman whose storage locker had been tossed and abandoned was anything but lazy. A lazy woman would never have created Patient Defenders.

"She's on the Roehner-Castillo board, but just nominally, I understand. Word is she hasn't been to a board meeting in a year, not since her father married his trophy wife and changed his will."

I turned right on Magnolia Street, pulled over in the middle of the crab apple tree–lined block. Not a magnolia in sight. But still, who wants to live on Crab Street?

Margo Roehner's house was a green wood affair with a deep sloping roof, built sometime after the Great War. Looking from the street, I'd have classified it as a cottage, but when I walked up the driveway, I could see the second story hiding its bedrooms and sleeping porches behind that sloping roof. Berkeley had a number of these charming houses designed not to overwhelm the modest lots allotted to them. Here any resident with sufficient pucker could fling open the casement and spit on his neighbor. No activity in these jowl-by-jowl bedrooms was quite private. No renewed passion or gastrointestinal malfunction not announced to the neighbors.

Once I'd lived for half a year in an aluminum-sided development somewhere in Jersey, where the little houses were this close. But privacy survived there, thanks to the depressingly same views out the windows and to winter and rain. Here in the Golden State the seduction of sun and straw flowers, bougainvillaea and balmy air made it hard to keep the windows closed.

I glanced up at the roof Margo Roehner had been rushing back to on Monday. It looked fine. Perhaps her workers had been more reliable than she'd expected.

I pushed the bell. Pereira was surveying the lawn. Was she toting up the years of scrimping and stock market luck before she could live somewhere like this?

"Shaggy," she said.

I raised an eyebrow.

"The yard," Pereira said.

Footsteps sounded on the stairs inside. Hurriedly I glanced around the yard. Pereira was right. The landscaping had been thoughtfully planned—rhododendrons against the house, Japanese maple in front—but they all needed trimming, like a four-month-old haircut with the bangs hanging in your eyes. And ivy, the bane of any serious gardener, threatened to creep over windows, mail box, suet feeders, doves, robins, red-breasted nuthatches, and, if we waited long enough, us. "The architectural equivalent of the Roehner-Castillo board meetings," I whispered.

It was a moment before Pereira grinned. "You mean, unattended?"

The door opened. Margo Roehner didn't look shaggy. She looked as if the energy of a six-footer had been compressed into her five-foot frame. In her tan corduroy suit with bombardier jacket she might have been as ready to deal with the public as she'd been Monday afternoon at her storage locker. But inside that suit all that energy was almost twitching. Her short brown hair had been finger-combed out of the way so often it stood in clumps. She could have been an October squirrel with more ungathered nuts than she could handle. Before I finished introducing Pereira, she snapped, "No. Look, I'm pressed for time."

"We'll only keep you a few minutes."

"Tomorrow I'll have all day."

Tomorrow Ott could be dead. "We'll be brief, really."

With an economic sigh she hurried us into the dark living room, which sat under that sloping roof. Here the dichotomy of landscaping and owner was answered. The room was a collection of carved straight-back chairs, weathered leather, floral couch so soft it was a temptation to leap in, and a green oriental rug that pulled the eclectic pieces into a whole. The effect must have been charming—before the window seat became a shelf for manila folders, before the coffee table grew covered with pamphlets, before the fireplace was blocked off by two stacks of cardboard storage boxes.

Margo scooped up the papers on the couch, pointed us to it, and perched herself on a leather ottoman.

"Looks like Patient Defenders has taken over your life," I said, glancing at the papers.

"It *is* my life. You wouldn't believe the need. People broadsided by illness. It can come out of nowhere. You're dizzy, you're weak, terrified, you don't know what's going on, and you've got to make the most important decisions of your life. And hassle your HMO." She looked directly at me, no hint of the palliative smile women are prone to. But then she wouldn't. She was the woman who had trained herself not to smile when her face had been paralyzed. "That's when you have to have a defender—"

"We'll be brief. There's a question about ACC's books. Did a private investigator named Herman Ott try to question you about it?"

"No."

"Are you sure?"

She sighed irritably. "I haven't answered the phone all week. These grant forms, they've got to be in the mail today. I've got two new employees who have to be paid. I had to stop everything Monday morning and hassle Roger to get my money out of ACC and into my own account—"

Pereira stared at her. "There are laws—"

"Sue me. Look, I don't want to sound callous about Bryant, but he couldn't have died at a more inconvenient time. I'm not going to let his death endanger hundreds of people who need Patient Defenders."

"Couldn't you have waited a week?" Pereira pushed.

"A week? Have you dealt with government? A month, more like it. People are dying."

"And if you miss the deadline and don't get your grant?"

"We can't go on. Not without paid staff, people you can count on when you end up in the emergency room at two A.M. Christmas Eve." Her lips moved in an odd, minimal way.

I wondered if she meant that to be a grimace and didn't realize that the residue of her facial paralysis had turned it into a meaningless movement of flesh.

"As I said, I'm really pressed—" She let out what in another person would have been a long, harried sigh, but that in her case was cut short because everything about her screamed, "I'm in a hurry."

Pereira was not impressed. "So," she said in a voice most people save for pets who've relieved themselves on the antique quilt, "how often did you check over the ACC books?"

"ACC?" Her tone mirrored Pereira's. "Please. If I don't get these forms all in order—"

"Should we take that as 'never'?"

"Hardly. When I came on to the board, before I made my investment, I went over those books. They weren't something I'd have taken home to Daddy, but they were legit. I told Bryant to get a good accountant, and I assume he did."

Pereira was unmoved. "And that was when?"

"About a year after Bryant founded it. I'd say three years ago."

"Have you checked them since?"

Margo Roehner looked around the room slowly, theatrically. "As I said, I'm pressed for time. So if you don't mind . . ." She reached for the doorknob just as the doorbell rang.

CHAPTER 27

MARGO ROEHNER DIDN'T GROAN WHEN she opened the door to Daisy Culligan, but only self-control kept her from it. If I'd dropped in on a friend and been greeted with shoulders hunched in frustration and a mouth crimped into the beginning of "Oh, no, not you too," I'd have been out of there before she could start spewing excuses.

"I'm really rushed," Margo said, unnecessarily. "I've got to get the grant papers . . . And the police are still here. They're just leaving."

Daisy patted Margo's shoulder. "So you're saying you don't want to go for coffee, huh?"

"Daisy! Every HMO is cutting back; they're tossing patients out of hospitals, giving outpatients appointments so short the doctors can barely figure out who they are, much less what complications they've got. Emergency rooms are zoos. I don't have time—"

"You want me to vamoose? Maybe take the cops with me?" Daisy shot me a grin.

It goes against my grain to leave a witness who wants me gone. But we'd asked what we came to ask. I wasn't going to get any closer to Herman Ott here. And I did have questions for Daisy Culligan, the woman who had driven Ott to the beach regularly always before dusk or sunrise. I could have taken her to the station, but she was like Howard, the King of Sting. They're delicate flowers on long, winding stems that get their nourishment not from the solid soil but from the air in which they sway and weave and bob when it suits them. Uprooted and plunked in pots, they shrink down and petrify. And they certainly don't answer questions.

But on a bench outside Peet's with latte in hand, they're likely to diffuse the seeds of their brilliance to the winds. And the cops.

"Peet's?"

"You're on."

Pereira called in for the beat officer to drive her to her car, and I headed the few blocks to Peet's. Daisy had a head start, but I still got on the coffee line before her. That's the advantage of driving—and parking—a patrol car.

I chose the one secluded bench at the edge of the courtyard. Ahead was Domingo Street, beyond were the tennis courts of the Claremont Hotel, and behind them was the great white shingle hotel itself, which holds court over this tony section of Berkeley like Queen Victoria keeping watch on her subjects. In the firestorm of 1991 in which twenty-five people died in the hills above, we all watched for hours as the fire jumped and scrambled down toward the Claremont, anxious for that one delicious bite that would fuel it for a leap onto the rest of the city below. Houses behind it burned, leaving nothing but foundation slabs and barbecues. But the Claremont had been saved. It had become a symbol of Berkeley's survival. Now the sun shone off its turrets and shingles, its porches and porticoes. I sipped my latte, ate the scone that was lunch, and thought how odd it was that my last visit to the grand old lady had been in the company of the last person I would have expected to find on the grounds, Herman Ott.

In the last place I'd have expected to find him.

My breath caught. Herman Ott in the Claremont?

I glanced over at the coffee line at Daisy Culligan and back at the hotel.

Could Ott be hiding in the Claremont? Why would he? If he was back in Berkeley lying low, it would be so he could keep after whatever he was after before he'd gone to the beach.

Yet—I was barely breathing—the Claremont was the last place we'd look for him. It was a spot neither his enemies nor his subjects would consider.

I was off the bench and looking for a spot to pour out my coffee when good sense slapped me. A witness in the hand is worth a bunch of hunches in the bush. Or the hotel. Daisy was coming toward me. If Ott were undercover in the Claremont, he'd still be there in fifteen minutes. Daisy, on the other hand, would not be sitting next to me, drinking a latte machiato, and sighing in pleasure.

"Daisy, you've had time to ponder those trips to Bolinas with Herman. What did he say?"

"Nothing."

"It's an hour's drive. Even Herman wouldn't call you for a ride and then sit in your car like a stone."

"Are you sure you know Herman?" She raised her machiato to her lips. I knew from experience it would still be too hot to drink, but Daisy kept the cup at her mouth, pretending to drink. Then she devoted a minute to dabbing the foam off her lips.

"Daisy, Herman—"

"Look, I said I don't know anything more." She lifted the cup, and this time she did drink. The coffee was still too hot. She pressed her lips together to keep from spitting it out.

I watched, holding my own latte in abeyance and wondering what it was that had turned chatty Daisy Culligan so suddenly taciturn. I tried another tack. Looking her in the eye, I said, "I heard about Damon, the hairdresser."

"Oh." I could almost see her changing mental gears and doing it with relief. In the new gear wariness battled pride, but it was an uneven skirmish. She pushed her curly gray hair off her face and grinned. "It was a nice tat, wasn't it?"

"Tat? You call your revenges tats?"

"Revenge is too mean a word. I'm not the Mafia. I'm just trying to bring a bit of balance into the universe. Life is so unfair. We've got such a bully culture, all these Goliaths stomping around so busy beating their chests they trample the Davids. And then the only thing they regret then is that their feet hurt. What I do is provide the occasional pebble for the occasional David. Or Davida." She looked me in the eye. "After all we women are the ones who get stepped on most. Tit for tat." She grinned.

I was amazed she was so open about her avocation. I sipped my latte, turning the paper cup so the coffee washed the foam and chocolate to the top, and watched Daisy out of the corner of my eye. "And what was the pebble you aimed at Bryant?"

"I didn't—"

I shook my head. "He wrecked your career because he was too self-absorbed to tell you the restaurateur screwed your predecessor. How much time, money, reputation did he cost you? You didn't sue him. He didn't bankroll you in your own café. You're living in two rooms, nice ones, but so small you have to use your stairs as a file cabinet." I sighed and indulged in another head shake. "You've got a grievance that makes the woman with the canceled hair appointments a piker. You are the Joe Montana of revenge. You could throw a Super Bowl–winning touchdown, and you're asking me to believe you just took a sack?"

She laughed.

"Was the tat Roger Macalester?"

"Roger?" She bobbled the paper cup. "I should be insulted. Roger? I did Bryant a favor sending him a guy with integrity who could also keep the office running. I did it for ACC. It galled me to take the chance of bailing out Bryant. I mean, I was married to the man. I knew he'd make a mess of ACC given the time. He had a great facade, but he was so self-absorbed he forgot anyone else existed. But Roger had years of credibility with the left; he's utterly committed to the idea of mediation. Roger was a gift."

I took that with a grain of salt. "So what *was* your tat then?"

"Why are you so sure . . ." She paused, took a long drink of coffee, and said, "Okay. You're right. What Bryant did to me was like sacking the quarterback. And I couldn't stay there on the ground after he ripped the ball out of my hands." She leaned in toward me in a posture I'd come to recognize as the Howardian Personification of Smug. "It was a delicate operation. If I planned a tat that was too endangering or too public, it could backfire. The ex-wife's always the first suspect, right?"

"Indeed."

"If Bryant got stung by any joke, a number of people would think of me."

People like Howard, she meant. The ones whose opinion truly mattered. "You had your reputation to consider."

"Exactly. And my own satisfaction. The tat had to be perfect. I mean it would be tacky to keep shooting off one try after another."

"You had your reputation—"

"So I kept in touch with Bryant and waited for inspiration. I'd been married to him long enough to know his moods, and I could tell he was getting more and more worried. I asked him what was the matter, but he just did what he always did: created a diversion. At one time I would have steered him back to the topic, but it's an effort and more than I'm willing to put into an *ex*-husband. So I asked myself, 'Why is he worried?' Here the guy's dressed in spiffy suits, driving a fancy new Jeep; he's a TV star of sorts. His mediations are going great. What's to worry about? Knowing Bryant and the procrastination method of bookkeeping, I figured it's got to be money. I concluded ACC needed money—no stroke of genius there. So"—she smiled, sipped, smiled again—"I called a couple of friends who had money in the ACC fund and got them to telephone Bryant and say they were thinking of making another, much bigger investment; they were anxious to; they'd heard such good things about the fund. But they were hesitating, not because of the fund but because of him, because"— she could barely control her grin—"they had heard he let down his own ex-wife, and now they weren't sure they could trust him." She pulled her thigh up onto the bench and turned so she could sit facing me.

"Now I'm going to prove to you how law-abiding a tatter I am. I didn't have my people tape their phone calls, so I only heard about Bryant squirming and wheedling secondhand. Still, it was lovely. That week I made my Dinners by Daisy clients meals they are still talking about."

"And Bryant, what did he do?"

"Just what I'd have expected, said he'd get back to the 'investors.' "

"And did he?"

For the first time an interior cloud darkened her eyes. "He died."

"When did your friends make these calls?"

"Three weeks ago. I mean, it wasn't like they called Sunday and Bryant was so distraught he raced up to Herman's office and shot himself."

I glanced up at the Claremont. "Did you tell Herman about this tat?"

"No. I don't know." She gulped down the rest of her machiato. "No, I'm sure."

"Honestly sure?"

"Yes." She stood.

"We're talking murder," I said, standing, facing her. "Herman's in enough trouble already without you lying about what he knows. I'm keeping an open mind about Herman. And when you, his friend, speak, I need to be able to believe you. Did you tell him about the tat?"

"No, really, I didn't."

I sighed. Of course I couldn't believe her. She could swear six more times, and I'd still be suspicious. I glanced back at the Claremont and said to Daisy, "One more thing."

"Yes?"

"The flasher pig poster in Margo's storage locker, it's yours, right?"

It was a moment before she relaxed enough to laugh. "God, I'd forgotten all about that. Margo kept it? She carried on so when I asked her to stick it in her storage. I was a middle-aged adolescent, she proclaimed. I could be using my time to help people instead of"—another silent skirmish ended in a shrug and a grin—"instead of taping it to the ceiling over the couch where a porcine husband of a client was known to philander. I understand it made quite an impression on the young woman beneath him."

I couldn't resist laughing too.

"Officer, I assume the pig's not part of your case?"

"Even the burglars didn't want it," I said.

Daisy shrugged, then looked questioningly at me.

I liked Daisy. What she was, how she lived were parts of what I loved about Berkeley. She was a real "Berkeley" type. Enough so that she'd harbor suspicion of the police. Even though she seemed to like me, even to trust me personally, she was edgy. Maybe it was just the political implications of being seen chatting with a cop. More than once, when I'd run into my friend Amy somewhere while I was in uniform, one of her friends had come up to her to ask if she was all right. Was I hassling her? had been the tacit question. "How can you be friends with a cop?" her friends had demanded later. "And they've never quite trusted me again," Amy told me.

"Daisy," I said, counting on the seduction of communal speculation, "think about Bryant. Suddenly he's forced to face those pesky financial problems he'd pushed out of his mind. Suddenly he finds himself sitting in his nice new Jeep, in his new clothes, planning to go to his new important job, and here's this nuisance of a financial problem getting enough attention that he can't go on telling himself that no one will notice. He's got to deal with it. Either he has to get money to pay back ACC . . ." I dangled the implicit question before her.

She stood. "Look, I've really got to go."

"Of course," I said. "I don't want to keep you if you're uncomfortable."

"No, no, it's not that," she said so awkwardly that she might have had a flashing *L* for "liar" on her forehead. She shot a glance behind her at the courtyard and then back at me. "Bryant couldn't have gotten a loan; he was maxed out with the Jeep and all."

I nodded thanks. It wasn't sharing the kind of purple secret that cements a female friendship, merely a pale pink offering, but it made me feel better about my place in town, about Daisy. And it was one of those pieces that lock together two big clusters of the puzzle.

Bryant could hardly borrow the money to pay back ACC, not without spotlighting his financial shenanigans there. So faced with that conundrum, what would he do? What he always did, create a diversion, the Big Mediation. For that he needed to bribe Cyril. But bribes take money. Money was the thing he didn't have. If he'd had money, he wouldn't have needed to bribe Cyril.

I chewed the last bite of scone. Maybe Bryant promised Cyril. Promised and didn't follow through. Maybe then Cyril moved Bryant to the Promised Land.

But why in Ott's office? And was the bribe, or the

pyramid, the reason that Ott was investigating Bryant?

I walked to my car and moved it across the street to the Claremont and headed into the lobby.

CHAPTER 28

THE LOBBY OF THE CLAREMONT Hotel is one of those areas more akin to a beautifully landscaped freeway than a room. Visitors in suits, jeans, dashikis stride purposefully toward waiting limos, passing turbaned guests heading for the decks and views of the gardens, tennis courts, and San Francisco Bay or sweatsuited guests rushing to the spa. The registration area seems no more than a little-used rest stop along the lush freeway, one that the Jaguars and Lexuses would speed by before they realized it. I glanced at the four-foot sprays of flowers, the sumptuous chairs. In this freeway Ott would be the broken-down jalopy spewing steam in the break-down lane.

Was I crazy to think of Ott staying here?

I checked the Claremont register. Ott wouldn't use his own name, of course, but he was an arrogant man, and it would amuse him to register as Andre Lamb, or N. der Cover.

I described Ott to the manager. In the dark suit he had been wearing Sunday, Ott would stand out here among the trendy business travelers and the healthy spa crowd. Had the hotel been in another city, the staff would have recalled Ott with disdain. In the dining room he would have resembled a small-town cousin exiled by his hosts to a hotel. But here he could as easily have been a Cal professor, a rich ex-hippie costumed for a lark, any of half the guys in town thumbing their noses at the thought of a dress code.

Neither the manager nor the dining room staff recalled Ott. Maybe I had been wrong about him. Maybe the Alexander Herman Ott who had had his chauffeur drive him to the airport in New York would fit right into the gracious life at the Claremont.

Or maybe he had holed up and lived on room service, the gracious equivalent of his habitual hot plate meals in his office. For one dinner he'd be paying what he spent on a week of hot plate specials. And how would he deal with the room service waiters? In egalitarian Berkeley people do have house cleaners. Here the problem is not overlooking Social Security payments; it's admitting you have a servant, not that that term is used, ever, for any service. The best of people are torn between being bourgeois or dirty. And to have a waiter bring food to your bedroom, put down the flower-decorated tray, and ceremoniously lift the lid from the entrée . . . I'd have given a lot to see Ott's reaction. "Do you have a guest who holed up in his room for days?"

"Officer, we don't monitor our guests' behavior."

"Could you check the room service orders?"

"For every single guest!"

"Did any of the waiters report odd behavior—"

"Officer, please. The staff here is used to odd behavior. Our room service waiters have delivered to nudity, orgy, and regurgitation."

I glanced around the lobby at a pair of tanned tennis players, a couple of tan-suited M.B.A.'s, a sprinkling of disheartened tourists in sweaters over summer dresses. To the clerk I said, "Keep an eye out. My guy is short, sallow, middle-aged, and may be wearing the kind of black suit an undertaker would use only for burial. He's—"

"Black suit?"

"Right," I said, drawn by his sudden attention. "He'll seem uncomfortable here, definitely out of place. He's got"—I raked my memory for any accoutrement Ott might have, nothing I knew of had been missing from his office—"well, he had a small silvery pin, about an inch high, a cross that comes to a point at the bottom."

"Like a sword? The cross, it's like a sword?" he asked excitedly.

"Right. Is he here?"

"You mean Reverend Ballinger?"

I was nearly holding my breath. "Does the reverend fit the description?"

"To a T. Or make that a cross."

"Is he alone?"

"He booked a single, but he has had company." He leaned toward me, then seemed to reconsider the indiscretion about to escape his lips.

"A lot of company?" I offered. "Young, rough-looking men?"

He nodded.

"His room number?"

Again he hesitated.

I lowered my voice. "You know I'm going to get it. Save me time, huh?"

"Two forty-nine."

"Don't warn him."

He looked abashed, but not as if the thought hadn't occurred to him.

"What do these rooms go for?" I asked almost as an afterthought.

"Hundred sixty-five for the hill view, hundred ninety-five with view of the Bay."

"Does that include use of the spa?"

"Oh, no, those services are extra. But the reverend does have access to the fitness center and our two Olympic-size pools."

"And room two forty-nine? Is that a hill or Bay view room?"

"Hill."

At least he'd shown some economy.

I took the stairs, rounded the corner, and stopped by those room number arrows that always take twice as long as you expect to decipher. Two forty-nine was at the end of the corridor.

From beside the door I knocked. Surely Ott wouldn't run his normal door-answering routine here, making me pound and holler till the neighbors noticed. I knocked again, but what greeted me was the familiar Ottian silence.

I knocked a third time. "Housekeeping." Ott, friend of the proletariat, would think twice before inconveniencing the maid.

Or so I thought.

"Please. Housekeeping," I squeaked. I had honed a certain skill at accents in my years of dealing with Ott. "Please, I will be in trouble. . . . Big trouble," I added. Olympian trouble, I could have said for all the difference it would have made to him.

Maybe Ott was out. Out to skulk in his normal terrain. I pounded a fourth time and waited. Perhaps he was sprawled on a better chair than he was used to in this room far above his element, looking out at the magnificent view of the East Bay hills. But where would he even get the money? Inherited from the mother whose funeral he boycotted? Or . . .

There were too many ors and question marks. I opted for a note on hotel paper.

It wasn't till I bent down to slide it under the door that I noticed the smell coming from inside the room.

CHAPTER 29

THE HOTEL WOULD SEND A senior staff member right up with a key to the room, I was assured. He'd be there in a minute.

Minutes stretch to years at times like these.

I had plenty of time to decide the smell oozing from under the door to the room "Reverend Ballinger" occupied was that all too familiar combination of blood and putrefaction. There were a dozen possible scenarios leading to this room: Ott had killed Hemming and now himself; Ott inadvertently had assisted the murderer and couldn't live with himself afterward; Ott was terrified of the murderer, had tried to hide out, and failed. It may not be Ott in there, I reminded myself every few seconds. Maybe Reverend Ballinger had a heart attack. Long enough ago to account for that smell?

From my cell phone I called the dispatcher for backup.

Inside the room the phone rang and rang till its demand echoed in my head.

A group of inadequately clad tourists exited a room halfway down the hall and headed for the elevator. They didn't notice me. Only the maid would have come to the end of the hall here. With the Do Not

Disturb sign on the door, she'd put off entering. Still, it was hard to believe that in a hotel of this caliber a body could lie unnoticed till it smelled.

The staff man arrived, knocked, called, gave up, and, muttering a plea about discretion, moved as far from the lock as possible to do the final deed. Once the door was unlocked, I had to give it the final shove to open it. It moved only a foot. The smell was overwhelming. I gagged and turned away, then forced myself back. Holding my breath, I peered in. The room was dark, curtains drawn tight.

"Flashlight?" I asked the staff man.

"No."

I wished I were in uniform with everything I could need hanging off me. I moved farther to the side, pushed the door harder. It gave an inch, then stuck, as if it had run into something.

I pushed again. It gave another inch. "Where's the light switch?"

One hand over his nose, he pointed inside the door.

I shifted to the other side of the doorway, stuck my hand inside and flicked on the light.

Blood was all over the rug, on the walls, on the bedspreads. Candles had burned to stubs. And spread thick on the rug were pigeons. Pigeons with their heads cut off.

Sacrificial birds.

Birds like Ott.

I jammed my lips together to keep from gagging. Behind me and down the hall the elevator door opened, spitting out two patrol officers. I swallowed hard and motioned them to wait outside. "Maybe all we've got is dead birds. But there's plenty of blood."

I started in along the wall, just as I'd done in Ott's office, here moving right, into the bathroom, then along the walls, poking under the bed, snapping open the closet doors. I'd been right: no corpses that hadn't once flown.

"What went on in here, Smith?" White asked.

I shook my head. "Could be ritual, could be slaughter for pleasure." One thing I was sure of: Ott hadn't set up this scene. If he had walked in on it, he was in more danger than he'd anticipated.

I called in for Inspector Doyle. He'd notify the watch commander. In half an hour one of the watch sergeants arrived at the same time as Raksen, the lab tech.

It was Raksen who spotted the crumpled paper under one of the pigeons. Torn from a small plain white pad, the word was almost unreadable under the blood. "Zeise," it said.

"Save it. It's important, Raksen."

Raksen grimaced in insult—as if he *wouldn't* preserve evidence?—but I didn't stop to salve his feelings. I took leave of the sergeant and raced downstairs to the hotel registration desk. The same clerk was still on duty.

"When Reverend Ballinger checked in, was he looking for another minister?"

"How'd you know? But he asked before he checked in."

"He was pretty insistent, huh?"

"I told him we can't give out information about our guests. I must have told him six times."

"And then he checked in. And hung around in the lobby?" On the lookout for Cyril or his followers.

The clerk nodded.

"When did you last see Reverend Ballinger?"

"About an hour ago. Right before you got here. Maybe fifteen minutes before."

"What was he doing?"

"Walking out with his men."

"Was he in front of them, beside them, what?"

"Right in the middle, like they were bodyguards. They were all around him."

"Did you hear where they were going?"

He shook his head. "They didn't speak at all. They just escorted the reverend out."

I stood stunned. My face must have gone stone gray.

"Ma'am, are you okay?"

"What? Yeah, sure," I lied. Herman Ott had been here fifteen minutes before I arrived. Brother Cyril's boys had marched him out of here while I'd been across the street with Daisy drinking a latte.

Ott, you stupid, arrogant bastard, you think about telling me what you're up to, change your mind, and get tossed in the frying pan with Ranger Zeise at Muir Beach. When you get yourself out of that frying pan, you're so sure you can outsmart Cyril, you can't get back to Berkeley fast enough to throw yourself into the fire and burn yourself to a crisp.

Or maybe you just sold out.

I knew that wasn't true. The "Zeise" note told me that. The odds of my convincing Inspector Doyle of that were about the same as Ott's living out the week.

When I got back to Doyle's office, Clay Jackson was sitting on a folding chair. His elbows were jammed into his knees. His dark face was compacted into a scowl. Had they been able to move, every ceramic rhino in the office would have turned tail and run. Eggs had stationed himself at the far corner of the inspector's desk from his partner. Inspector Doyle was leaning back in his leather chair. His skin hung from his face as if it had just been pasted to his bones. I wondered when he had last slept.

"Gone!" Jackson snarled. "Damn Cyril. Asshole strolls through the lobby and out the Claremont like he's Jesus on Palm Sunday. Then he vanishes—'gone' like he's been risen up to heaven."

I glanced at Eggs, ready for him to look down his long, bony nose at Jackson, shake his head, and say, "Your theological history is a little spotty, Brother Jackson. Haven't you forgotten there was a week between Palm Sunday and Easter?" But Eggs's face was a carving of disgust.

"Whole damn case's going nowhere," Jackson added.

I closed the door and leaned against it, brushing off chair-getting motions from Eggs. This was no time to bring up the subject of Ott. "Maybe Cyril's gone back to Monterey. Or on to his church in Modesto."

Jackson shook his head. But I persisted. "He had to go somewhere. Why wouldn't he go where he knows? Unless he's been driven out of there."

"Both those places, Smith, the brother's a model citizen. Word is he preaches in his storefronts, and that's it. He runs a circuit: in the pulpit in Monterey Friday nights; here to hassle us on Saturdays and Sundays; preaches in Modesto Monday night. No complaints either place. Not even parking."

"Does he husband all his venom for us?" Eggs demanded.

"Sad but true. And if you all paid attention to his schedule, you can see that by this time in the week he doesn't exist. Gone from Modesto. No sign of him in Monterey." Jackson slammed back. The folding chair quaked, and for a moment it looked as if Jackson would go banging into the wall.

Doyle had a translucent violet rhino in his fingers. He was tapping it hard against the desk. "And getting the weekend rate at the Claremont."

Jackson's fists tightened. "Special collections," Jackson growled. "Asshole bilked his followers good." Jackson had handled a couple of clerical frauds before he came to Homicide-Felony Assault Detail and one assault on a sticky-fingered minister since. He had forced himself to meet with the devastated parishioners afterward. "It's not so much the money," he'd told me, "though these folks can hardly afford it. It's the trust. Some of them will never trust again. Might as well've been their god that shucked them." When I asked how he could be so definite, he just said, "I *know*, Smith." I picked up the leader of the windowsill herd and fingered him intimately. "Jackson, don't you think Cyril's schedule is peculiar?"

Deliberately Jackson nodded, as if he were a teacher with a particularly slow class. "The weekend in Berkeley?"

"Right. Sunday, Cyril's big business day, why devote it to Telegraph Avenue?"

"Because Sunday's Telegraph's big day and the asshole's more after raising hell than saving souls."

"But why? Doesn't he have much of an investment in his little congregations elsewhere?"

Jackson's face pinched tighter in disgust. "Two storefronts. Nothing in any of them."

"Not even chairs?"

"Zilch."

"Maybe his followers levitate," Eggs offered.

"Did he ever have chairs or equipment?"

"Altar, candles, statues, the works. But they're gone."

"What does he drive?"

"Van. So, yeah, Smith, he could haul a bunch of folding chairs and paraphernalia everywhere he goes. But they're not in his van when he carts his flunkies up to the Avenue to raise hell."

"How about the ACC storage locker? Bryant was bribing him, paying him off with something. There's no record in the ACC books. So maybe the bribe is space in his storage locker."

Eggs shook his head. "Smith, you are suggesting a rather modest price for giving up rights to Telegraph."

"We know Bryant was paying him off with something. We know Ott was checking up on Cyril. We can deduce that Cyril was involved in something unsavory." Something Ott discovered and I hadn't.

"So, Smith, you're suggesting Bryant's payment was sealed lips," Jackson said.

Eggs looked confused. "Keeping quiet about whatever Cyril was up to but not giving him space in the storage locker?"

I shrugged. "Either or both. It's probably no big thing to Bryant. Still, someone did break into Margo Roehner's unit right beneath it."

"But if Cyril knew Bryant, he'd get the key and"— Eggs hesitated, abashed—"the key wouldn't work because he'd be at the wrong locker and he'd be sufficiently angered to break in. And once he got inside, he'd realize he wasn't in the ACC place—"

"Right," I said, "and he'd have no interest in the Patient Defenders boxes of records, so he'd just make a mess and leave."

Jackson was smiling. "But like we said, the dude's no dummy. Maybe he figures out his mistake and finds his way upstairs and leaves his chairs. Or something better. Worth a look."

I stood up.

"Before you go, Smith," Doyle said, "what about Ott?"

CHAPTER 30

JACKSON AND EGGS DIDN'T MOVE, except to resettle in their chairs. With Doyle, they stared at me.

I took a breath. "There was a note in the Claremont Hotel room in Ott's handwriting—"

"He *left* a note? Among the slaughtered pigeons?" Eggs demanded.

Ignoring his sarcasm, I said, "I know his handwriting. The paper said 'Zeise.' It proves Ott was at the beach when Bryant was killed. It proves he's not the murderer."

"You've got a pretty big leap of faith there, Smith." Doyle clicked the little violet rhino's heels against the desk.

"Zeise is the ranger at Muir Beach, the one who told Ott not to camp overnight Sunday night. He spotted Ott there again Monday morning and was sure Ott had defied him. He probably was professional but hardly overly gracious that second time. Ott didn't note down Zeise's name to get together for coffee later." I waited till Doyle gave a grudging nod. Neither Jackson nor Eggs bothered.

"The only reason for Ott to write down that name was to prove he was there"—I checked to see that Doyle was still with me—"so he could give it to me to

check. Which meant"—I raced on before any of them
could interrupt—"he at least *suspected* there was
something he'd need an alibi for, right?"

"Dude *knew* he'd need an alibi," Jackson growled.

Doyle sat silent. His face revealed nothing but ex-
haustion.

"Look, guys, if Ott had been hiding out at the
beach, he could have done it well enough to avoid
being spotted. He wouldn't have prowled the parking
lot in his mustard yellow trench coat. But he made
himself suspicious enough that the ranger had to deal
with him because he suspected something would happen in Berkeley in his absence—"

Doyle smacked down the rhino. "Smith, I
hardly—"

"And since Ott had spent his time here going after
Cyril, it follows that he suspected Cyril was involved
in whatever happened."

"And so," Doyle said, "you're saying that Ott got
himself back to Berkeley. Somehow he uncovered
Brother Cyril in the last place you'd expect an itiner-
ant troublemaker—"

"Ott called me to the Claremont Sunday afternoon. The site was his choice. I figured he'd just
picked a place where none of his cronies would see
him with me."

Eggs laughed. "So, Smith, you flattered yourself?
Ott wasn't thinking about you at all, right? He was
just having you up there because he was there anyway,
spying on Cyril?"

I brushed over Ott's insult and Eggs's righteous
amusement. "It explains the black suit. Cyril wasn't
registered under his own name. The hotel manager
checked every entry for the past two weeks. There

was no way for Ott to know what name he was using or what room he was in. So Ott dresses as a man of the cloth and asks the staff about other clergy, and when he can't get an answer, he checks in and waits in the lobby till he spots Cyril or one of his thugs and follows him. Or vice versa."

"Jesus, Mary, and Joseph, Smith. The scenario could be: Ott and Cyril both had rooms because they planned it that way. Ott walked out with Cyril's thugs because he's one of them."

"But why—"

"Smith, it's all speculation. Nothing's changed except we know Ott's loose in Berkeley."

My hands balled into fists. "No, we know Ott *was* in Berkeley," I said slowly, deliberately. "We certainly don't know he's loose. He left the hotel surrounded by Cyril's men. If Cyril's got him, he's not loose."

"No need to patronize us, Smith."

"I'm not, Inspector. I'm just trying to get you to see—"

"What I see, Smith, is"—his face was red, he seemed to be forcing himself to take a breath—"you found Ott. Your part of this case is done."

"But, Inspector, Ott's still—"

"We don't know what Ott is. But there's no more call to focus on him separately." Before I could speak, he said, "No more call. No more budget. If what you say is right, when we find Cyril, we'll find Ott."

"He could be in the locker."

"Maybe he left another note there." Jackson's voice was cutting. I looked over at him, my old buddy from Homicide. He met my gaze, but his face was a wall.

Doyle took a deep breath. "Smith, I knew I should never have put you on this case. You're too close. You can't be objective."

I felt paralyzed, as you do in a dream. The key fact was right out there somewhere, but I couldn't reach for it. I was so close. No one knew Ott like I did. There were things they'd miss, key things. I couldn't say any of that. On the desk the herd of rhinos plodded motionlessly in their endless journey to where they were. "Inspector," I said, sounding dead calm, "I've been in the storage units. I took Margo Roehner's report there. It'll be easy for me to see if Cyril could have mistaken her unit for ACC's."

Doyle shrugged. "Fine, Smith. Go with Jackson. But then you're back on patrol."

CHAPTER 31

"THE ASSISTANT'S GOT A BUG up his booty. Why all of a sudden?" It was a rhetorical question Jackson was throwing out to avoid the awkward subject of my being taken off the case. He had made it across town to Storit Urself with a series of turns and fast pickups that would have impressed me if I were allowing myself any feelings at all. Not only had he avoided the major red lights on University, San Pablo, and Sixth Street, but he'd maneuvered the side streets like a pinball, never once getting caught at one of the intersection fences the city erected to thwart drivers. I had followed him through the gate at Storit Urself, bounced over the speed bump, and parked in front of the four-story prefab building in this village of the unwanted.

"Last I talked to him," I said as we headed to the elevator, "I'd have listed Macalester as depressed. He was bemoaning Bryant killing ACC and undermining the mediation concept with his duplicity. The idea of mediating between citizens and bureaucracies or corporations—faceless entity mediation—was Macalester's baby. He saw it as saving the world and—"

"And Hemming pictures it as pocket lining?"

"You could make a case for that. Macalester wouldn't have disagreed. So what's he up to now?"

"From the looks of it, he's already up there in the storage. He must have had wings on that hog. Didn't even bother with a helmet." Jackson pushed the elevator button. "Maybe we should have gotten a warrant."

Automatically I groaned. "Right, and devoted the entire afternoon to paperwork."

He lowered his voice. "So, I call Mr. Cooperative Macalester and tell him we need to go by the storage unit and we'll swing by his office for the key."

I almost smiled. *Assuming* permission, making Macalester scamper uphill to object.

"All of a sudden Macalester's coming here anyway. He'll meet us."

We rode up silently, and when the elevator door opened, I headed out ahead of Jackson. Macalester might be nothing but bad-day jumpy, but if he was on the edge, he'd be less confrontational spotting me than he'd be with Jackson. Male cops used to worry whether they'd have to protect their women partners; they never considered situations like this. I made a quick right and strode down the stark hallway, past door after metal door. All the units looked alike—mausoleum slots for stuff. If Cyril had got off on the wrong floor, he'd have forced Margo's tiny lock and been inside staring around in disbelief before his mistake occurred to him. I knocked on the door of 307. "Roger? Jill Smith here, and Detective Jackson."

"Come on in." Was his pitch a bit high? Nervousness? Exertion getting here?

I eased open the door. The space looked like something out of Dickens. A ten-by-fifteen box. No

ceiling light, just two camp lights stuck on the plywood walls. Macalester standing by the far wall in
front of cardboard boxes and hastily organized piles
of cloth and papers. Sweat shone on his pate, and his
little ponytail glistened. The whole place smelled of
dust and something I couldn't name. "You've been
cleaning up?"

"This is the attic of last resort. You could have
spent all day hunting through things the way they
were." It was the kind of light statement with a
twinge of sarcasm typical of our earlier interview, but
now it sounded neither easy nor loose.

"So you don't mind us looking through it, right?"
Jackson asked, before heading for the piles.

I motioned Macalester closer till we were huddled
near the door. "Roger, look, I've been something of a
slob all my life. I know from panic cleanup. These
piles of yours, they're an open book to me. Save me
some time. What are you covering up here?"

Macalester backed away, hands digging into his
jeans pocket. "I'm just trying to help."

I softened my voice. "Roger, half the time witnesses cover up, it has nothing to do with the crime.
Officer Jackson and I are dealing with murder; if
you've been stashing a couple joints here, we don't
have the time—or the inclination—to deal with that."

"I don't do drugs."

Maybe. Macalester was an old lefty, but there was a
conservative strain to him. I could picture him refusing meat, saturated fats, or drugs. "Okay. Just tell me
what you're hiding here. You didn't kill Bryant, so
you've got nothing to be afraid of."

He looked at me, raised an eyebrow; then he
laughed.

Sometimes it worked; sometimes it bombed. I shrugged and walked over to Jackson, who was scanning the last box. "Pottery. Shaving mugs."

"One of our members' overstock." Macalester stayed put. I considered moving between him and the door but opted for readiness instead.

"And the rest?"

"T-shirts, assorted clothing, lamps, penal codes, papers, more papers, blankets, old phones, and the like," Jackson said.

I stared at the piles. There weren't many for a room this size. "Why did Bryant bother getting a storage unit?"

Macalester just shrugged.

I looked more carefully at him, the personally conservative lefty. "You don't ride your motorcycle without a helmet, do you?"

He flinched. "I thought you were only interested in murder!"

"Do you? Ride without a helmet?"

"Of course not. But what do you need to know for?"

Jackson had stopped sorting and stood, legs apart, arms crossed.

"Where is your helmet? It wasn't on the cycle downstairs."

"I left—I didn't—"

"It's with your personal things, isn't it?"

He didn't answer in words, but his slumped shoulders and quick glance toward the door shouted: Sleeping bag and box of clothes out back.

"As I said, Roger, we're interested in the murder; we're not housing police. We don't care that you've been living in here."

"I'm not now," he insisted. He must have looked just the same when he was five, backed into a corner, arms hugged tight against his ribs.

"Where are you living?"

"A motel."

"That's a big step up." And an expensive one. "How come?"

"Bryant. He gave me the money. It was temporary. He was going to let me stay in his place after he left. Till his lease ran out."

"Why that generosity? All of a sudden?"

Macalester hesitated, mentally fingering a lie, tossing it away. "The big shots from Washington. Bryant didn't want them to think his assistant was a street person. Looks bad when you trust your organization to someone you pay so little, particularly if you haven't paid him in months. Temptation's too great."

"And was it?" Jackson's voice seemed to come out of nowhere. Macalester had forgotten he was around.

"No. Honestly. No," he sputtered.

"Tell me true."

"Really." If Macalester could have disappeared in the corner crack, he'd have been gone.

"Are you sure," I asked, "that Bryant got you out of here because he was afraid of the Washington guys? Maybe he had something in here he didn't want you to see?"

"I don't—"

"Think."

"Well, I guess, maybe. I mean the motel money, it did come out of nowhere. It's not like I asked. I'd never have thought of asking, much less asking Bryant."

"So he just offered. When?"

"Saturday."

"Saturday," Jackson repeated. He didn't say aloud, "the day Brother Cyril arrived in town."

I looked at Macalester, standing now away from the wall, looking like the guy who ran the office at ACC, like himself again. I smiled. "Roger, you are not naive. You didn't believe Bryant about the Washington threat, did you?"

He allowed a little smile.

"And you had a key for here. You'd made yourself a copy, right? Any sensible person would."

Still smiling, he nodded.

"And so you came back here—didn't you?—to see what Bryant had here. How could you *not* check it out?"

"Yeah."

"What was it?"

His smile bloomed and died. "I figured it must be something bad, maybe illegal, but not . . . Kaldane."

Jackson whistled.

"Kaldane?" I asked.

"Kaldane," Jackson said, "is a pesticide. It's so toxic it's illegal to transport it in a private vehicle." He stared at Macalester. "Lucky for you you had that motel room. You spent time in here with that poison, who knows what of your parts would never have fun again?"

Macalester glared at Jackson. "Very funny. And chauvinistic. What about the Mexicans whose fields this stuff lands in? What'll happen to them? Did Bryant think about that? They're not going to be asking for mediation when their children are deformed, so what did he care? Just steal the toxins up here, sell

them for a fortune down there where they don't have
the EPA watching out, where they don't care if they
maim their field-workers and let the runoff poison
their water supply. And what about us, Officer, when
we get our fine vegetables from Mexico, what do you
think we'll be eating?" His face was white with rage. I
could imagine this discovery pushing him over the
edge and him squeezing Bryant's neck till his bones
broke. I wouldn't have blamed him.

Roger had talked about Bryant's destroying ACC.
Few things would do it faster in Berkeley than the
news that Bryant was smuggling toxic chemicals to
Mexico. People across the political spectrum would
be disgusted. Nixon might have been rehabilitated,
but a man who foisted poison on unsuspecting field-
workers and into the mouths of his neighbors' children—never.

CHAPTER 32

JACKSON HEADED OFF TO THE manager's office. I considered the onerous and probably futile project of interviewing other renters, hoping someone had seen the Kaldane making its way into the storage unit. I wondered how many of them would be scurrying to cover up questionable items in their own units. If Margo Roehner had thought about it before calling us when her unit was broken into, would she have ditched Daisy's pig poster?

Later I would take Roger Macalester to the station for a formal statement, but I wanted to observe him here in the storage unit. He had come here voluntarily at least twice, but that was before Jackson's comment about the toxic effects of Kaldane. I suspected Jackson knew no more of the specific effects of the pesticide than I did. Macalester didn't realize that. He was looking decidedly twitchier than he had two minutes ago. That was to my benefit. A nervous subject is a careless subject.

Still, decency bade me open the door wider and let in the minutely fresher hall air. "Do you know for a fact Bryant was selling the stuff in Mexico?" I recalled Griffon's hinting at that.

"Where else?"

"Did he go to Mexico often?"

"Not that I know of. But he wouldn't advertise it, would he?"

"The smart smuggler has a valid reason for going over the border," I said. "He's not trying to hide his travel, just the illegal reason for it."

"Well, our hero Bryant was better than smart. There's no record of his trips south. I know; I checked. And that blond accountant cop, what's her name?"

"Officer Pereira."

"Pereira, she just went over the books. Ask her if there are any tickets to Mexico charged."

"Bryant could have paid his own way."

Macalester laughed—the sarcastic laugh of the unpaid employee.

I took a breath, a shallow one. That smell in here I couldn't quite name, was it pesticide, or had I psyched myself instead of Macalester? Either way I was impatient to get out. "Bryant Hemming is a very convenient scapegoat for this smuggling. The man is dead."

"Maybe that's why he's dead."

"Maybe not. Who else had keys here? You and—"

He flinched but caught himself before responding. "The board?"

"No. It changes too much, and there are too many flakes on it. If we gave them keys, then those keys would have been all over Telegraph. There wouldn't have been room for me to sleep in here."

"So who? Just Bryant and you?"

He stood, his fingers moving together and apart. It was a moment before I realized what he doing, squeezing and releasing a squishy orange ball that wasn't there. Just as the wise smuggler wouldn't hide his trips, Macalester would consider which holders of keys he wanted us questioning. He would put as much thought into his answer as an innocent man trying to recall facts he hadn't expected to be asked. It meant his pensive period wasn't telling me anything. "Who, Roger?"

"Just Bryant and me."

"What about you, Roger? Have you been over the border?"

"Sure. And when I get tired of the staterooms on my cruises and grand tours, I opt for a change of pace and camp out here in the four-star storage unit."

"Have . . . you . . . been . . . to . . . Mexico?"

"What do you think? Taking BART to San Francisco's a big investment."

I took another breath. Maybe the stench was just coming from Macalester's attitude. "Look, Roger, you're telling me someone was smuggling Kaldane into Mexico but no one went there. You're too sophisticated to think you're not a suspect. Give me a real lead to someone else." "Give me a lead" could be translated as "I realize the interview is over. You're free to go."

I stepped back to let Roger pass and was so immersed in the routine of giving the scene a final survey that I almost missed his statement.

"What?"

"You wanted a lead; I'm giving it to you. I drove down here, like you said, to see what was going on. But I didn't come up to the unit."

"Ump." My request had been a throwaway line. I had expected no answer; what Roger seemed to be giving me was the closest thing.

"The reason I didn't come up here," he insisted,

looking a bit miffed, "was that I saw them downstairs, headed up here."

"Saw who?"

"A tall, skinny guy in the shadows. I couldn't see his face. But he stuck an arm out, and the light hit it. The arm, it was tattooed."

"Describe the tattoo."

He shrugged. "I just remember tattoo. I didn't pay that much attention because"—he paused for so long I suspected he was paying me back for my dismissal a moment ago—"the guy with him was Herman Ott."

He had my full attention now. "Ott? When did you see him here?"

"Last week. Sunday."

"A week ago Sunday?"

"Right."

A week before Ott disappeared he had come here to Bryant Hemming's storage unit. "What was Ott doing with the tattooed guy?"

"Racing ahead of him, batting him away, like a canary with a tomcat on his tail."

"Did they say anything?"

He started to shake his head and stopped abruptly, leaving his pigtail quivering as if it were the part of him eager to divulge the answer.

"Roger, Bryant is dead. It's too late to protect him," I said, giving him the opening to divulge in righteousness.

He took it. "Okay. Here's what I heard. The tattooed guy said, 'It's okay with Hemming.' Ott turned toward him—he was sort of running—and shouted, 'Poison. It's poison!' "

"And then what?"

"That's it. I was at the end of the building. There

was no way I could get closer without coming out into the open."

I swallowed my disappointment. "And they'd told you what you wanted to know."

Roger shook his head, this time slowly, pointedly, his face sagging with despair.

"Did they come out of the building carrying anything?"

"Nope."

"How long were they inside?"

"Five minutes max."

Ninety-nine-point-nine percent they never got into the storage unit. Copying the entry code to Storit Urself was one thing; getting the key to an individual unit another entirely.

So Ott was on to the Kaldane. If he had been a decent citizen, he would have called us. But in he trotted himself, without even the sense to stay under cover. The man was arrogant to the point of idiocy. To the point of death.

There were only two practical possibilities for the tattooed man. I tried the better of them. "Roger, was Griffon the man with Ott?"

Roger jerked his head toward me, eyes wide with confusion. It was a moment before he said, "No, of course not. Griffon doesn't have tattoos."

"Griffon the tattoo master is a blank canvas?" I couldn't restrain a grin.

"Yeah. Too pure, too scared of error, above displaying anyone else's work, take your pick. A shrink would have a field day with him, right?"

"So, Roger, was the tattooed guy one of Cyril's guys?"

"Yeah. I couldn't give you a name. But he had a

black T-shirt and muscles so blown up they looked like water wings. And one of those little tin crosses."

I leaned back against the wall, recalling *A Fair Deal* and Howard's and my questions about it. "This last mediation was not the kind Bryant normally did or that you set up for when you had the idea. Your specialty, and Bryant's, was mediating between aggrieved individuals and the looming bureaucracies that drive them crazy, right?"

"Exactly."

"But this one was between Serenity and Cyril, parallel individuals. How come?"

"Bryant said it was high-profile."

"But how did he even get the idea?"

"Griffon suggested it."

Griffon! Did the man have his talons in every facet of this case?

CHAPTER 33

JACKSON WAS OUTSIDE THE MANAGER'S office nodding as the manager spoke. From the looks of the two of them, Jackson was downwind of a rant. He put out a hand and was beside my car before I'd stopped it. "I'll be rolling in a minute. Back to do the paper on this." He lowered his voice. "Anything more from Macalester?"

"Says it was Griffon who suggested the mediation with Cyril."

"For a dude who just wanted to stash his cash in ACC, he raises a lot of questions."

"Just what I thought. First he's searching Ott's office, then he's telling me to check on Hemming's trips to Mexico, and now this, telling Hemming to mediate Cyril and Serenity. What's with him? I'm going to swing by his place on the way back to the station."

"Hey, Smith, Doyle said—"

"I'm just tying up a loose end from here."

His brow lowered. "Do what you want. You're going to anyway. But don't pull my name into it." He turned and walked back to the manager before I could answer.

* * *

The Chartreuse Caracara was not open for business. I knocked, identified myself, and knocked again. Griffon probably never would have opened the door if he hadn't forgotten he was wearing leather-heeled shoes. And if I hadn't had years of experience listening for sounds witnesses didn't want me to hear, I might have missed that soft tapping on his floor.

"Griffon, we have an agreement!" I called through the metal door. Cooling my heels in the putrid alley wasn't making me a more cheerful servant of the people.

The door opened about five inches. The crack revealed Griffon's long, emaciated form. As before, he was dressed in a white turtleneck. I glanced at his wrists. No tattoos emerged from beneath the sleeves, but there was a subtle outlining along the veins on his talonlike hands. Behind him the wall of hearts and claws and skulls and dragons seemed to mock his plain white attire.

"How come you're not tattooed, Griffon?"

"Styles change. I can't afford to be passé."

I flashed on the 1950s furniture in one of the furnished houses I had lived in as a teenager. The dated blond wood had been an indictment of my father's irresponsibility, my mother's passivity, my own need for the right answer that was anywhere but in that room. "What about your clients? They're out of style all over their bodies."

"It's not their craft," he said, talons wrapped tighter around the edge of the door. "Is this what brought you out here in such a huff?"

"Your not answering my knock created the huff. Mind if I come in?"

"We can talk like this."

He was within his rights. But I started segment scans of the room, looking for anything I hadn't seen before, like cartons, cases, or bags that might contain Kaldane or drag marks on the floor where they'd been pulled away from the door. "You suggested to Bryant that he mediate between Brother Cyril and Serenity Kaetz. Why?"

"Publicity." His shoulder dropped; I hadn't realized how tense he'd been before. Before he figured I wasn't after whatever he didn't want me to find.

"How did you know Brother Cyril would be willing?"

"Worth a try."

"Had you dealt with him before?"

"Him, no. I've done a couple of his guys' backs. But before you ask, we didn't talk about him. Didn't talk, period. So if you're looking for info on Cyril, I don't have any."

"*Au contraire.*" I turned and left. I didn't mention the drag marks on the floor or the box he had forgotten to drag out of sight. The one that remained at the start of the marks had stenciled on the side: "Brede Mortuary, Modesto, Cal."

I wrote my report in the car, whipped into the station to drop it in Jackson's IN box, and raced out without running into Doyle. No point in dealing with his outrage prematurely. I was already back in patrol. What more could he do to me? Suspend me? No point in . . .

I stopped for pizza on the way home. It had been another of those days when I couldn't remember when I'd last eaten.

Howard was in the bedroom, sitting cross-legged against the headboard of the California king. He had been hiking in Tilden Park with a friend and two black Labs. He was still in shorts though it was much too cold now; mud spattered his calves; his sweatshirt was smeared with brown lines of questionable origin, his normally bouncy red curls were sweat-matted, and his freckled face had that outdoors glow. He leaned over, stuffed my pillow against the headboard for me, and grinned as I settled in.

As if nothing had happened.

"You find Ott?" he asked, so easily I wondered if he had forgotten our tense talk of yesterday or just chosen to believe things had worked out. Whichever, I hadn't seen him this relaxed in days.

As Howard guided the first hot, dripping pizza slice (pepperoni, anchovy, Greek olive, and feta cheese) to his mouth like a veteran driver backing an eighteen-wheeler into the loading dock, I eased into recounting the events of my day: Serenity Kaetz telling me about Daisy and Margo; Pereira discovering Bryant Hemming's little pyramid scheme at ACC; board member Margo's ignorance of it and her anxiety to get me out of the house so she could get her grant forms in the mail and make Patient Defenders a formidable force. When I came to Daisy Culligan's tat with her friend's hairdresser, Howard nearly choked.

"Irreverent cop anchovied to death?" I said over his guffaws. "He went laughing, I'll tell them."

He plopped the pizza back in the box, downed a

swallow of beer, and nodded happily. "Daisy's such a pro. No low blows, no dirty tricks. She's got an eye for the ridiculous, and she goes with it," he said admiringly. "If the victims complain, they look like poor sports—"

"Which they are."

Howard grinned. "Right. And lucky for Daisy because keeping secrets isn't her long suit. She's blown one or two great revenges that way."

"Too bad! I'll bet by now half of Berkeley has laughed about Damon, the hairdresser." I pulled a pizza slice free and chewed slowly. Howard stretched out his long legs, and when he spotted me watching, he wiggled his flipperlike feet at me. I took another bite of pizza, hating to let go of this moment. I couldn't bring myself to tell him about my scene with Doyle, that I'd been tossed off the case. What I said was, "I suppose you heard about Ott and Brother Cyril at the Claremont with the dead pigeons."

Howard nodded. No smile when it came to Herman Ott. "So where is Ott now? Off with Cyril?"

"Looks like it. They had him surrounded when he left." Before he could comment on Ott, I launched into the scene at the Chartreuse Caracara and Griffon. "So there he was, gargoyling the door, hiding cartons from Brede Mortuary, Modesto, C-A."

The pizza was on its way to Howard's mouth. He stopped it halfway. "Mortuary? There's nothing he ought to be getting from them. Mortuaries, Jill, taketh away; they do not giveth."

"Or selleth. You think he was decorating the dead?"

"Hands-on practice, and you can bury your mistakes?" Grinning, Howard thrust his palms into the mattress and swung himself up straighter. He barely noticed the pizza box rock precariously in reaction. We had sat here so often eating pizza, hashing over cases, fingering each other's minds. In the last six months alone we'd had gone through three bedspreads.

"I checked with Monterey PD. They've had reports of missing Kaldane. So Cyril brings the Kaldane here to the storage locker. Griffon hears a rumor about something dangerous in the ACC locker, breaks into Margo's locker by mistake—"

"Or maybe it's Griffon who's got the Modesto connection." He stuck the crust in his mouth and chewed. "Know a guy. Vice. Loan to Fresno."

Translated to empty-mouthed English, that meant when Howard had been on loan to the Fresno Vice Squad, he'd met a guy on loan from Modesto. He could ask him to contact Brede Mortuary. "No. This is too tricky to bring in somebody from outside. I'll drive down first thing tomorrow."

"What about Ott?"

So much for avoiding that issue. "I'm off the Ott hunt. Doyle's sending me back to patrol."

Howard didn't speak. He just stared.

"Doyle says it's because I fulfilled my mission, so to speak. I did find Ott at the Claremont, even if he got away before I got there."

"But?"

"The real reason? He says I'm too close to Ott."

"Too close." His mouth barely moved. His voice was so low I wasn't sure I'd heard the words.

I hadn't let myself register the import of those words, not till I saw it drawn on Howard's taut face. Too close to him, too far from us. Someone we can't trust—officially. Anyone who heard about my removal, who heard "too close" would know better than to trust me.

"Did he say it in private?" Howard grasped at the hope.

"In a meeting with Eggs and Jackson."

"Oh." He reached over to wrap his arm around my shoulders. It hung suspended awkwardly because of the distance.

It felt like a stranger's arm, on a stranger's shoulder. On the shoulder of a woman who would never again sit downstairs in a room filled with cops, eating six different kinds of take-out, griping about the old patrol cars with the seat backs that ride at forty-five-degree angles, about drug dealers who slither out of town to their mansions to the south, about the city council, and the protesters. About Ott.

Later, when I remembered this moment, I was surprised the air didn't feel cold or hot. But the truth is it just felt thick, stiff, unmoving, like the eye of a hurricane, the still point before the fury takes the opposite direction.

Then the air moved again. I leaped forward over thoughts and mournings I'd come back to later. "It's okay. The police 'family' doesn't matter to me like it does to you."

"Jill, it'll blow over." His fingers dug into my shoulder. "You've got friends who'll go to the wall for you."

"I can't ask them to do that."

"They won't wait to—"

"No, Howard. Listen. The truth is the idea of police family doesn't comfort me; it binds me."

His eyes glistened.

Why had I come home? Why hadn't I just taken myself somewhere where I wouldn't hurt him? I might as well have said *he* didn't matter. I scrunched over next to him and pressed my head against his shoulder for a moment. When I started to speak, I wasn't looking at him but straight ahead, at the green walls and white trim he had painted in this house he loved filling with the "family" he'd made for himself. Desperately I tried to explain. "Howard, lots of people go to a job, have work friends, and come home. We've got other friends."

"Just friends," he murmured. "Not family." He swallowed and swallowed again before he went on. "This house, it's the only place I've ever been home. This is my city; it matters to me to take care of it. The force, it is family. Family"—the word squeaked out—"where they can't just walk away."

They could walk away, of course. Just as I could. Suddenly the old urge burned within me; I yearned to jump up, run to the car, make a right on Ashby and another right on Route 80. To drive into the dark and unknown. To leap onto the magic carpet just as Howard's mother had time and again.

I looked over at Howard, his face now pale. We were using the same words but speaking different languages.

"Why don't you just find her—your mother?" The words were out of my mouth before I realized it. "Finding people is our business. Why don't you initiate a search?"

"Based on what?" He pulled back as if attacked. "I know nothing about her. No Social Security number—"

"Surely, she must have one by now."

"Surely? With Selena there was no 'surely,' not about anything."

"But—"

He rammed his fists into the bed and shoved himself away. I tossed the pizza box to the floor.

"Let me tell you about Selena, Jill, and then you'll know *surely*. When I was eight or so, she took me to sign up for summer camp. The camp woman insisted she needed Selena's Social Security number on the application form. Selena laughed. 'Oh, that. I forgot that years ago,' she said. The woman wasn't amused. And she wasn't going to let me go to camp. So Selena said she'd 'search her files in her home office'—this from a woman who used her cardboard moving boxes for tables. When we got outside, she took me for an ice cream and assured me I'd get to camp. Then she went back and filled in the blank with a Social Security number."

"Maybe you could—"

"No, Jill. She made up the number. She'd had to ask the kid at the ice cream counter how many digits were in a Social Security number."

"Still, we could notify other departments. They could keep an eye out for—"

"For who? I don't know what name she goes by. Selena Bly is only one of the names she used when I was a kid. Selena Howard was another. Who knows how many she's created since? I can't swear to her birth date. Jill, it's like—it's like I made her up." His voice was as raw as the wound he'd reopened.

I wanted to reach out to him, but I knew I couldn't comfort him now. I was too suspect. "Why—"

"Why do I care? Damn good question. She doesn't— No, don't tell me she does. You don't know;

neither do I. Maybe . . . This is how I remember her. From one day, a summer Thursday. She was wearing a light blue dress with big blowzy red flowers. I'd spotted it in a secondhand store window because the flowers and the vine reminded me of a horror movie we'd just seen. It was big on her, but we both loved the horror dress. Her arms were freckled—"

"Like yours."

He started, then looked down at his arms and nodded vacantly as if the connection hadn't occurred to him. "But in that dress they looked tan and strong, like Jane in an old Tarzan movie. Like she was so strong she could grab me and swing off on a vine into a magic land only she could see." He was still looking down. "Then she would open it up so I could see it too, and I'd be . . ."

Safe?

". . . home." He swallowed. "With her a trip to the grocery was an adventure, looking for peas was a game, the people in the checkout line concealed nefarious secrets we made up on the way home."

"It must have been like living with a fairy on a magic carpet—"

"When I was a little kid, yeah. By the time I was ten it was living with someone who thought she was a fairy, and I had to watch out so no one pulled her magic carpet out from under her and left her to crash onto the road in front of a truck."

"Oh, Howard." I clambered up and pulled him against me, wishing I were big enough to wrap around all of him. He shuddered, and I pressed harder against his body. His breaths came fast and shaky, and I tried to calm them with my own. I ached for the little boy he was. I wanted to squeeze out the years of dread and loneliness, to give him a base so secure and strong nothing could hoist or push or drag it away.

But that base was the police family, and I was the one yanking it away.

It seemed like an eon before I could force myself to speak. "Howard, do what you have to, but make it clear to the department that you have no connection to my case; I'm in this on my own. Let everyone know you have no part of Herman Ott. You warned me to be a team player—"

"You don't need to buy the team ethic. You just need to win the game for them." His fingers wound through mine. "It's hard to complain about a guy who's holding the ball in the end zone."

Forestalling comment, Howard insisted, "Brede Mortuary. You were figuring Griffon was taking the Kaldane there." There was a false buoyancy to his voice. "What about Bryant's trips to Mexico? Now you're saying he was *not* smuggling the Kaldane to Mexico?"

"It was a reasonable possibility." My own voice sounded distant, as if I were listening to a stranger playing a role. But, at least, I was still in the play with Howard. "You can make a bundle selling pesticides down there. Even ones that are banned here can go for a bunch of pesos on their black market. Running outlawed pesticides to the San Joaquin Valley is not the same gold mine, but it's a damned sight easier. No border searches to worry about, no one wondering why you've come and gone so often."

"If you spend every weekend in Modesto, people may wonder about you, but they're not suspecting illicit or illegal pleasures." Howard summoned up a grin. "Griffon's hardly too honorable to run toxins, but why should he take the chance?"

"So he can finance his upscale tattoo parlor on Union Square."

"San Francisco's Union Square?" Howard whistled. "Now that's taking a giant step up."

"Indeed. It would be a risky and expensive move, but it could catapult him into next year's 'in' thing. He could turn out to be one rich needle man." I let my hand rest on Howard's thigh as it had a thousand times, felt the familiar warmth of his arm against mine. In a minute I'd think about how I'd be getting to Modesto tomorrow, how I'd handle the Brede Mortuary, but not yet. I'd always been a planner with my eye half a mile ahead, weeks into the future. Now, suddenly, I wanted to remember this moment, to feel not only Howard's warmth, but the bedspread beneath us, the air cold against my untouched side—

Howard glanced at his watch. "And you saw Griffon, what, two hours ago? Before you went back and met with Doyle?"

"No, after."

"What do you mean *after*?" The life was gone from his voice.

"I had the meeting with Doyle. He agreed I should go to the storage locker with Jackson, and sign off the case after."

"*Before* you went to Griffon's? You were officially taken off the case and you went ahead to Griffon's anyway?" He grabbed my arms and stared me in the face. "Jesus Christ, Jill, what's the matter with you? You're not just tossing your career away: you're throwing it in Doyle's face. I can't believe you." He stared at me for another long moment, picked up his wallet, and walked out the door.

I heard his truck start up, a low, distant rumble. It was only then that I realized how truly alone I was.

CHAPTER 34

FIGHTS WITH HOWARD WERE AWFUL. Some people righteously insist you have to "get it all out," be good at battle, glory in topping your lover, stripping him bare of defenses. For them that must be like racing first across the finish line. For me, there aren't winners, just losers walled in separately by animosity too volatile to touch.

Fights were bad, but the worst was having Howard stalk out. And being left here. I wanted to stalk out, to slam door, to burn rubber. . . .

But you feel like a jerk stalking alone. Instead I called Laura Goldman. It was eight o'clock. Eleven in Pittsburgh. I tried the station. She'd been gone for hours.

If she'd come up with something on Ott, she'd have notified me. All I would get for disturbing her at this hour was grief.

She might be in bed.

If so, she wouldn't have far to reach. I dialed.

"You've reached eight-nine-two—"

"Goldman! Answer the phone!"

The recording ended.

"Goldman, Jill Smith here. It's important. Look, if you're just not answering . . . I'll call back, even later. Or the fire department, I'll ring them up and say I'm your neighbor and there's smoke coming from your kitchen again and I know that you're a rotten cook and maybe there's nothing the matter but—"

"Okay, okay, Smith. God, why didn't I ask for a single room at that convention? How could I know they would pair me with a nocturnal lunatic?"

"Sorry. But it really is important."

"And nothing in my life is of consequence?"

"Goldman, I roomed with you. I know how much time you spend snoring away. I could keep you up for a month and you'd still be ahead of the game."

"Ah, the authority on healthful living. Next thing you'll be reorganizing my diet. 'I know how many vegetables you eat, Goldman. You could eat just chocolate for days and still be ahead.' Well, Smith, did it ever occur to you I might not be sleeping? I could be entertaining. The drought in my sex life that rivaled my grandmother's buddy Sister Joseph Martha might have been coming to an end. And just at the moment fireworks were to explode and I was reminded I was the hottest stuff west of the Susquehanna, what do I hear? 'Goldman! Answer the phone.' "

"If he loves you, he'll get it up again."

"So crass, Smith. And may you have a romantic night too."

"Small chance. Howard's . . . out. So, Goldman—"

"Okay. I was going to call you in the morning." She yawned theatrically. "Now I'm sitting up. So, you remember I told you there was a huge fight between Alexander—your Herman Ott—and his father that ended with Alexander stomping out—"

"To the Iberia Airlines gate at Kennedy Airport. Do you know what caused the crisis?"

"Hang on." Goldman was never one to condense a good story. "You'll recall your Ott came from the union of Herman Steel and Ott Mining. His father was Ott Mining. I checked the papers for mine disasters, but there was nothing about the Ott mines. So I went on to other things. Leads petered out like veins in a mine."

"Goldman!"

"Here's my mistake." Goldman's voice was tight, her tone suddenly somber. I realized she hadn't been so much playing with me as stalling. "I'd forgotten that earlier Otts had bought up mines from outsiders. So they owned small mines as far away as Kentucky. Far enough away that cave-ins wouldn't make the local papers. Mines small enough that disasters wouldn't be reported beyond *their* local papers. The cave-in in question occurred outside Wheeling, West Virginia. The shaft that collapsed was reinforced with beams made of a steel alloy instead of wood. It was an experiment that could have revolutionized mining. Could have saved some of the steel mills that were going under, including Herman Steel. Instead it killed thirteen men."

"Omigod! Why? Surely steel is stronger than wood."

"Maybe. But when the ceiling in a mine begins to collapse, the wood beams give way slowly, and, Smith, you can hear them creaking. When steel goes, it's silent—no warning. Those miners were crushed where they stood."

"Oh, God!" No wonder Herman Ott couldn't stay home, in the family manison built on corpses.

"Smith, that's not the whole thing. The reason behind the cave-in never came out in the papers."

"You got it through the Sister Joseph Martha connection?"

"Right. Distantly. I'll spare you the trail. But the story is that Alexander's father was hot to use the steel. The plan was within governmental safety standards at the time. The Otts of course were more familiar with the properties of their steel and their alloys than the government was. Alexander's father wasn't sure this alloy was right. He was going to test the beams in a played-out mine. You know, simulate the type of stress you'd get in a working mine. He was working on the plans, but apparently he got sidetracked by a new business venture. Or by a new mistress. Whichever, the steel beams were sent to a working mine, and Ott senior was too distracted to notice. Until the men were dead."

It was a moment before I said, "And ostensibly nothing changed for the Otts of Pittsburgh?"

"It was just another mine disaster. A risk of the business."

"Thanks, Goldman."

"Sure. If I come up with anything else, I'll let you know. Don't call me, Smith, I'll call you."

"Right," I said, almost too subdued to answer. "Sorry about the hour. Just one more thing. Was that mine case considered by the local Historical Review Society?"

"Yeah. How'd you know?"

"Crack detective work. And because I found a printout of a newspaper article from the Internet on Ott's floor the day of the murder."

"And that means?"

"That you're not the only one who discovered the mine tragedy. Someone brought it to Ott's attention."

"How?"

"That's the jackpot question." Slowly I put down the receiver. I was picturing the scene just as Inspector Doyle would. Bryant Hemming stalking into Ott's office, newspaper in hand, threatening to expose Ott as the child of bloodsuckers. Ott would have remembered his father tossing aside the lives of his workers for the sake of his career or his loins. Ott, who had investigated some facet of ACC, who had been to the storage unit, would have looked at Bryant Hemming with disgust. He'd have seen a man who'd just tossed aside ACC, endangered the small savings people had invested there, and was on the road to undermining the mediation project because of his connection with the Kaldane. Ott would have looked at Bryant Hemming and seen his father.

In that state even I could picture Ott shooting Hemming.

But if he didn't shoot Bryant Hemming? How did he react when he saw the article that pulled the rug out from under his life?

Anyone else would have kicked in the door, slammed the phone into the wall, screamed till his throat closed. Herman Ott walked out of his office and left the dead bolt off.

If Bryant Hemming didn't bring the article, who did? Who set out to unhinge Ott, drove him off, and used his office to kill Bryant Hemming?

I raced out of the house, slammed my VW into

reverse, squealed the wheels, drove to Ashby Avenue, and turned right. For the first time this evening I felt free. It wasn't as if I'd keep on and make another right onto Route 80, but it was movement. The pain and fury were still back in the bedroom, and I was doing something.

Going to the last place I had a legitimate reason to be.

CHAPTER 35

At night shops are closed on Telegraph Avenue, their gratings down over windows that all too often have been smashed in riots. Cars find more inviting thoroughfares. Doorways are littered with guys who inhaled or injected away their brains in the sixties or seventies or eighties or the new homeless, "downsized" onto the street. In the entrance to Ott's building one of them nested, head covered against the cold night wind.

Behind me an engine picked up speed. I reached for the building door, stopped, glanced warily behind me. For the first time in years I was relieved to find the vehicle coming was not a patrol car.

I turned back toward the building where I had no business being. Disobeying an order is grounds for suspension. If Kovach or one of the other guys discovered me when he swung by for a check on Ott's office, Inspector Doyle could not ignore it. He'd have to suspend me.

Suspended from the department. The thought was like a slap in the face, the sting all too real. I stood with my hand on the door. I hadn't crossed the line yet; I could turn around, drive home, take a bath, sleep, wake, and report for patrol. Nothing would be changed.

A mitt of fog rubbed cold across the back of my neck.

I opened the door and walked across the threshold and pulled the door after me. It closed with a bang.

The door had been unlocked. It always was. Who would the owners of this building bother keeping out? Paper detritus banked the corners of the lobby. My steps reverberated like drumrolls on the stairs and the landing as I made my way around the second-floor to the next flight of stairs and Ott's office. Of course no one in any of the offices–cum–illegal living units opened a door to check me out. The Unabomber could have been typing his manifesto on the landing and residents would have stepped over him and never remembered his face.

The crime scene tape was gone from Ott's office.

I squatted to peer under the door. Dark. The door was unlocked. I pushed it open and waited. "Police!"

No reply. I reached inside, switched on the light, and repeated the call. Silence. My gun was in my fanny pack, but I didn't draw it out. Both rooms were empty, but the startlingly, un-Ottian tidiness in the bedroom after our search had dissipated. The floor wasn't covered shin-high in a homogeneous swirl of clothes, magazines, and God knows what, as it had been when Ott was in residence, but clothes were in pillow-size clumps on the floor, interspersed with a couple of take-out plates and beer cans. What amazed me was not that any of Ott's cohorts or clients had come in after we'd left, but that the place wasn't wall-to-wall snorers right now. Everyone on Telegraph knew Ott was gone, and despite its numerous drawbacks, as a crash pad Ott's office was superior to a doorway on the Avenue.

In the hallway a door banged. I froze. Another door shut. One of the tenants using the bathroom across the hall. My hunched shoulders dropped. Nothing to worry about *this time*. But I didn't have forever in here.

I stood in front of Ott's scarred wooden desk as I had so often, picturing his office as it had been then, as it would have been right before the murderer walked in. Had Ott been expecting him? I pictured Ott inside here while his entry ritual unfolded. During the minutes I habitually spent pounding at his door had he been shoving papers into his desk helter-skelter, or was he normally so organized that he had had just one sheet to refile and then spent the next few minutes sitting back in his patched Naugahyde executive chair enjoying my performance outside?

I started rifling through Ott's desk. His files of course were at the station now. But it took only the ill-folded copy of the *Express* that had been stuffed into the side drawer to give me the answer. Ott *had* been surprised.

So the killer walks in unexpected, flashes the mine disaster article in his face, and then invites Ott to go birding? Not quite.

I moved around the office, going through the file cabinets once more. I squinted out the sooty window into the black air shaft and glanced at the holder where the gun had been stashed. I came up with nothing I hadn't noted Monday—because his files weren't here.

I had written down the cases in those files, the one he had kept without identifying names: a report of vandalism on the street sellers' display tables, a T-shirt theft, the flowerpot theft—I stopped. Stolen flowerpots *and* chemicals. Ott had been investigating stolen agricultural chemicals! Pesticides.

I sat in his decrepit chair. I had had things backward. I'd assumed that someone hired Ott to investigate Bryant and that led him to Brother Cyril. But it had been the other way around. Ott's starting point had been the pesticides. Someone—probably totally unconnected to this case—had hired Ott to investigate pesticides stolen in Berkeley. That would have led Ott to find out where they were being transported for sale and to discover Brother Cyril going there—to Modesto. Then Ott convinced one of Cyril's followers to take him to the storage unit.

Outside, a door slammed. My breath caught. I sat dead still, listening to the footsteps coming closer till another door squeaked open and banged shut. Then I realized I was breathing again.

Ott had checked the locker a week ago. Did that mean Cyril moved a new shipment every week? Why not? Why would he stop a good business with one shipment?

I pictured Brother Cyril, the milquetoast of a man. Now it was clear what kept his thuglike disciples loyal: the tried-and-true promise of salvation, cash. With a weekly run of Kaldane, there would be ample money for everyone. Cyril had stayed in the Claremont, but the disciples probably had their own castles elsewhere. No wonder we'd never found a communal hideout.

And we hadn't wondered what they had been up to in Berkeley, as we normally would have, because we figured we knew: They were creating a hassle on Telegraph.

The ACC locker, I realized with a start, was the bribe. Bryant had let Brother Cyril hide his Kaldane shipments in the locker. In return Cyril had accepted the mediation decision. Cyril had given up his place on Telegraph, which was just a cover for the drug running anyway. Jeez, the man must have spent his days in his expensive hotel room laughing.

It was so easy to imagine Daisy or any of the ACC members killing Bryant Hemming. If Ott hadn't been on his way to Muir Beach when Hemming was shot, I would almost have included him. I slotted him in as the killer as I ran through the scene in my head.

Bryant Hemming was a head taller than Ott, fifty pounds heavier, and in better shape than Ott had been any time since his high school football picture. But it'd be Ott glaring at Hemming like a lion at a weasel, Ott demanding confession, restitution, the naming of names.

And Hemming? He'd be wheeling, dealing, trying to haggle and charm. When none of it worked, he'd do what he always did: assume the problem would go away.

Ott would pull out the nine-millimeter and click off the safety.

Hemming would laugh, a little forced but still arrogant. "Ott, you're not going to kill me."

"This is fraud, grand theft, endangering the public safety, Bryant. When your new backers in Washington hear about this—"

Hemming would shrug. "Ott, Ott. Given the choice of you or me, who do you think they'll believe?"

Maybe they'd have gone another round or two, with Ott deigning to mention the law or the prospective testimony of the ACC members and Hemming laughing at the picture of Serenity Kaetz or Roger Macalester facing men in five-hundred-dollar suits; or Daisy, the aggrieved ex-wife, still whining about missing the knock of opportunity two years ago; or Margo ranting about emergency rooms with half her face hanging flaccid; or Griffon. . . . Here Hemming would have thrown up his hands. "Move out of the way, Ott. I have a plane to catch."

And Ott—or Daisy, Margo, Griffon, Roger, Serenity?—would have shot him. Hemming would have fallen back through the doorway, landing as we'd found him on the bedroom floor. The killer would have stood, stunned, for minutes till the outrage and frustration dissipated enough to realize he was a murderer.

"I didn't intend to kill him," he'd say later. "Bryant drove me to it." Maybe he'd be embarrassed at that cliché defense. But the irony was he'd be right. Bryant Hemming had pushed the people who trusted him and lied and finagled, and when they tried to nail him down, he evaporated. He had in fact become the personification of the bureaucracies he railed against.

I savored the moment. No longer was I worried about noises outside; instead, I felt the tacit protection of this shabby, dark, uninviting building.

I leaned back heavily in Ott's mustard desk chair. Strips of tape that covered the tears and cracks in the Naugahyde cut into my arms. I shifted, but there was no decent way to sit in this chair. I almost laughed. Of course this seat was awful. For Ott, it would have been improper to have his chair be better than the miserable wooden seats he offered his visitors.

It was cold in here, a stale cold that preserved the smell of Ott's bitter green tea, of dust and the limp salty crackers he kept beside his little fridge, the reek of dirt and sweat that settled in the coats of his unwashed clients, the remnants of urine, excrement, blood, and decay that were Bryant Hemming's epitaph.

Understanding the motive brought me no closer to the killer or to Ott. But when I knew how Ott left the office here, I'd have them both.

What would have so unnerved him as to make him forget to lock his dead bolt? The combination of the mine disaster article and the rare chance to see a yellow-billed loon? Was that enough to discombobulate Herman Ott? Maybe.

I thought I heard the building door open. I cocked an ear toward the hall, straining to note the distant pat of feet on the stairs. Still quiet.

Think! Herman Ott was on Brother Cyril's tail. Cyril had to be on Ott's. Ott hated to "give" anything to the police, but if he'd gotten evidence of Brother Cyril running pesticides, he would have wrapped it in ribbons for us and announced it to the newspapers, TV reporters, anyone who would listen.

Cyril would be on guard, jabbing back, threatening him. And Ott was too savvy to dismiss the threats of a man who figures he represents the Almighty. Suddenly Ott gets an offer to disappear. He can spend the night at Muir Beach, then creep back into Berkeley and attack Brother Cyril from behind. A golden opportunity. But he's got to move fast if he's going to get to Muir Beach by dusk. He doesn't, after all, want to miss the rare loon.

How long had Ott planned to stay away? Had he hung around Muir Beach waiting for his driver to come get him? That driver was all of a sudden a murderer and had more pressing problems than ferrying Ott home. Still, Ott wasn't miles from civilization. From Muir Beach he could have walked fifty yards to a house and asked to use the phone. Maybe then he saw the newspaper coverage of the murder or heard Jason Figueroa's report on TV.

I smiled. Once Ott heard that, he'd have stayed hidden on principle, the principle of not helping the cops. And the certainty that he could solve the case before the Berkeley police did.

He'd be right, because of course he knew who had driven him to Muir Beach.

And that person was someone he wasn't so eager to turn over to us.

Footsteps? I leaned forward, listened. Were those feet moving up the stairs? I switched off the light, moved into the bedroom, and kept my eye on the door.

I stood behind the bookcase as I had before. But now I felt as if a cold hand had clasped the back of my waist. If Kovach came through the office door, I was stuck. No excuse. No escape. I felt like Bryant Hemming as he backed through the doorway into here and realized there was no way out.

The door handle turned.

I held my breath. This was no casual nocturnal visitor. Ott's associates couldn't be that quiet.

The door opened slowly.

He looked around, then walked over to the file cabinet and pulled open the drawer.

"Police!" I said. "Hold it right there!"

He didn't hold it. He ran.

CHAPTER 36

"Stop where you are," I yelled after him into the hall. He kept moving down the corridor, feet slipping on the slick floor as he rounded the corner. By the time I reached the stairs he was running up. Logic would have told him to race down and out of the building and onto the street where everyone would be his friend and no one would be anxious to tell the cop where he'd gone. But panic has its own rules. When you're going all out, you're too frantic to trust yourself step after downward step. Instinctively you go up with the stairs in front of you where you can see them, push off if you have to. Adrenaline takes care of the climb.

At the top he banged forward into the wall, bounced off and onto the dark, narrow flight of stairs to the roof.

My breath was coming in gasps. I pushed off the wall and up into the rickety staircase, moving by instinct in the sudden blackness. Above, the door opened, the dim light of night outlining him as he flung himself forward.

I caught the door before it slammed, skidded through the opening, stopped dead, and listened. If he'd been a pro at this, he'd have been still too. Or

already over the edge onto the next roof. He was neither. He was running across the gravel.

"Hold it where you are, Roger," I shouted as I
raced after him.

He leaped for the rim. With a final burst of speed I
grabbed him and brought him down.

I put him in the holding room downstairs in the
station. Macalester glanced around the tiny room,
settled himself on the pine bench, glowering at the
thick metal rings to which we clasp the handcuffs.
The elevator doors—the jail express—made up one
wall. The room had that dingy finality of an old
downtown train terminal filled with people anxious to
get out.

Macalester's denim jacket was sweat-damp, and his
ponytail lay like a dead eel on his back. Another old
plaid flannel shirt poked out under his jacket.

I reran in fast forward my mental tape of an outraged Ott shooting Bryant, this time slotting Roger
into the Ott role. No problem there. His motive put
Ott's in the shade. Could he have had a key to Ott's
office? With the number circulating on the Avenue,
he'd have been embarrassed not to. "You were in
Ott's office. What were you looking for?"

"I wasn't—"

"Roger! Do you want me to list the laws you've
broken? This is your last chance here with me. And I
am completely out of patience." When I booked him,
I would have to admit I had been waiting in Herman
Ott's office. I needed Roger to provide me with a
touchdown. Otherwise my suspension loomed large.

"Roger, let's cut to the chase. You were looking for

something in Ott's office. Here's your choice: You can tell me what you were after and leave me satisfied or you can stonewall, piss me off, and have the entire Homicide team combing through your life." I paused, watching his opaque brown eyes flicker from side to side as if looking for a way out. "Getting an answer now will also put me in a much better mood. You'll appreciate that later."

He screwed up his elfin face, puckered his lips, then shrugged. "Okay."

"You were searching for?"

"Copies Ott made from the foundation books."

"The same books Officer Pereira went over?"

"Yeah."

I was tempted to point out that if there had been an irregularity, Pereira would have found it. "Why?"

"Ott caught the entry; I figured you might."

"Entry?"

Again his eyes flickered back and forth. It was too late to back out now; the best he could hope for would be to shoot me down a wrong path.

"Entry?" I insisted.

"It was just a lunch," he muttered, suddenly enshrouded in second thoughts.

A lunch! I wanted to shout. *You don't kill over a lunch!* Why was he worried about something as inconsequential as a lunch anyway? A lunch paid for by ACC. Unless it was at a spot where he shouldn't have been, doing business he shouldn't have been doing. "The meal at Chez Panisse," I said.

He cringed. "I took two friends. The whole thing came to over a hundred dollars. I don't know what came over me to charge it to ACC. I just didn't want it to get out. I'll look like such a—"

"Liar?"

"Hey, I'm confessing. What more do you want?"

"The truth. Roger, you are a miserable liar. All you're doing now is ticking me off. You and your friends are not the lunch at Chez Panisse set. I'll bet you've never even been there," I baited.

"Sure I have. Upstairs. You want to know what it's like? Want me to describe the two gigantic flower sprays, one just off to the right of the stair landing, the other on the bar? Want to know where we sat? In the back room beyond the booths or in the front room between the bar and the sleeping porch? Want to know what the bathroom is like?"

I waved off the offer. A description of the men's room wasn't going to do me much good. In any case, he'd said enough. "I believe you—"

He smiled smugly.

"—that you've been there. Not that you've been there with friends." It wouldn't have occurred to him to go with friends or to charge it to the foundation.

But clearly he *had* been there. He *had* charged it to ACC. If the meal wasn't with two friends, who was it with? "When was this lunch?"

"I don't—"

"Roger!"

"Last week."

It took me only a moment to recall what had happened in the world of ACC since then and whom Roger Macalester would legitimately take to lunch at Chez Panisse. "So, it was you, Roger, not Bryant, who negotiated with the conservative investors."

"Yeah," he said, hanging his head. "But like Bryant said, if they wanted to invest their money in our projects, all the better for us." He looked so relieved I could barely keep myself from laughing. He was so caught up in this cover-up that he'd clearly forgotten he'd taken their money not for investment purposes but to pour down the bottomless chute of the pyramid.

That I would ignore for the moment, in favor of the bombshell he was hiding. "You paid for the lunch. So, Roger, the conservatives weren't courting you, as you made out. They weren't begging; you weren't deigning to take their money and accepting it as contributions to the investments ACC supported. You were going after right-wing money for ACC."

I was braced for a flurry of righteous denials, the waving of outraged arms, flailing his twenty years of card-carrying leftism at me. Roger Macalester just grinned.

I glanced around the small dark anteroom. It was the best Roger Macalester would see for a while.

His fleecing of right-wing contributors for the ACC pyramid was fraud. He'd do time (a small price to pay for a guy already spending his nights in a storage locker). And he'd come out a cult hero on the Avenue.

Once he started telling me about luring the smug and greedy with promises of profit and social acceptance, he could barely move his lips fast enough. It was opening night of a performance he would give again and again at every coffeehouse on the Avenue for years to come. The man was elated.

I was not. I didn't know how much of what he said was true. But one thing I was sure of: if Herman Ott had uncovered that scam he would never have considered turning in Roger Macalester to us. "Ott knew, didn't he?"

Roger nodded.

"Roger," I said, sure of the answer already, "what should make me think you did not shoot Bryant?"

"Kill him? Why would I kill him? Things were bad before he died, but once he left town and I was in charge, I could have salvaged ACC. The new contributors, that's what that was all about. I would have gotten our members' money back. Everything would have been okay. It all would have worked out if fucking Bryant hadn't gone and got himself killed. God, it's just like him."

"Smith." One of the dispatchers stuck his head in the door. "I'm doing you a favor, on my break."

"Yeah?" I said.

"You've got a message from Howard. And Doyle's in his office. He wants to see you."

CHAPTER 37

A SUMMONS FROM DOYLE. I had nothing near the touchdown I needed to face him.

And Howard waiting for a callback. Was he home, or in a bar somewhere, or halfway to Nevada by now? And still furious?

I took Macalester upstairs for booking and headed for one of the phones off the squad room. One sergeant sat behind the window, pencil in one hand, phone propped to ear. The squad room itself was empty, and the electronic hum of the copy machine, the coffee machine, the computer—the chorus of the nineties—seemed louder. An empty box on the table held the crumbs of cookies, doughnuts, scones— something sugary, something I would have liked. Something that was gone now. I picked the phone by the window, dialed, and stared down into the alley as it rang.

"Where are you?" I asked when he answered the phone.

"Modesto. With a couple of the guys I met in Fresno."

"Modesto, home of the Brede Mortuary?" The man was a saint. A saint in a bar, from the sound of the music and laughter behind him. "I owe you."

"We'll talk about that later."

I couldn't read his voice on that. Not the normal lascivious "playful," but nowhere near as furious as when he'd stormed out of the house hours ago. Later, indeed. "What did you find on Griffon?"

"Well, Jill," he began, chuckling. Now I could fill in the "relationship" blanks here. This call wasn't a statement that he had reconsidered his position re: me and the department. He just had something too good to keep to himself. "Too good" was definitely what I needed now. He said, "Seems Brede, the owner, has a brother."

"Brede, the brother?"

"Brede, the ne'er-do-well brother, who is a mortician too."

"It must take talent to be a failure as a mortician when your own brother owns the place."

"Some got, some don't got. Anyway, Brede, the brother—it didn't take long to get him to come clean. For someone else, the maneuver might have been an effort, but well, it's such a kick to con a con man. And Brede, the brother, is the kind of hotshot who's got irons in every fire in town. All he needed to hear was police, and he was so busy looking over his shoulder he just about decapitated himself. I don't know what his big-ticket scams are—selling corpses, scooping up the gold from their fillings?—but Griffon was a mole-hill compared to the Alps he was hiding."

"Howard! What was our molehill up to? Was he Brother Cyril's front man, selling Brede, the brother, the Kaldane?"

"Brede's a seller, not a buyer."

"Griffon was driving to the valley to buy something? From a mortuary worker?"

"You got it. Jill, you remember those tattoos he did, the ones that were supposed to shine?"

"Yeah."

"Seems Griffon heard that tattooists from Asia created shine by mixing their ink with human fat. Theory is the body keeps rejecting the foreign fat and the rejection process creates the shine—like a layer under a scab that's pulled off too soon."

"Yuck."

"And not cheap. Problem is, getting the fat. Even friends who have excess aren't about to undergo medical procedures to spiff up their buddy's tattoos. But corpses don't complain."

"So Brede sold Griffon dead fat."

"Right. Said he offered him formaldehyde and embalming fluid too. Brede thinks Griffon's a loon. Says he doesn't care what Griffon pokes under his skin as long as he can turn a profit."

"Does it work, the shine?"

"Brede doesn't think so. But Griffon was real hot on the idea. It'd make him the king of the tattooists."

"Outshine the competition?"

Howard groaned, but I knew he would have said it himself if he'd thought of it first.

"It would," I said slowly, "give him the leverage to open his San Francisco shop as long as he could keep the source secret."

Howard didn't respond. Then he said, "By rights I should have called this in to Eggs or Jackson or Doyle. I called you at home, where I figured you'd be, since you were off the case. I'm not asking what you're doing at the station—"

"I'm taking the gluteus contraband in to Doyle right now. He's waiting." A choral groan rose in the bar there in Modesto. I wondered what game was on cable there. "Leave me a message about when you're coming home, okay?"

"Right," he shouted over the noise. He didn't want to discuss that either.

The front phalanx of the rhino herd had been ambushed, they lay on their sides around Doyle's IN box. Doyle was on the phone. He motioned me to sit. He wasn't talking, just listening. He also wasn't looking at me. Nor offering me the latest addition to the herd for appraisal, amusement, or in some cases silent amazement. Even in the world of ceramic rhinoceroses, his raised eyebrows had often said, there's no accounting for taste.

But now he grunted into the receiver as if I no longer existed here.

After what seemed ages, he put down the receiver, and muttered "CHP. They picked up Brother Cyril."

"From the APB?"

"Emissions. His van was stinking up the road from here to Albany, which is where they got him."

"Ott?" I was holding my breath.

"Not with him. No pesticides, no Ott. Just eight punks and Cyril. Cyril ranting up a storm about justice, and vengeance being his, and Sodom, Gomorrah, and Berkeley."

My shoulders tightened. "The pesticides aren't in the storage lockers anymore. If Cyril doesn't have them, where are they?" I flashed on the hotel room in the Claremont, the dead pigeons on the bloody carpet. "And Ott? What'd he do with Ott?"

"Ott! Jeez, Smith, what is it with you and Ott? I

take you off the case, and where do you go? Ott's office. I gave you an order, Smith, a direct order. You spit in my face. You've come to the end of your rope. You—"

The phone rang. "Yeah? . . . Delaware? . . . Yeah, right." He glanced at me and then away. "Tell him I'll be right down." The phone was barely in the receiver before he was out of his chair. "The ACC headquarters on Delaware, it's on fire. I'll deal with you later."

I was already racing out the door.

CHAPTER 38

THE OLD WOODEN WATER TOWER that housed ACC was burning like kindling. Flames shot through the first-floor siding and out the first-floor windows. One fire engine was parked on Delaware Street looking oddly anachronistic in front of the nineteenth-century buildings. A second stood around the corner on Fifth Street. Firemen had emptied the houses that abutted the windmill. The residents stood on the wood-plank sidewalk across Delaware Street, the blinking red lights from the patrol car alternately revealing their panic and blacking it out.

I raced through the fire lines. "Hey, lady, get back!"

"Police!" I yelled, leaping over a pulsing hose. I spotted Eggs and Jackson standing behind the fire lines, nodded, and kept moving.

Steam rose from the building, like the backlash of water tossed in an overheated frying pan. Firefighters guided and hung on to their hoses, as if control bounced from one to the other. Water poured into the house, and the house spit it out.

There was no ladder to the second floor.

I looked around frantically for Doyle. "The second floor," I yelled above the jumble of the water and machinery, the engines and brakes of incoming cars. "Have they checked up there?"

"Not yet."

"That'd be where Cyril would stash the pesticides, where he'd leave Ott. No one goes up there."

"Ladder." He pointed to the left as firefighters steered it through the courtyard path. In a minute the front of the building was obscured by a wall of water. Then the ladder went up, the firefighter went up, and another minute later she came out with Ott. "Clear the street."

I walked in step with the paramedics. Somehow I expected Ott to look as sooty as the building walls, but as the paramedics shifted him onto a gurney, he was paler than I'd ever seen him.

"Ott," I said, putting a hand on his shoulder, "you're going to be—"

"Who did this to you, Ott?" Inspector Doyle demanded. Eggs was behind him.

"Pesticides," he croaked. "The room's full of them." He swallowed, squeezed his eyes shut a couple times to clear the soot. "Toxins," he forced out, "enough to bankroll . . . agribusiness for . . . a month."

"Eggs," Doyle said. But Eggs was already halfway to the fire captain. To Ott, Doyle repeated, "Who did this to you?"

Ott's eyelids flickered. His lips moved slightly, then stopped.

"CHP's got Cyril. You're in no danger," Doyle assured him. "Tell us who did this?"

Ott's eyes opened, then narrowed. His hazel eyes flickered to the left and back. He was thinking. Dammit, the man was scheming.

"Ott!" I wanted to shake him. "I saw the hotel room and the decapitated pigeons."

"Cyril." Ott swallowed hard. He focused not on me but on Doyle. "Cyril's got twenty, maybe more guys. Some armed." He swallowed harder, as if calling up his last drop of internal moisture. "Semiautomatics. Converted. The back of his van, it's an arsenal." He pressed his lips, worked his throat till I thought he might choke. "He believes . . , pipeline to . . ." His eyes flickered upward. Then he reached a hand toward Doyle. "Battling cops, it's how he gets his followers."

Doyle moved back, already half turned to move on the information.

I bent closer to Ott. "What about Bryant Hemming? Did Cyril kill him?"

Ott's eyes closed.

"Enough," the paramedic said. "We've got to move this man."

I kept pace with the gurney. "Ott, who took you to Muir Beach?"

Ott groaned and turned his face away.

I leaned closer. "Ott, you were dealing with a better-natured killer than a pain in the ass like you deserve. If he'd had any sense, he would have just tied you up and stuffed you in the attic overnight."

Ott's eyes flickered. I could tell it pained him to leave me the last word.

The paramedics lifted up the gurney and slid him into the ambulance.

"You believe all that, Smith? You, the expert on Ott," Doyle said as the ambulance pulled off.

"Everything he said, Inspector. But—"

"Clear the street. Come on, move it! This stuff's poison," the fire captain yelled.

"Smith," Doyle said as we moved back, "you found Ott. Ott—maybe the smoke got to him—but he was helpful. If that stuff blows up, or the smoke's toxic, he'll have saved people." We were next to my VW. Doyle leaned against it. His mouth twitched as Ott's had done, and when he looked over at me, I could tell he was forcing himself. "Smith, you came within a hair of being suspended. In my office I was going to . . . This saved you."

My breath caught. I hadn't allowed myself to speculate on that other issue he hadn't gotten to.

"Do the paperwork later. Go home, sit on your laurels. That's an order."

"But, Inspector—"

"An order! Smith, you don't have any leeway. Go."

I climbed into the bug and drove away from the fire. Ott had been helpful, all right. Too helpful. Ott, who would normally gag before *giving* us anything, was using his last bit of spit to croak out what he knew. He had focused our attention on Brother Cyril, but he'd never actually said Cyril was Bryant Hemming's killer. When that question came up, the chatty Ott was suddenly too weak to speak.

I turned left on University, heading up between Indian restaurants, groceries, sari shops. Of course I believed Ott. He wasn't stupid enough to lie. No reason to lie for Brother Cyril.

The light at San Pablo turned red. I jammed on the brake. I wasn't watching the road.

We'd given Ott a free play with Cyril. By the time Ott told us about Cyril's weapons and threats, we had already told him Cyril was in custody. As for the pesticides, the firefighter who rescued him had seen them. So Ott had given us zip.

Then why had he bothered with that performance, the smoke screen at the fire scene? For someone he cared enough about to protect, I guessed. For someone he respected. For the person who understood the lure of the yellow-billed loon, the person who had driven him to Muir Beach and killed Bryant Hemming. If mere murder were insufficient reason for Ott to turn in the killer, I'd have thought using his office and luring Bryant there because Bryant couldn't afford to ignore Ott would have infuriated him. But not enough to call us.

I knew that, and there was nothing I could do about it. I was off the case. I didn't have a touchdown, but I'd gotten close enough to the goal line to grab some credit—if I didn't blow it now.

Once Howard and I had vied for who would someday occupy the chief's office. Now I was almost out the door.

If I cared about my job, I would go home.

Doyle would still be at ACC. I hung a U.

CHAPTER 39

DELAWARE STREET WAS BLACK. SOOT shrouded the Victorian houses and shops. On the patrol cars and fire engines, pulser lights burst on and off, turning one area after another the color of dead meat.

Doyle was gone. I must have passed him on University after I made my U-turn.

I hung another U and headed back to the station. I'd have ten seconds to convince Doyle. Once he got his mouth open, that "later" he'd threatened me with would have arrived, and he would be talking only suspension.

It was after midnight, the roads were nearly empty. The wind swatted the VW like a giant going after a fly. I clutched the wheel. There had been times, driving across the Bay Bridge, when I'd had to brace my arms and elbows to keep from being blown into the next lane. Tonight wasn't that bad. It wasn't late enough in the year for that. In December or January, maybe. Still, now, to my left in the middle of University Avenue the wind yanked baby trees almost out of their soft dirt mounds.

I ached to be speeding in a patrol car, lights and sirens clearing my way. There was no reason for the killer to wait now, and common sense told me Bryant

Hemming's wouldn't be the last violent death. Even the few minutes it would take to convince Doyle could be too long.

Damn Bryant Hemming. If he hadn't disregarded his ex-wife's career, if he had been a whit less righteous, if he'd even hinted she should look twice at the restaurant owner's record, Hemming would be alive now and his biggest problem would be deciding at which Washington cafe to make a reservation.

But he had brushed aside any concern for Daisy. And her particular revenge on Bryant—her tat—set off alarms in the minds of the people she recruited to make her calls. They had been put into the position of declaring to Bryant that they didn't believe they would get their money back. After that, they couldn't help asking themselves if it could be true. *If he undermined his ex-wife so matter-of-factly*, they'd have wondered, *how can I trust him with my money, my future?*

It's a long leap from there to murder, Doyle would say.

I left my car double-parked on the street, ran to the side door, and took the stairs two at a time. At the squad room table, a patrol officer and the guy he was interviewing stopped silent as I raced past, on through the night-dim file room, and around the corner to Doyle's office.

"Inspector! Herman Ott's sending us on a wild-goose chase. Brother Cyril didn't kill Hemming."

He glared up at me. "Smith, do you under—"

"I'll tell you who the killer is. She's been wound tight for days; that's over. Tonight she's through; nothing's holding her back." I waited, the only sound in Doyle's office my short, hard breaths.

Doyle clenched his teeth together. He ached to

explode at me, but he couldn't—not for the moment. He gave me the smallest of nods.

"Margo Roehner—"

"Jeez, Smith, you *would* have to pick the one with the most influence."

"And her lifework riding on getting her money out of ACC. She needed to get Patient Defenders' money back; Hemming was going off with it."

"Fine, Smith. But the killing was in Ott's office. Roehner barely knew Ott."

"She's Daisy Culligan's friend. Daisy Culligan told *me* about Ott and their nocturnal trips to the shoreline. She enjoyed telling me, Inspector. It's too good a story to keep to herself. I can hear her telling her friends, wondering what Ott was doing overnight in the marsh, him insisting on staying through dawn. Dawn—bird time. Margo's enough of a birder to fuss about red-breasted nuthatches; she'd pick right up on that."

"So?"

"So she knew how to lure Ott out of his office for a few hours. Then she left a message summoning Bryant Hemming to Ott's office. Hemming knew Ott was investigating him; he didn't dare ignore a call supposedly from Ott."

Doyle looked down and away, trolling for objections. "The newspaper article on the mine disaster, what about that?"

I was gaining. "Part of Patient Defenders' service was combing the Internet for medical information. Carnegie-Mellon University is in Pittsburgh; there's a lot of medical research in Pittsburgh. Margo would check those papers."

"So she just happens to come across the article on the Otts, is that it, Smith?"

"Right, it is. But what that article does is remind her about Herman Ott, who—like you said—she doesn't know well but knows a lot about from Daisy, from Roger Macalester, and probably from Bryant Hemming himself. She is on the ACC board. She's organized Patient Defenders, gotten together a grant proposal. She's used to planning. She figures: Get Ott out of the office; confront Bryant; get the Patient Defenders' money. Then Bryant will fly out, Ott will drag back from Muir Beach disappointed about missing his yellow loon but no worse for wear, and everyone will be happy."

"And?" he said, no less skeptically.

"Bryant blew her off. So she shot him."

"Smith, jeez, what you've got here is theory. You're talking about a woman with connections, one who kicks up a fuss as a vocation, and you want to accuse her of murder with no more evidence—"

"She focused everything on getting her grant forms in the mail today. That's the only thing that held her together. Now—"

"No! Smith—"

"Inspector—"

"No. Smith. I'm not telling you to go home. I've already said that. Here's what I'm saying now. I gave you an order; you ignored it. Smith, you are suspended."

CHAPTER 40

I SPED ACROSS SHATTUCK, DARING my colleagues, my *former* colleagues, to pull me over. The radio was so loud it shrieked. When I came to Ashby, I yanked the wheel right, west, toward the freeway. Another right there, onto Route 80, and I could keep going for three thousand miles. Going to anywhere. Free as Howard's mother. I reached for the radio knob, but I had already turned it up as high as it would go. Something country was playing, something I didn't recognize. No matter. The words were a blare that blotted out thought. I stepped harder on the gas. One more light and I'd be on the freeway.

The light at San Pablo was red. I sat, tapping my foot hard against the clutch, cursing Doyle, angrily shoving away thoughts of Margo Roehner, and Herman Ott and his effort to protect her.

I was suspended. I could drive to Chicago and come back for my hearing and be reinstated as if nothing, much, had happened.

And forget about Margo Roehner spinning out of control now.

What had I said of Bryant Hemming? He hadn't considered the rule of holes: When you're in one, quit digging. I had buried myself chin deep already. One more shovelful . . .

The freeway would still be there in an hour.

Margo's house was dark. Someone had said it was designed to pull knees to chest and burrow its head forward, squeezing its girth into a small package on its small Berkeley lot. Now it looked dark and tiny among the bigger, blacker houses on either side. Her station wagon—the suburban warrior's car—stood at the ready. I ran up the short driveway, onto the porch and peered through the glass in the door. Now I could see a dim light in the living room. Not a good sign. Her Patient Defenders grant application must be done and in the mail. Nothing was holding her now.

I knocked and rang the bell. Margo's nine-millimeter was in an evidence locker, but guns are like tattoos: The first one's a big decision; after that it's easy to add to the collection.

The porch was a terrible place for cover, with narrow columns of glass on either side of the door and casement windows forming the east wall of the porch. Those, plus the living room windows on the far side of the door. I found myself hunching my shoulders forward as if that would make a difference.

I pushed the bell again, heard it ring inside, waited, knocked four heavy blows. Then I stood dead still and listened, straining to block out the whipping of branches and catch the muffled sound of slippered feet.

The house seemed to scream its silence against the

roar of nature outside. A high-pitched moan broke the air. A tree scraping on a window?

The door opened, and I had no idea whether that low wail could have come from Margo Roehner. When I had first seen her at her storage locker, she had stood small and trim. She had reminded me of a Chinese tomb warrior, single-mindedly prepared to defend her emperor through eternity. Then she had stood squarely in front of me and faced me head-on, foot tapping impatiently. She had already murdered Bryant Hemming.

Now she stood staring at me. She had a gun, all right, but it wasn't aimed at me; she had it braced against her temple.

Without speaking she backed into the living room. I shut the door and followed, afraid a misstep could kill her.

She was wearing a brown shirt and black slacks, clothes much too thin for this cold room. But she wasn't shivering. Her awkwardly placed hand wasn't even shaking. She was beyond that.

There was a glass next to the leather chair where she'd been sitting and a brandy bottle on the credenza in the dining room behind. How like Margo to be too organized to die leaving an open brandy bottle on the floor.

Now she planted herself behind the chair and waited.

"Margo, why don't we sit down—"

"No."

"You don't mind if I do?" Better we both should have been in chairs or on the sofa, like friends gossiping. I had been hostage negotiator on the department team; now I felt myself slipping into that role. I propped myself on the sofa arm and tried to relax my face, to emulate a calm that would spread across the room. Then I moved to infiltrate her passionately held belief. Ideally it would become not hers but ours. Purposely I spoke in the present tense. "Margo, you are providing a vital service with Patient De—"

"I had a friend who died of pneumonitis because the emergency room doctors diagnosed the flu and sent him home. If he'd had a Defender—"

"Still, Margo, murder? It's a big step for a nice middle-class lady like yourself."

"Bryant would have destroyed Patient Defenders. He would have let people die."

"But not from malice—"

"Ha! He wouldn't have given it that much thought. He was too caught up in his own fucking importance. Just like the doctors. I gave him a chance to explain, there in Herman Ott's office. I never planned to kill him; I just needed my money back. I had two new employees and no way to pay them until I got the grant money. If they quit before the grant evaluators checked us out, Patient Defenders would be in chaos, I'd look like an incompetent and a liar, and we'd never get a cent. 'Show me how you're going to pay me my money, Bryant,' I said. Do you know what he told me?"

"What?"

"It wasn't his problem anymore, he said. 'Take it to Roger,' he said. Smug little bastard. He was just about to start toward me; his hand was out; he was going to shove me out of the way." Margo glanced at the brandy glass. Her small, skewed face twisted at the mouth. "I didn't squeeze my eyes shut or look away when I shot him. I felt I owed him that much. It turned out I owed it to myself. You should have seen his incredulous expression when I pulled the trigger. He never thought I would follow through."

"I guess he'd spent too much time looking at his own example."

Her hand tightened on the gun. "I'm not going to tell you I'm sorry. Not about him. Just about—"

"I know." My heart was racing; I struggled to keep my face calm. This was the crucial point. I had to express thoughtfulness, concern. "It's a shame now he'll have beaten you. I guess the HMOs will be glad when you're gone."

She gave what might have been a laugh, except that she couldn't laugh. Her mouth just pulled to the side. I wondered how many times men like Bryant Hemming had looked at her and dismissed her, an odd, disfigured woman, of no use to them. I wanted to look away as they must have done.

Margo's hand quivered slightly, but it wasn't shaking. Her legs were not braced. I did a handstand once in a yoga class, and for a moment, by a fluke, I was so balanced I couldn't move my legs back or forth, couldn't get down. I had been so in control that I had no control. Margo was like that now, balanced stiffly between life and death. In a moment she would crash down, one way or the other. In the case of my handstand, the teacher had nudged my heels, and my legs had dropped easily forward into safety.

"Margo, you can shoot yourself. I'm not going to stop you. But if you do, you lose control of everything that follows—"

"That's what death is."

"Right. But you shot Bryant for a reason. For a cause. You've still got a choice. You can take the high road, admit you're guilty, and make your trial a forum on the medical system. Tell the world that the self-important do get punished. Let people know about HMOs with gag orders on nurses, with doctors ruled by the bottom line; let people know why Patient Defenders is vital. By the time your trial is over, you'll have a committed successor to take it over."

She didn't move.

"Bryant Hemming made a mess and walked out on it." I was almost holding my breath. "Don't be like him, Margo. People need you. Do what you expect of doctors; hang around to clean up your mess."

It was her decision. There was nothing I could do now. A whiff of brandy cut through the icy air. I forced myself to look away from Margo, to give her privacy to decide. Pictures flashed in my mind: the bullet exploding into her eye; her face half gone; her body folding lumpily, bloody, to the floor; the paramedics arriving; Eggs and Jackson on the scene; Doyle eyeing me, shaking his head. I wasn't breathing at all.

Slowly I leaned forward and put out my hand for the gun.

CHAPTER 41

"IT'S HARD FOR THEM TO complain when you make the winning touchdown," Howard had proclaimed. True on the gridiron, perhaps, but not with the Berkeley Police Department. Inspector Doyle arrived to read Margo her rights and take an official statement.

"I'll need your report, Smith, before . . ."

"Before?"

"Before I sign you out on suspension."

By the time I finished the paper on the case and left the report in Doyle's IN box, it was nearing dawn. Doyle must have come back to the station from Margo Roehner's house, but I hadn't seen him.

I walked out into the charcoal gray morning. The fog was damp on my face, the air deceptively still as it is before the winds of morning gear up. All thumbs, I fiddled with the zipper on my jacket. Birds squeaked and chirped, whistled and squawked—a clamor that's charming when you're standing at the window with your lover's arm around you and a cup of coffee in your hand. Now I felt as if those birds were squabbling for space on my shoulder, eager to snap their talons on my ear, hang from my hair, and run their claws down the blackboard of my eardrum.

It was a suitable mood in which to visit Herman Ott.

Ott owed me. He could start paying off with a flock of answers.

I drove to Alta Bates, thinking that a room here would provide the best day's accommodations Herman Ott had had since he left Pittsburgh. I hoped he was on one of the upper floors so I could pause by the picture windows and watch the rising sun begin its daily quest to pierce the fog. If I spent enough time with Ott, I could stop at the window on my way out and see patches of bright blue bay rippling in the fresh sunlight, the San Francisco skyscrapers glistening as if they were dew-covered, the red towers of the Golden Gate Bridge hooking the last shred of fog. If Ott had any sense, he'd aim to stand there too.

But he didn't, of course. And I never got to the fourth floor. Ott had already checked himself out.

The man owed me! I slammed out of the hospital, strode furiously to my car, raced through the thick gray dawn to Telegraph, left my car in a red zone in front of Ott's office, and stalked into the building. God damn him. I took the stairs two steps at a time, only sorry I didn't have an ax with me to trash his office.

But I was too late. Ott's friends or enemies had already done a number on the place. Clothes and newspaper, books, a pizza box, paper cups and crushed malt liquor cans and empty bottles of rotgut covered the floor. A tornado could have mistaken it for a trailer. But for the liquor detritus, the chaos in the bedroom might merely have meant Ott had moved back in. It was his office that shouted the truth.

Never had I seen a file drawer left open, papers piled on the desk, as much as a dust ball on the floor. Even after we had searched the files and the lab tech left a film of print dust on every surface, the room was still tidy. Now file cabinets were toppled, desk drawers yanked open, and Ott's mustard-colored Naugahyde chair had been slashed in the few places where it wasn't already taped together.

On the seat was a dead pigeon.

I found Ott curled up in a yellow wad on the backseat of Emma, the Studebaker. He probably hadn't been asleep for more than a couple of hours. Exhausted, probably. I banged loud on the window.

Limp blond strands were matted to his forehead. His round, sallow cheeks were wrinkled from sleep. As his hazel eyes opened, his thin lips automatically curled.

Before he could greet me with his customary snarl, I said, "You owe me big time!"

He closed his eyes.

I banged the window so hard I thought it would break. "So, Ott, your friends—the Angels of Righteousness—trashed your office. What are you going to do, call the police?"

His eyes snapped open, and he was halfway to sitting up before he realized how much he'd given away.

So he hadn't seen it. He'd just anticipated the danger.

"God damn it, Ott, if you had just told me about

Cyril and the pesticide when you called me up to the Claremont—"

He mumbled something through the closed window.

"What?" I shouted, giving the window another bang.

He rolled it down an inch. "Couldn't," he mumbled.

"You couldn't?" I screamed. "Why the hell couldn't you?" Behind me in the apartment building a window opened. A guy shouted. I ignored him. "Why, Ott?"

"Because, Smith, I wasn't going to leave you that bombshell."

"*Leave* . . ." I could have wrung the rest of the explanation from him, but I knew him too well to bother. I shook my head. "It's like Leonard said, we've all got our price. Ott, I thought yours was protecting your people. I was wrong, huh? You knew about the toxins. You weren't about to tell the police at a time when you wouldn't be around to monitor us as we investigated. And you couldn't do that Sunday night, could you? Because between the time you called me and the time you got to the Claremont, Margo Roehner told you about the yellow-billed loon sighting."

Ott's lips pursed so tight he looked as if he'd swallowed his mouth. "Get out!" he growled, overlooking the fact that I was already out.

I went on. "And so you spent a night in the sand looking for the yellow-billed loon. And where is that loon? That loon, Ott, is where it always is: in Alaska."

Ott's face flushed pink. He shoved himself up higher on the seat and leaned toward me. "Get . . ."

"Ott, I took a lot of shit because I believed in you. No one else even entertained the idea that you might be innocent. Because of me, you are sitting in your own car instead of on a jail slab!"

He gave an odd little bouncy movement with his low sloped shoulder—his version of a shrug—and said the last thing I expected from him. "You're right." Then, as if the admission amazed him as much as it did me, he added, "You're not a cop anymore; what is it you want from me?"

I stood there at the carport, staring blankly into the Studebaker. It didn't surprise me that Ott knew I'd been suspended. It just shocked me to hear the words, to realize that I was no longer a police officer.

"Nothing, Ott. There's nothing you can give me." I turned and walked back to my Volkswagen bug and sat in the driver's seat, feeling the closeness of the little car, the silence without the dispatcher's voice sending out patrol officers, tracking chases, without the little give-and-take of those in the know. Suddenly I longed to banter with Eggs and Jackson, to watch Inspector Doyle shepherd his rhino herd to the side of his desk. I longed for Pereira to gobble down the rest of my scone before I had decided I was full. I longed for Howard. Oh, god, Howard.

A whirling cold emptiness expanded within me.

It would have been easy to "get" Ott, with a comment about his chauffeured ride to Kennedy Airport or a comment on his father. But like him, I have principles. I will never mention the Hermans and the Otts of Pittsburgh, nor think of him without picturing the smiling little running back on the Monongahela Mongeese team.

And I will never ask Daisy Culligan if it was Her-

man Ott who suggested her clever tat against Bryant
Hemming. He merely wanted to know what was in
the ACC books he couldn't get at. Even Ott couldn't
have foreseen that it would lead to Bryant Hemming's
murder and Margo Roehner's destruction.

The fog had thinned to that gauzy gray that makes
the hills look Japanese and promises hidden spots of
beauty and silence. I drove slowly west toward Howard's house; I was almost to Ashby Avenue before I
shifted out of second. The sky was the same murky
battleship color that pales the orange and vermilion
leaves. It wasn't till I saw the looming brown shingle
and the empty driveway that I realized I wasn't ready
to see Howard.

I drove on to Ashby Avenue and stopped at the
corner. I could turn right and right again at the freeway, as Charles Edward Kidd would have done if he'd
owned a car. As my great-uncle Jack's neighbor Mrs.
Bronfmann had done that day when she'd climbed
onto the crosstown bus and the Spanish exchange student had caught her eye. As Howard's mother had
whenever hope or terror or maybe whim had teased
her forward.

I've thought of the contrast between Howard's
mother and mine. My mother spent her life clutching
on to the small acorn of security she could find in
each new house and town to which her dreamer of a
husband led her, putting her best foot forward toward
the neighbors as if this house or job would be the one
that would take root. She clung to her hope against
the sea of fact and fear and common sense that surrounded her. Howard's mother floated above it all.

When I'd last visited my parents in their retirement apartment in Florida, their days were filled with golf and bridge, their nights thick with the fear that inflation would make their payments too steep. My mother cashes the checks I send, but I doubt she spends them. And Howard's mother, Selena Bly, is she worse off? I sometimes wonder when they land in their final places if there will be a hairsbreadth of difference between them.

I turned right, up Ashby, away from the freeway. Spikes of sun pierced the fog and glistened off the Claremont Hotel's white turret. I hung a left and wound up into the hills till I came to a pullout on Grizzly Peak. I opened the door of my familiar little car, stepped out, and looked down at Berkeley from a different angle.